Michael Nicholson has been an independent filmmaker since the mid-1970s, writing, filming, directing, editing, some animations, and selling his films of various lengths to Australian television over the years. Nicholson has also written various books and has had several art exhibitions. He is married to Fatma Beyen, an architect from Istanbul, and they have a daughter, Melissa, who has a bachelor's degree in filmmaking.

To my wife, Fatma, and my daughter, Melissa.

Michael Nicholson

THE MOSAIC ESCALATOR

The Front And Back Cover Paintings
And Design By Michael Nicholson.

AUSTIN MACAULEY PUBLISHERS™
LONDON * CAMBRIDGE * NEW YORK * SHARJAH

Copyright © Michael Nicholson 2024

The right of Michael Nicholson to be identified as author of this work has been asserted by the author in accordance with sections 77 and 78 of the Copyright, Designs and Patents Act 1988.

All rights reserved. No part of this publication may be reproduced, stored in a retrieval system, or transmitted in any form or by any means, electronic, mechanical, photocopying, recording, or otherwise, without the prior permission of the publishers.

Any person who commits any unauthorised act in relation to this publication may be liable to criminal prosecution and civil claims for damages.

This is a work of fiction. Names, characters, businesses, places, events, locales, and incidents are either the products of the author's imagination or used in a fictitious manner. Any resemblance to actual persons, living or dead, or actual events is purely coincidental.

A CIP catalogue record for this title is available from the British library.

ISBN 9781035840182 (Paperback)
ISBN 9781035840199 (ePub e-book)

www.austinmacauley.com

First Published 2024
Austin Macauley Publishers Ltd®
1 Canada Square
Canary Wharf
London
E14 5AA

"Whatever happened between the free and the obediently confined?"

Chapter 1
Hiking Around Uluru

It's like a dream... We're dreaming... It's dream time, Jonathan thought to himself as he looked at Uluru through the window. "It's a dream," he whispered.

"It's not a dream. It's a 'monolith'... a huge rock," Yvonne said.

Jonathan stared at Yvonne, her slightly dreamy frown turned into a beautiful smile as she gazed back at him.

The students climbed out of a minibus holding their backpacks and bags at 5:30 am. The sun appeared over the Central Australian horizon and the bus drove away leaving them standing on the roadside of the Uluru-Kata Tjuta National Park. There was only the rock and the thought of time and space. You couldn't miss it since Uluru was one of the most famous landmarks on earth.

"Are you really our guide? I must be dreaming," Jonathan mumbled as he looked directly into the eyes of Yvonne.

"You are not dreaming; I 'am' your guide. I am nearly a full-blooded Australian aborigine. My father married a white nurse, and thus I have a bit of Anglo-Saxon blood in my veins, but I am still your Aboriginal guide, nonetheless."

They were four university students in their early twenties on a trip to Central Australia and all of them were from Melbourne, except for their guide Yvonne, who was from Alice Springs.

They gazed at the rounded curve of the rock. "It almost resembles a giant planet embedded in the ground, with just the tip showing," Jonathan observed.

"Christ, look! A dingo!" Cathy exclaimed in scared excitement. A large dingo emerged from the scrub and then stopped in the middle of the road. Cathy scrambled to unzip her backpack and fumbled for her camera.

A larger tourist bus sped towards the dingo as it turned to run away, but suddenly, for no explicable reason, turned again and froze. The bus skidded, the horn blared, Cathy clicked her camera, and in the confusion, the bus hit the dingo. Through the camera lens, Cathy saw the dingo thrown to the gravel roadside. Japanese tourists inside the bus peered out the window in horror.

The dust settled and momentarily there was silence. A dingo pup emerged from the scrub searching for its mother and in dreaded anticipation the sorrowful yelping interrupted the silence. It was a miserable situation.

The driver's door of the red tourist bus was flung open, and a large man jumped out cursing his luck. He knelt over the body of the dingo and felt for a heartbeat and glanced at the small amount of blood splattered on his bull bar. Finally, he grabbed the dingo's rear paws and dragged it back into the scrub. Cathy looked at the red tourist bus, framed by Uluru. Through her lens, it looked like the huge red rock had windows with Japanese tourists crowded against them staring out.

The large man returned to the bus, and as he clambered back into the driver's seat he stopped and looked at the group of astounded students.

"Well?" he growled in a matter-of-fact way. "I tried to swerve; it's the dog's fault. I'm sorry…"

He slammed the door shut and the rear tyres skidded in the gravel leaving another cloud of red dust as the bus drove away at high speed.

Not wanting this mishap to ruin their trip, Jonathan ran into the scrub and within seconds, emerged holding a whimpering dingo puppy.

"Oh, you poor little thing," Cathy moaned in sympathy as she went to Jonathan's side and started cuddling the sad animal. "You come with us."

"And we'll call you Azaria!" Jonathan said, trying to alleviate the sad situation. He hated that the trip had started like this. They were all there for an adventure, and he was determined to make sure this trip went well. The group paused awkwardly, and Jonathan held his breath, but then everyone broke into spontaneous laughter.

"Don't be stupid Jonathan," Cathy replied. "We'll call her 'Zara'!"

After strolling along the path for an hour directly below the huge imposing Uluru, only the dingo pup scampering between their feet reminded them of the unfortunate accident.

They had met their guide, Yvonne, for the first time that morning, when they refused to join the much larger tour group that was planning to climb Uluru.

Their tour organiser, Ian Harrison—who was already climbing the rock—had hastily arranged an Aboriginal guide to walk with them around the base of the rock.

"You don't really need me," Yvonne said as they passed another sign explaining where they were and how many kilometres they had covered. "Everything is clearly marked, and these notices tell you more than I know anyway."

"Forgive me, but you give us a feeling for the place, Yvonne," Sebastian clarified quickly. He could hardly stop looking at her. Maybe it was her beautiful smile, her slightly curly hair, or even the rhythm of her walking style that Sebastian felt drawn to. Sebastian was tall and handsome and was responsible for galvanising the group to refuse to climb Uluru on the grounds it was offensive to local aborigines. Ironically, Sebastian was an American now living in Melbourne.

The other two male students were no less impressed by Yvonne. Jonathan, the stockier of the two, had gotten the group together. He was a tech wiz in electronics and computer technology and a natural leader. He wore rimless glasses and had a ruthless, but pragmatic sense of humour. Kim, who was from Taiwan, had a tough wire-like frame, was incredibly intelligent and light years ahead of everyone. He was very knowledgeable about history, and his mind was encyclopaedic.

"I'm not offended if you climb my rock," Yvonne explained patiently. "It's a rock, and it's been here for millions of years, and is no different to any other rock."

"Yes, but it's common knowledge that some elders don't like people violating their sacred sites," Sebastian politely argued.

"No, Sebastian," Yvonne refuted. "They're scared tourists will fall off it. Do you understand?"

Eager to keep the peace to ensure they would enjoy this trip, Jonathan spoke up. "Anyway, I don't think we should sit too close to the rock in case one of the other students falls on us."

Cathy laughed. "I agree to that."

They decided to rest and have breakfast. The hot sun had replaced any morning chill and the shade of the various gum trees only mildly alleviated the heat. "I didn't pack these cans," Sebastian mumbled as he unzipped his heavy backpack and started urgently searching the large pockets. "This isn't my pack."

He pulled out a wallet and opened it. "It's Mr Harrison's! And he must have mine. Here's his mobile phone."

The others looked over in puzzled interest as Sebastian uncovered a pouch of compasses and assorted navigational equipment. "And Ian probably discovered this on top of Uluru," Sebastian concluded aloud.

"Zara! Come back here!" Cathy called out as the dingo puppy scurried through some shrubs towards the rock. "I'll give you a sandwich." Cathy followed the puppy right up to the face of the rock.

Her heart skipped a beat, and her throat suddenly contracted as she blinked in disbelief at what she saw. The head of the dingo puppy had seemingly gone into the rock. Then it came out again as it continued sniffing around.

Cathy couldn't believe what she had just seen, and then it happened again. This time the entire puppy, except its wagging tail, passed into the actual rock.

Cathy instinctively lunged forward and grabbed the tail and with the momentum her hand also momentarily went into the rock before she pulled the puppy out. Zara was fine and the rock appeared as solid as before.

A cold shiver raced up Cathy's back, and she sat down to compose herself as her heart began to beat fast, and she carefully crawled backwards still clutching the puppy. Cathy then grabbed a stick and threw it at the rock, and the stick disappeared into the rock.

"Where's Cathy?" Yvonne asked, looking around. The boys were immersed in Ian Harrison's backpack and weren't paying any attention, so Yvonne stood up, strolled into the scrub, and soon found Cathy standing rigid in shock. "Cathy…?"

"What's happened?" Sebastian enquired as Cathy and Yvonne appeared. "Are you all right, Cathy?"

Cathy stood there stroking the dingo pup.

"Watch this," Cathy stated as she grabbed a stick and threw it at the rock. The stick disappeared into the rock instead of bouncing off. Suddenly, the puppy struggled free and rushed off to fetch the stick, and before their very eyes, the puppy disappeared into the rock completely, gone, vanished.

…Are we dreaming? Is this a dream? Jonathan wondered. "This can't be…" Jonathan said as he adjusted his rimless glasses. "It's solid rock."

"I think we should get out of here," Yvonne urged. "Let's get back to the track and go home… I do not understand what I've just seen. I'm sorry."

"Not so fast," Kim replied calmly. He strolled over to the exact place in the rock where the dingo puppy had disappeared. "There must be a reason for this."

Before anyone could do anything, Kim put his hand into the rock, then his arm, then his head and shoulders, and then just as quickly pulled them out and looked at the rest of the group. They all stood aghast with their eyes wide open in surprise.

"It's a cave of some sort in there, quite well-lit," Kim stated in a matter-of-fact way.

"But you went through solid rock!" Sebastian spluttered out with a quiver in his voice.

"Well, it felt like thin air," Kim said. "Not solid rock at all, I promise." Kim walked right into the rock and disappeared completely. The rest of the group stood motionless.

Yvonne started to cry. "I'm your guide, and I'll be in so much trouble."

As she sobbed, Cathy put her arm around her. "No, no, it's not your fault at all," Cathy said as she also began to cry.

No one knew what to do least of all Jonathan who was supposed to be the leader of their group, not to mention the one who'd planned this. His immediate thought was to get help but what would he say? We need the police here; someone has walked through solid rock?

'Bip, bip… bip, bip… bip, bip'. The eerie silence was broken by the distinct sounds of a text message from a mobile phone.

"Ian Harrison's phone!" Sebastian replied in relief, as they ran the short distance to their backpacks. He fumbled through their tour leader's belongings; grateful Harrison had left his mobile phone. Some in the group had agreed to leave their phones on the bus, so they wouldn't be spending their time looking down at their hands rather than looking up at the enormous rock. He switched on the text message and read it out aloud.

'ENJOY THE VIEW!'

"Who's it from?" Jonathan enquired as they looked at each other mysteriously.

Sebastian tapped a few buttons to reveal the sender. "It's from Harrison's wife," he replied.

They quickly solved the puzzle. Mrs Harrison was back at the main camp and had obviously sent a text message to her husband knowing he was by now on top of Uluru with the rest of the class and probably enjoying the panoramic views.

"Well? Come on Sebastian!" Cathy ordered angrily as they walked back to the rock face. "Call for help."

"Yes, yes," he replied, fumbling to make a call.

Just as he began to find an emergency number on the mobile phone, they heard the dingo pup yelp along with Kim's familiar nonchalant whistling. Cathy pointed her camera at the rock and through the viewfinder she saw Kim emerge from the solid rock smiling and holding the puppy. She took an amazing photograph of Kim seemingly half embedded in rock.

"You're safe," Yvonne sighed in relief as they crowded around him.

The dingo pup played around happily, oblivious to the science fiction dilemma that had unfolded. Sebastian tapped away on the mobile phone and put it to his ear as he looked blankly at the others.

"Hullo? Mrs Harrison?" he said politely. "It's Sebastian here… no, nothing's wrong, I've got your husband's mobile phone by mistake. The backpacks got switched and a few of us didn't climb Uluru after all," he explained. "So, when we meet up at the end of the day, I'll give it back. Yes, we'll see you this evening. Bye." He turned off the mobile phone and looked at the others with a judgmental frown.

"Well? She would have thought we were all mad if I told her Kim had walked through solid rock!" Jonathan claimed.

Kim, meanwhile, had used a long stick to poke around the apparent hole in the rock. After a while, he discovered the height and width of the mysterious opening, and it was about the size of a garage door. He placed a couple of tall sticks on each side, so they knew where the entrance was since they certainly couldn't tell by looking at it. Visually it all looked like solid rock.

"There must be some logical explanation to all of this," Kim said to the others. "Since clearly we've all witnessed it."

"But you're the only one who's been through it, Kim," Sebastian argued. "So only you have experienced it."

"Well then, I'll give it a try," Jonathan offered as he stood up and walked over to the area between the sticks.

"No, don't, Jonathan!" Yvonne protested. "As your guide, I demand of you…" Her voice trailed off in resignation as Jonathon walked through the rock and vanished. Everyone stared in silence at the rock. Moments later Jonathan stepped out nodding his head.

"You're right, Kim, it's just a cave in there…" he announced.

"Maybe it's an optical illusion of some sort," Sebastian suggested. "After all, there are lots of caves in this rock, are there not, Yvonne?"

"Well, yes… of course," Yvonne replied uneasily. "Everyone knows that…"

Sebastian then bravely strode through the rock and returned before anyone could even blink or protest.

"Yep. It's a cave," Sebastian concurred.

"All right then," Jonathan announced. "Let's all go in and explore… how can that offend the Aboriginal elders?"

"Oh, I get it," Cathy replied curtly. "We shouldn't climb over Uluru, but we can climb 'into it'. How convenient."

"So then who's coming?" Jonathan enquired confidently as he picked up his backpack. Kim and Sebastian followed him, and the three of them strolled into the rock and were gone.

"Oh, dear, and I'm the guide, I guess…" Yvonne said as she looked at Cathy. And, with those words, Yvonne and Cathy picked up their backpacks, held their collective breath and marched through the rock after the three boys.

Chapter 2
Hiking Inside Uluru

"Well, here we all are then!" Jonathan declared as Cathy and Yvonne emerged through the rock wall. "And at least it's nice and cool in here." He flapped his wet shirt that was clinging to his sweaty chest. Kim and Sebastian, meanwhile, grabbed a few sticks they had thrown inside and placed them against the cave wall to mark the exit.

"Where's Zara?" Cathy asked. "We can't leave her by herself." At that moment Zara suddenly scampered through the rock waving her tail and Cathy picked her up. "Who's a lovely little puppy?" she said, cuddling the dingo.

"Now listen," Yvonne said, raising her voice causing a small echo. "We're in this cave for two minutes, and then we're out of here!"

"Yes, yes," Sebastian replied defensively. "Anyway, anyone can leave whenever they wish…"

"That's odd," Kim whispered, studying one section of the smooth cave wall. "This dent in the rock here appears to be from a bullet."

"How can you tell that?" Jonathan asked.

Everyone leaned in, taking a closer look.

"Well, this appears to be a spent cartridge shell," Sebastian said as he stooped over and picked up something from the cave floor.

"It's from a 303," a World War II rifle," Kim concluded confidently.

"Hmm… let's go outside and look at it under natural sunlight," Jonathan suggested, heading for the exit that was marked by the two sticks.

"Why would someone want to fire at a cave wall anyway?" Kim wondered.

Jonathan reached the exit and collided with it. "Ouch!" he gasped and staggered back holding his bloodied forehead. Everyone blinked and immediately Sebastian went for the exit with his arms outstretched.

"What's going on?" he shouted, bouncing off the cave wall. "It's solid rock!"

Cathy and Yvonne glanced around in a panic as Kim started running his hands along the cave wall.

"Where's the exit? It's gone!" Cathy screamed as they all started frantically touching the cave wall. "We're trapped!"

"What should I do?" Yvonne whispered to Jonathan as she patted her handkerchief over the bloody gash on his forehead. "I'm supposed to be your guide."

Jonathan's eyes rolled back, the cave started spinning, his legs went to jelly, and he slumped to the floor of the cave. The strange echo of Cathy saying, 'What a hero…' was the last thing he heard as he fainted.

Cool water splashed on Jonathan's face. He blinked his eyes open and stared up at Yvonne's smiling face.

"He's coming to!" she called out. "Jonathan, hello, are you alright?" Her hand gracefully dabbled a wet cloth over his brow. "You've been unconscious for over an hour…"

Jonathan started to think more clearly. He realised he was lying down on the floor of the cave with a backpack under his head. "We're still inside the cave," he muttered. "Didn't you find the exit?"

Kim emerged from deeper inside the cave with Cathy.

"No, Jonathan, we haven't found a way out," Cathy said with an air of mystery. "But this cave goes on a fair way and Yvonne thinks it might lead to another exit."

"Yes, I know about caves in Uluru," she said. "And some go in at one place and come out at another… So I've heard. So maybe this is just one long cave that leads to an exit on the other side of the rock. I can't be sure though."

Jonathan slowly sat up and looked around. He felt achy from lying on the rough stone floor.

"We tried Ian's cell but there was no network service," Sebastian lamented as he held up the phone. "But that's hardly surprising since we're encased in rock."

"Well, I'm okay now," Jonathan said, getting to his feet and concealing his abject disillusionment. "So all we can do is walk along this cave, I guess."

Kim glanced around. "This cave seems to be man-made."

It was a comment that began a train of thought and Jonathan soon realised he was right. It was almost a perfect sandstone cave. It stayed the same height and width as they hiked, and it didn't have any roughness or craggy sections like normal caves. And then there was the low light the entire time, as if the surface of the walls glowed with subtle sunlight, just enough light for everyone to see clearly.

"Hmm... It's 5:00 pm," Sebastian said, looking at his watch. "They'll be waiting for us at the base of Uluru."

"I'll be in so much trouble," Yvonne bemoaned. "Regardless of whether it's my fault or not."

"It's no one's fault," Cathy responded. "We're all to blame for walking into this thing."

"Have you noticed this cave is becoming spherical?" Kim asked, running his fingers along the wall. "And it's getting smoother and silvery in colour?"

They all reached out for the wall and realised it was looking less like a cave with every kilometre they covered. "Shoosh," Yvonne said. "Can you hear that?" Everyone stopped and listened intently to a deep vibrating twang. "It sounds like a didgeridoo for crying out loud!"

Sure enough, the sound of the Aboriginal instrument echoed ahead of them in the cave.

"We must be near an exit!" Jonathan concluded. "There must be a corroboree of some sort!" He imagined they would come upon a First Nation dance ceremony at any moment as they continued.

"We'll be home in time for dinner!" Sebastian exclaimed, and they all started running for the exit, their collective excitement growing. The deep resonating sound of the didgeridoo became increasingly louder. Finally, they rounded another bend in the tunnel and slowed to a walk as they entered a large room.

"What is this?" Cathy exclaimed in confusion. They stopped and looked around in bewilderment. In the middle of the cave was a television set with a screen on every side.

"It's some sort of television cube," Kim whispered.

"Maybe we're in the foyer of an exclusive hotel," Jonathan suggested as they all inspected the room more closely.

Playing inside the television cube was an Aboriginal man, sitting in the outback scrub playing a didgeridoo. The sound echoed throughout the cave.

"This is so familiar to me," Yvonne said confidently, studying the indigenous artwork on the walls. "It's a story from our Dreamtime, handed down over many generations from the Pitjantjatjara and Yankunytjatjara tribes who own the area around Uluru, the Anangu people."

Yvonne pointed to a painting on the wall. "The old hairy man holds a large bark shield and painted on it are the symbols of all the tribes around Arnhem Land showing unity."

The sound of the aborigine playing the didgeridoo resonated in the background as Yvonne moved on to the next painting on the wall.

"But the Diprofodon and Genyornis, large ancient animals, grab the shield and run into a cave, and this work here shows the old man telling his two sons to chase them and bring it back," Yvonne continued. "On their journey, they stop at a waterhole, and then they notice the roof of the cave is like the stars and the universe and the sky gods direct them to the place where they find the two ancient animals holding the shield and…" Yvonne's voice trailed off.

"And what?" Cathy asked in anticipation.

"And…" Yvonne's voice faltered. "And I don't understand this final artwork…"

"Well, what do you think it may be?" Jonathan asked.

"I don't know," Yvonne whispered. "Possibly it shows they are given a choice or something," Yvonne said vaguely. "Look, I'm a guide, not some brilliant indigenous art historian."

"Okay, okay," Jonathan said. "You've explained a lot already. That's great, really."

"Incidentally," Sebastian inquired. "What type of animals are a Dipro-thing and a Geny-whats-you-call-it?"

"Oh!" Yvonne's eyes brightened. "A Diprotodon is a giant kangaroo, about three metres high, and a Genyornis is a giant emu. You see, it's all myths and legends passed down from my ancestor spirits."

Above the wall, Jonathan noticed what looked like Egyptian hieroglyphics.

"Let me see Harrison's phone."

Sebastian handed it to him. "But there's no network service," Cathy said, stepping closer.

Jonathan opened a book application on Harrison's phone. "Yes," he whispered.

"What?" Yvonne asked hopefully. "Is there service?"

"No, but I remember Harrison saying he has a dictionary about Egyptian hieroglyphics." It was almost as if Harrison had expected them to find the Egyptian script on a wall. He pointed at the writing on the wall.

"What does it say?" Sebastian asked.

Kim and Jonathan spent a few minutes trying to translate it. Jonathan figured it out first.

"It says 'friend'."

"I don't like the sound of that," Sebastian whispered.

"No, it's a positive message," Yvonne said. "That's a good thing. I feel safer."

Cathy grabbed her camera from her backpack and stood back from the group. They formed a semi-circle around the television cube, with the artwork, and hieroglyphics on the wall behind them.

"Smile," Cathy said, pressing the shutter.

The flash momentarily illuminated the large room. Then something strange and unexpected happened.

A rumble of thunder echoed from the television cube. Everyone looked at the screen and watched the aborigine continue to play his didgeridoo in the vast red sandy plains of the outback, and above him, the sky split, and it started to rain.

"What are those? They appear to be people with wings fluttering around above him," Yvonne said, her beautiful brows furrowing deeply.

Jonathan sensed that somehow there was a connection between Cathy's camera flash and the thunder and rain on the television. "Well, I think we should move on," he said, breaking the silence. "Maybe the exit is just around the next bend."

"Did you notice that these indigenous paintings are almost luminous?" Kim observed as he tapped the wall. "They're not painted on as such. They seem almost like neon signs…"

"Yes, I know," Yvonne nodded in agreement. "It's quite odd really."

Zara, the dingo pup, began barking at the television cube and then scampered into the tunnel on the other side of the large room. The group picked up their backpacks and with Jonathan leading the way, followed her into the tunnel, the sound of the didgeridoo slowly fading into the distance.

Chapter 3
Slipping and Sliding

The tunnel seemed to be endless. The temperature was pleasant enough and the light, though slightly dull, was bright enough, and the walls still gave off a mysterious silvery glow.

"This walking is getting easier by the minute," Jonathan noticed. "In fact, it feels like we are going downhill…"

"And the surface is getting shinier," Cathy added. "It's as if we're walking inside a large stainless-steel tube of some sort."

Ahead of them, the dingo pup started to slide. Then Yvonne, whose shoes had very little tread, also began to slide, her feet slipping out from under her.

"Wow… oh!" Yvonne exclaimed as she lost her balance. "This is like walking on ice."

"Hold on," Sebastian warned. "This tunnel is descending more and more!" Just as his feet slipped, everyone lost their footing, tumbling on their tails and beginning to slide downhill.

"It's like a water slide!" Sebastian said with an edge of excitement. "Maybe we should hold hands, so we don't get separated."

"Yes, yes," Jonathan said, grabbing Yvonne's hand. "Let's keep together. This is so weird."

They soon caught up to the dingo, and Cathy reached forward and lifted the pup onto her lap as they all whizzed down the shiny tunnel gaining speed. This peculiar sensation of sliding was both magical and exhilarating.

"It must be around supper time, and we've still got lots of sandwiches," Cathy said, reaching inside her backpack and breaking off some bread for the dingo pup. "I wonder how far we have travelled?"

"According to the step counter, I have attached to my ankle," Kim said, studying the figures on the counter. "I estimate we walked about seven kilometres today from the entrance of the rock to the spot we started sliding."

"I think I can calculate it," Jonathan said, reaching into his backpack for his laptop. It was moderately tricky because they were still sliding downhill. "The compass on my laptop has been recording the direction we've travelled the whole time. We've been going north, slightly north-east, on average."

"Are you sure that compass is accurate?" Sebastian asked suspiciously. "Remember, we're below solid rock."

"Who knows what the magnetic force is like down here?" Jonathan said. "I could be completely wrong, but I think we're about midway between Uluru and The Olga's." He double-checked the compass, and suddenly the needle started spinning rapidly. "Uh-oh."

"Uh-oh?" Cathy gasped. "Why did you say uh-oh?"

Jonathan picked up the laptop mouse and pressed it against the wall of the tunnel.

"What on earth are you doing now?" Yvonne asked.

"I've been doing a test on how fast my mouse moves on my computer pad when I'm at home," Jonathan explained. "And I've connected a tiny speedometer to the ball in the mouse."

"And so, by running it along the wall, you think you can estimate the speed we are sliding?" Sebastian probed in admiration.

"Yes, that's right," Jonathan said proudly, studying the figures on the screen of his laptop. "And, right now, it shows we are travelling 120 kilometres an hour!"

"Well, that's what it feels like," Sebastian said, his hair blown back. In fact, they all had a similar hairstyle now from the speed, including the dingo pup whose tiny wind-swept ears were now pointed horizontally backwards.

"Here Sebastian, have a tuna sandwich," Cathy said, pushing the sandwich into his mouth. "You're so clever."

"And there's more," Jonathan mumbled with a mouthful of sandwich. "If I combine our speed with our direction from the compass…" He tapped a solitary key defiantly. "There! It says we are approximately 850 metres underground going downhill at an angle of forty degrees and still heading in a north, north-easterly direction."

"I feel great!" Yvonne called out loudly. "This slide is wonderful." They all nodded in agreement as they whizzed down at breakneck speed.

Sebastian began to fall asleep. One by one the others started to doze off with their heads resting on each other's shoulders or backpacks. Jonathan closed his laptop and fell asleep.

Occasionally the dingo pup looked up at attention, as if she was on honorary guard duty, but then put her head back into Cathy's lap.

"Only in extraordinary states of consciousness can one be aware of, or attuned to, the inner dreaming," Yvonne whispered into Jonathan's ear. Her eyes closed, and along with the others, she fell into a deep sleep in this strange tunnel speeding along ever so smoothly.

Chapter 4
Think Tank

Jonathan's deep sleep was interrupted by the strange sound of a tiny harpsichord playing *Waltzing Matilda*, the alarm on his watch. He opened his eyes and switched it off.

"Oh, it's 7:00 am," he said, stretching and accidentally elbowing Yvonne. "We're slowing down!"

Everyone began to sit up and look around. They were still speeding along, but the gradient appeared to be levelling out.

"Hmm, we've slept for over eight hours," Kim said. "We must have travelled a long way."

"One thing is for sure," Sebastian said, standing up and looking as if he were snowboarding without a snowboard. "Uluru will be crawling with search parties by now." The tunnel finally completely levelled out, and they stopped sliding. The dingo pup jumped out of Cathy's lap and started sniffing around. Everyone stood up and stretched.

"Okay then, let's start walking for a bit and then stop for breakfast," Jonathan suggested. Everyone nodded in agreement, put on their backpacks, and began strolling along.

"We've got enough food and water for a couple of days," Cathy estimated. "And then who knows?"

The floor of the tunnel became a bit rougher offering a good grip for walking. The silvery colour remained on the walls, lighting the way. They hiked for about ten minutes and after a long curve, stopped in disbelief.

"It's a World War Two Japanese military tank!" Kim exclaimed. "What's it doing here?"

It was about the size of a Land Cruiser and was in pristine condition. Jonathan knocked his knuckles on the solid steel exterior, the clunking sound echoing down the tunnel.

"Hello? Anyone inside?" Jonathan inquired in trepidation. "We are here in peace."

"'We are here in peace?'" Sebastian mocked.

"Hey," Jonathan said. "One of those Japanese soldiers from the Imperial Army could be inside. Maybe they don't know if the Second World War is over."

Cathy laughed, unsure if he was joking.

Sebastian stepped up beside Jonathan and tapped on the tank. Nothing happened. Soon they all began examining it more closely and Jonathan and Kim climbed onto it and tried to open the circular metal door, but it was firmly fixed shut.

"Look at this everyone," Kim said, using his penknife to remove some sand from the corners of the metal tread. Everyone knew Kim had a considerable knowledge of Japanese culture and the Second World War, in particular. "It's a mixture of red sand and arkosic sandstone." He held out his hand and Jonathan inspected it closely.

"What's arkosic sandstone?" Jonathan asked.

"It's what Uluru is made of," Yvonne said. "It's a sand that contains feldspar, quartz and mica."

"Exactly," Kim said. "Which means this tank came down the same tunnel."

"Oh, I see," Jonathan nodded.

"Smile everyone," Cathy said, readying her camera to capture the scene. At that moment, the metal door on top of the tank suddenly swung open and the smiling face of a Japanese boy popped up. Cathy snapped a photo, capturing everyone's surprise.

"Hello!" The boy said. "I'm Charlie."

"We're friendly visitors," Jonathan said immediately and gave a courteous bow.

"I know you are," Charlie said, offering a confident smile. He climbed out of the small round metal hatch and stood on top of the tank. "Do you want to come with me?"

"To where?" Sebastian asked.

"To meet my parents," the boy said excitedly as he jumped onto the ground. Everyone glanced at each other and shrugged their shoulders in agreement.

"Sure," Cathy said, wanting to put the boy at ease. "My name is Cathy. This is Yvonne, our guide, and Sebastian, Jonathan, and Kim."

"We've been on holiday in Central Australia," Jonathan explained.

"Oh… Well, I've never been to Central Australia," Charlie said. "But I know all about it… and the big rock, Uluru…"

"Well, Charlie, show us the way," Jonathan said, scratching his head, perplexed but intrigued. He picked up his backpack, and they all started walking.

"How old are you, Charlie?" Cathy inquired, taking him by the hand.

"I'm eight years old, and I have an older sister," Charlie explained enthusiastically. After walking just fifty metres, they rounded a slight bend and the tunnel opened into an enormous cavern, kilometres high and wide. They stared out at a most unbelievable view, motionless, their collective breath taken away.

"This is so beautiful," Jonathan muttered in amazement. "It's unreal!"

They were standing atop a rise that was covered by an almond tree orchard in full blossom. Further down the hill was a large traditional Japanese village nestled next to a calm lake that stretched as far as the eye could see.

"And look at the sky!" Kim exclaimed, gazing up in astonishment. "It's like the universe set in stone!" The roof of the enormous cavern was about five kilometres above them, and an array of illuminated rocks dotted the ceiling like stars, bright lights twinkling over the vista and creating daylight.

"Okay then, Charlie," Jonathan said. "Let's meet your parents."

They began descending a perfectly manicured path through a forest of trees covered with white blossoms towards the village. "These are Somei Yoshino trees," Kim said after mentally paging through his photographic, encyclopaedic mind.

"You would know that," Cathy commented.

Even though they were in an underground cavern and there was no sunshine, the trees were beautiful. They could see people going about their daily routines, working in their gardens, and shopping at a market in the middle of the village. Others were riding on bicycles and several small fishing boats floated calmly near a jetty. As they moved closer to the village, people came out of their houses to stare at them, and it was clear they had not seen visitors for a very long time.

"How long have your people lived here, Charlie?" Kim asked with an air of nonchalance.

"My family have been here for over eighty years," the boy answered. "It's like a paradise for me."

It was abundantly clear that they were no longer in Central Australia.

Chapter 5
The Formal Tea Ceremony

Charlie's mother shuffled into the room dressed in a silk white kimono holding a tray of ceramic cups and teapots. Everyone sat quietly on the tatami mats with their legs crossed around a low wooden table. No one really knew what was going on, but the women's kindness calmed them a little bit.

"We rarely have formal tea ceremonies these days," she said, placing the tray on the table. "But this is clearly a special occasion. My name is Akia. Ah... here is my husband now," she said, as Charlie's father slid open the rice paper door and smiled.

"Hello and welcome. I'm Charlie's father, Bepo," he said, eagerly shaking everyone's hands and bowing courteously. "Please feel free to eat up these delicacies my wife has prepared, you must be hungry."

Cathy hungrily grabbed a crispy tempura. "Hmmm, this is delicious."

"After this tea, I will show you to your rooms," he said. "You can freshen up and relax with an 'ofuro'."

"That's a hot bath," Kim whispered to the others.

Jonathan looked around, and realising no one else was going to ask the pressing question, he spoke up. "Um... where exactly are we?"

"Well, we're miles under Central Australia," Bepo smiled. "Don't worry, you're quite safe. My father would like to invite you all to his place for an official dinner. He is very old but quite lucid. He will explain everything."

"I'm a skilled practitioner at serving *cha-no-yu* or hot water for tea," Charlie's mother said, adding some powdered green tea. "It's a traditional ritual influenced by 'Zen Buddhism' although, usually, we're happy with Lipton's."

"I see..." Sebastian said. He turned to Bepo. "Do you have a phone so I can call my parents?"

"A phone?" Bepo laughed. "Here? Didn't you hear what I said? We're underneath Australia."

"But we have families who are worried!" Cathy said.

"What is going on?" Yvonne whispered.

"My father will explain everything over dinner," Bepo said. "Just relax and freshen up. Please, trust me."

The group realised there wasn't much to be gained by arguing. They continued with the formal tea party and ate as many of the delicacies as they could.

After about fifteen minutes, Charlie's mother concluded the tea ceremony, and they all stood up, thanked her, and bowed, as Charlie excitedly showed them to their rooms, which were located on the other side of a large courtyard.

"Wow! This is five-star!" Yvonne said walking around the large guest room. "And look at this private courtyard, it's so beautiful," she said, admiring the *bonsai* and shaped shrubs amongst the raked pattern pebbles.

"Oh, look," Jonathan said. "A TV!" He reached for the remote control and switched it on. On the screen was a cricket match between Australia and India. No sooner had he sat down when Sebastian flung open the door.

"Jonathan! Quick!" Sebastian called out. "My room has a television! It's showing today's cricket live!" He glanced at Johnathan's TV. "Oh, you already know."

"Switch to channel 3, it's the news," Kim said entering the room. Jonathan fumbled with the remote control and soon found a news broadcast.

A reporter, standing at the base of Uluru, conversed urgently, "As we've been reporting, search parties have found no sign of the missing students from Melbourne who vanished yesterday on a walk around the base of Ayers Rock, properly known as Uluru."

"Well, this proves we're not dreaming," Jonathan said.

"Shoosh!" Cathy said. "Listen!"

"We believe a handkerchief has been found that belongs to one of the missing students," the reporter continued. Behind him were the two sticks leaning against the rock wall and Cathy's white handkerchief. "This handkerchief, with Catherine Swift's name on it, was found here. With me is the ranger from Uluru-Kata Tjuta National Park, who was first on the scene. Sir, can you tell us about these footprints?"

"Yes," the stocky ranger replied. "We're sure that these shoe prints match the shoes being worn by the missing students and the Aboriginal guide. The footsteps appear to stop at the rock and disappear, almost as if the group somehow climbed the rock."

The reporter glanced up at the rock. "But the rock wall is too steep to climb, isn't it?"

"That's correct," the ranger nodded. "And that is the mystery of it all. Now we're treating this as a possible homicide."

"We'll bring you updates from the scene when they arise," the reporter said. "In the meantime, here is the finance news…"

"Homicide?" Cathy gasped. "Our parents will be horrified!"

"There's still no network service," Kim said, glancing at the cell phone.

"Yeah, because we're underground," Sebastian said, "But the TV works, very strange."

Yvonne shrugged. "He said we're underneath Central Australia. It doesn't make sense, none of this does."

Kim glanced around the room. "Try that phone," he suggested, pointing at a telephone next to the bed.

Jonathan immediately grabbed the handset and tapped out some numbers.

"It's ringing!" he said in surprise, as everyone looked at him. A voice answered and Jonathan held his breath, his heart pounding. "Hello? Who is this?"

"Hi, it's me, Charlie."

"Oh," Jonathan said. The others looked at him eagerly. "You can only make outgoing calls to other houses around the village," Charlie explained.

"Oh, I see," Jonathan said. "Okay, thanks."

Their silence was broken by a knock on their door. Yvonne opened it to find a very old man standing there, in a well-used waistcoat over suspenders.

"Hello. I'm Wally," he said. "I'm the stockman from Alice Springs. I've been watching your story on the news just now."

"Oh," Yvonne said, shaking his hand. "Come in, I'm Yvonne Makepeace, the guide."

Jonathan stood up and shook his hand. "Nice to meet you. Bepo just told us all about you and his father, Tohru."

"Oh, did he now?" Wally muttered, sitting down. "It was his stupid decision eighty years ago that put us all down here."

"You mean to go into the tunnel like we did?" Sebastian asked.

"Yes," Wally said. "You see there is nothing wrong with this place. In fact, it's like a five-star resort, and we can get whatever we want. But there's no sun! We don't have sunshine. God I miss the sun."

Cathy poured him a cup of tea. They all sat around as he told them about life underground. "You are the first ones to come through the tunnel since we arrived here. Through no fault of your own, you may have upset the balance."

"What does that mean?" Jonathan asked.

"It means that something drastic might happen to reset the balance."

"Oh, really?" Jonathan glanced at his friends who were all looking uneasy.

"Has anyone tried to escape?" Kim finally asked.

"Escape?" Wally barked. "You don't need to escape. You can just ask to leave. And of the few thousand people living down here, several have left." His voice trailed off.

"How?" Jonathan asked.

"Well, the Hawaiians help. But then you never come back. None of them have ever been seen again. It's uncertain what happened to them."

Everyone looked at him in confusion.

"Hawaiians? What has Hawaii got to do with all of this?" Cathy asked. "I don't understand."

"Okay," Wally said. "It's like this. We have this settlement here of about a few thousand men, women, and children, Australian, Japanese, and aborigines. And we're on the banks of an enormous lake of pure water… but way over there is an island we call Hawaii."

"Are the people there friendly?" Sebastian optimistically inquired.

"'Businesslike' is how we describe them," Wally said. "And they deliver us anything we want. For example, back in 1962, we asked for television, and we all got black and white televisions."

"So you ask these businesslike Hawaiians if you want to leave, is that it?" Kim responded in puzzlement.

"Yes, exactly like that," Wally said. "And they take you to their island, and we never see you again."

Kim frowned. "Do they kill you?"

"Not as far as we can detect. We believe you go on a journey, a long journey." Wally interlocked his hands. "That's what we've been told by the Hawaiians. But where to, we don't know, and they refuse to say."

"Never to return here though?" Sebastian asked.

"That's right," Wally said, sitting on a sofa. "Nonetheless you move on. And so that's that."

Everyone sat in silence. The dingo pup suddenly leapt onto Wally's lap and made herself comfortable. The silence continued.

"So how come you have a suntan Wally if there's no sun?" Yvonne asked.

"Well, if you study the ceiling of this enormous cavern, you will notice it's made up of all types of amazing stalactites and aquamarine gems, and during the daytime they are very bright, creating daylight. When the sun sets above-ground, the stones darken, and some luminous ones twinkle like stars, creating the illusion of nighttime. Also, each house here has a solarium, which helps."

"Oh," Yvonne replied, nodding her head.

"Anyway," Wally said, getting to his feet. "Why don't you join my family for a barbecue lunch tomorrow if I'm still alive? If you think this traditional Japanese house is good, you should see ours!"

"We would love to," Sebastian said. "You look very much alive, Wally."

Chapter 6
Dinner with the Grandparents

Everyone sat quietly with their legs crossed on the tatami matting around a low wooden table. At the head of the table sat Charlie's grandfather, Tohru. He was a regal man and was dressed in a Japanese Imperial Army uniform. The low sound of *Wadaiko* drummed from the stereo, creating an air of suspense.

"I propose a toast to our Australian guests," Tohru announced, holding up a small glass of 'Sake'. "Cheers."

"Cheers," they all responded in unison, politely sipping the sake.

"Hmm… this sake tastes earthy," Sebastian said to Tohru. His wife, Charlie's grandmother sat beside him, dressed in an emerald satin Houmongi, or kimono, the fabric decorated with gold edging and ribbon.

"My son and daughter-in-law have spent all afternoon preparing this banquet," she confided to Cathy. "And Charlie wants to be the waiter."

"Your menus," Charlie announced, entering the large dining room dressed in a dinner suit. He was clutching a bundle of folders, and his hair was neatly brushed back. He grinned as he handed the menus to the guests one by one.

Tohru smiled and looked around the room. "Let me tell you a story. In March 1943, I was flying with the Zero Fighters of the Chitose Air Corps, but our mission was not to bomb Darwin. Instead, five of our fighters had tanks hanging below our planes, and we flew well into the interior of the Northern Territory and dropped them."

"Didn't the tanks get damaged when you dropped them?" Kim asked.

"No," Tohru replied, raising his eyebrows. "Some landed on their sides, and we had to roll them upright, but they landed on trees or soft red ochre sand, and they 'all' worked fine. Everyone in our large planes, except the pilots, parachuted down and joined the tanks. The planes flew back to the airbase in Papua New

Guinea, and we drove the tanks to Ayers Rock, Uluru, and all of this was done under the cover of night."

"Let our guests choose their meals," the grandmother said, interrupting him. "Charlie! Take their orders."

Charlie produced a pad and pen and stood poised at attention behind Cathy.

"Let's see," Cathy said, scanning the choices. "Um… I'll have the chicken on bamboo skewers with Yakitori sauce and spring onions, please."

Charlie scribbled away. "What will you have Jonathan, the *Tonkotsu* Noodle Soup?"

"Yes," Jonathan replied, slightly startled. "With blanched snow peas and two poached eggs, please Charlie."

"We'll have the *Maki-Zushi*, rolled sushi, please, and seaweed spread with rice," Sebastian said, ordering for him and Kim.

"Oh!" Yvonne said nervously, realising everyone was looking at her. "Um, I will have what Cathy is having."

Tohru looked at Charlie and gestured impatiently. "The usual Charlie, raw fish and Sushi-Meshi, the vinegared rice." Charlie finished scribbling into his notepad and disappeared out the door.

"Anyway," Tohru continued, "We were on a secret mission, and we had instructions directly from the emperor to capture the heart of your country… Uluru!"

He thumped his clenched fist softly on the table, shaking the sake in the glasses.

"So your convoy of five tanks made it to Uluru?" Sebastian asked.

"Yes. There was no one to stop us but a small tribe of aborigines, some Anangu people, locals." He glanced sympathetically at Yvonne, who avoided eye contact. "So we captured them without force."

"You had no resistance at all?" Kim inquired, tapping his fingers on the dinner table in time with the background beating of the Japanese drum, the Wadaiko.

"On the contrary, two truckloads of armed white people arrived on the scene. They were local stockmen and their wives, not soldiers. But they had sighted our tanks, and they knew about the bombings in Darwin. They added two and two together."

The door opened and Tohru looked around to see Wally standing there.

"Ah, Wally, I was just talking about you. Sit down, you know the story well."

Wally shuffled in and sat on a chair. He was way too old to sit cross-legged on the floor, getting up being the problem.

"What happened then?" Jonathan asked in amazement. Tohru picked up his glass of sake, glanced at Wally, gulped it down and then rolled the glass along the table.

"The full moon illuminated the night," he explained, his eyes became distant as he started to recall that night back in 1943.

The convoy of five Japanese tanks rumbled along noisily, the soldiers running behind, herding fifteen handcuffed Aboriginal prisoners. They could see the headlights of the two Australian trucks in pursuit.

"Keep close to the rock!" the commander ordered in Japanese. "We might lose them."

Behind the tanks, the first of the trucks sped up, the tires bouncing over the shrubs and trees that the tanks had flattened. The driver, a tough stockman named Wally, glanced at his wife beside him. He turned and yelled at the men standing in the back of the truck.

"Hold on tight! We're gaining on these people! Take a potshot!"

One of the men put his shotgun to his shoulder and pointed it towards the Japanese tank, the moonlight illuminating their path. He fired and a bullet pinged off the rear of the tank.

Inside the tank, the commander looked around quickly. "Tell the front two tanks to circle around behind them!" He ordered. Two tanks swerved away from the rock, snapping trees and branches in their path as they rumbled away into the darkness.

Inside the truck, Wally laughed. "This beats wild boar hunting!" He pressed harder on the gas, gaining on the Japanese tanks. He didn't notice the two tanks breaking off from the others.

The commander inside the tank was ready. "Okay. Let them have it." Suddenly, the rear tanks flipped into reverse, turning on a sixpence, rotating one hundred and ninety degrees. The tank stopped, directly facing the oncoming trucks.

Inside the truck, Wally gasped.

The Japanese commander grinned. "Fire!"

"Jump!" Wally screamed, grabbing his wife as he threw open the door, leaping out of the truck. The men and women in the back jumped off the truck, narrowly missing being blown to smithereens.

The tank fired and the truck exploded, the petrol igniting it. The fireball lit up the night, flames catching onto trees and shrubs, creating a bright glow in the immediate area.

The second truck slammed on the brakes and reversed. In the confusion, the Aboriginal prisoners broke away from the Japanese tanks, escaping the soldiers. They shuffled into the darkness, still handcuffed together. They seemed to vanish into thin air in the night shadows of Uluru.

The driver of the rear truck skidded his vehicle around, ready to flee. His eyes widened in surprise at the sight in front of him; two tanks that had broken away from the others, the truck's headlights illuminating them.

"Oh, dear," Wally, the driver whispered, glancing at his wife. "We've had it."

They clambered out, throwing their hands up in the air, and soldiers were on them in seconds. One soldier aimed his flamethrower at the truck and fired. The truck was instantly engulfed in flames, and its gas tank ignited, creating a booming explosion as another fireball lit up the night.

The commander emerged, staring at the Australians who'd jumped from their trucks. "You are all prisoners of war! We have formally taken control of Ayers Rock in the name of the emperor of Japan!"

Wally glared at the man. "Over my dead body!"

"If that's what you want," the commander yelled angrily. "Place him against the rock and prepare the firing squad!"

Wally was blindfolded and pushed to the rock face of Uluru.

The full moon and the burning trucks illuminated the commander's grinning face.

"I have a better idea," the commander announced in broken English. "I will run you through instead!" He laughed, raised his bayonet, and sprinted towards the blindfolded truck driver.

Wally shook his head, dislodging his blindfold. The moon reflected off the shiny blade of the bayonet, its sharp edge point coming towards him. At the last moment, Wally jumped out of the commander's way. He expected to hear a 'clunk' as the bayonet hit the rock.

To everyone's amazement, the Japanese commander disappeared into the rock, his body vanishing as if the rock was made of air.

The commander glanced around a cave, utterly bewildered. He had no idea what had just happened. Laughter echoed across the cave, and he glanced up at the fifteen aborigines, still handcuffed together. Confused, he fired a shot that ricocheted off the cave wall. He jumped backwards and emerged outside into the fresh air. He stared at the rock, realising he had somehow walked through it.

"What sort of rock is this?" the commander shouted. "Drive a tank into it!" There was some hesitation, and then he repeated his order. A tank turned and sped towards the rock. The commander watched in shock as the tank passed through the rock wall, disappearing inside it. The commander scratched his head and gathered his soldiers.

"Maybe this rock is hiding Australian soldiers," the commander said. "We must invade it and take them out!"

He started screaming orders, and before long, the entire convoy of tanks, Japanese soldiers, and Australian prisoners entered the rock.

Inside, they easily recaptured the aborigines. The commander found a tunnel and ordered the soldiers to follow it. The Japanese Imperial Army set off along the tunnel. On finding no end to it, they turned back, but to the commander's shock, the exit had sealed up.

In frustration, the commander butted the cave wall, but it was solid rock. They were trapped inside Uluru. Tohru finished his story and sighed.

"You were the commander!" Jonathan realised.

"Indeed, I was," Tohru nodded.

"Is this your bullet?" Jonathan asked, placing the bullet on the table. "We found it in the cave."

Tohru put on his glasses and inspected it. "Yes, that is my bullet."

He went pale, as did Wally looking on.

"So, sixty years ago, you found the same hole in the rock as we did," Jonathan said, as Charlie and his parents entered the dining room with plates of Japanese cuisine.

"Smells delicious!" Cathy exclaimed, fumbling for her chopsticks. "I'm famished."

"Enjoy!" Tohru said. "And help yourself to more sake."

As everyone began to eat, Yvonne looked up. "Did you come across a large cavern with a TV set in the middle of the tunnel?"

"Did we?" Tohru laughed. "I was driving the front tank, and I crashed into it! My tank was dented, but not a scratch on the television cube."

"Was there an aborigine playing a didgeridoo in it?" Yvonne asked.

"As a matter of fact, yes," he said. "And so we decided to release the aborigines from their chains, and they celebrated by performing a corroboree. It was quite fantastic."

"So that television cube was there sixty years ago?" Kim asked.

"Yes, and none of us had even heard of a television, let alone a television cube." Tohru continued scratching his head. "We simply thought the Australians must be an incredibly advanced nation, except our Australian prisoners of war hadn't seen one either. It was all very strange."

"And then your convoy of tanks, soldiers and prisoners, started sliding, right?" Sebastian asked.

"Indeed, we did," Tohru nodded, scooping more steamed rice onto his ceramic dish. "And we all came out where you did, except there wasn't any village, only some Aboriginal tribes."

"What?" Yvonne gasped, dropping her chopsticks. "There were Aboriginal tribes already here?"

"Yes. Apparently, they had come down the tunnel hundreds of years ago, even thousands, according to legends," the grandfather said. "And settled here. They were pleased to see the Aboriginal prisoners we freed since they were all Anangu people from the same tribe."

Recognising it was the same tribe as Yvonne's, everyone looked at her. Her smile faded and frowning, she glared at Tohru.

"So where are they now?" She demanded.

"Well, their descendants are living in huts up the other end of this village," Tohru said. "And the Australian families are there too." He sat back and smiled. "In fact, Wally here, the truck driver I tried to bayonet, lives there too. And he's over ninety years old now, like me. There are thousands down here, it's like an alternate civilisation, but our housing is all mixed around, and we all get along well."

The dinner party continued until fatigue caught up with the students and the old men, and they adjourned to their rooms.

Chapter 7
Can You Believe the TV News?

"This sake is too strong," Kim said, as he lay sprawled out on the sofa. The others laughed, taking a seat around the room and watching the television.

Jonathan had the remote control and was surfing the channels in search of the news. Charlie entered the room with a tray of coffee and after-dinner mints.

"Good man, Charlie," Cathy said eagerly. "Exactly what we need."

Charlie had a strange look on his face as he left muttering something about the two old men locked in deep discussion about the bullet they had been given.

Jonathan flipped the channel to ABC as a current affairs program started.

"The mysterious disappearance of four students and their Aboriginal guide in the Uluru-Kata Tjuta National Park has continued to grab the attention of the nation," the reporter said. "But this mystery has deeper implications. One of the students is one of Australia's most gifted students specialising in computer technology and mathematics," the reporter explained.

"That's me!" Jonathan said, sitting up abruptly. They all gazed at a recent photograph of him on TV. "I'm famous now!"

"Shut it, just listen!" Cathy snapped.

Jonathan turned up the volume of the television.

The reporter continued: "I have with me here in the Canberra studio the federal minister for telecommunications and the attorney general. But first I spoke to Jonathan's parents this afternoon. Here's what they had to say." The reporter turned to a large screen that showed him and Jonathan's parents seated together in a TV studio.

"My parents," Jonathan whispered, suddenly feeling a wave of sadness.

"Thank you for agreeing to talk to us under these unfortunate circumstances. Firstly, do you have anything you would like to say if your son Jonathan is watching?"

"Yes," Jonathan's father said, leaning forward. "Please Jonathan, please contact us if you can, any way you can. We want you home."

The reporter leaned in. "We have been told that he carried a very advanced laptop computer with him. Can you tell us anything about it?"

"Well, yes," Jonathan's dad said, adjusting his glasses. "It's modified for his specific studies. It was supplied by the government because of his exceptional talent."

The reporter nodded. "Did your son give you any indication that he might have his own plans?"

Jonathan's mother teared up. "What do you mean 'his own plans'?" She suddenly became agitated. "What are you suggesting? My son tells me everything!" She shook her head, "Most things anyway. What sort of holidays do you conduct in Central Australia? I want my son back!"

"Thank you for your time. Minister, what is your reaction to this criticism?"

The minister folded his hands. "Well, I can assure Jonathan's parents that the Northern Territory police and the rangers at Uluru-Kata Tjuta National Park are doing their best. And I can assure the public that the government is taking this very, very seriously."

"Is it true that the computer that Jonathan has with him has a GPS chip and the chip shows that the laptop is somewhere inside Uluru?"

"Now listen here!" the minister interjected angrily. "That is only hearsay and rumour."

"Well, Attorney General?"

The attorney general looked uncomfortable. "Well, if it shows such a thing, then it must be faulty equipment. Uluru is made of solid rock. No computer could be inside the rock."

Kim laughed. "But it is!"

"I mean there are some caves," he said. "But they have all been carefully explored."

The reporter nodded. "Thank you for your time. I'm sure this story has a long way to go. And now to finance. A conference of chartered accountants in Adelaide…"

Sebastian turned off the television and looked at Jonathan. "Is it true? Does your laptop have a tracking chip?"

"Yes!" Jonathan said, jumping up. "My laptop has just about everything. Oh, I hope it still works."

"Me too," Yvonne said, as they pondered their situation with mesmerising silence that was suddenly shattered by Charlie bursting back into the room.

"What have you 'caused'?" he screamed angrily, "Wally and Grandpa Tohru just had simultaneous heart attacks and are 'dead'!"

The students snapped out of their silence and scrambled after Charlie, across the courtyard and back into the dining room to find some people crouched around the bodies of the two old men lying on the floor.

A beautiful young Japanese woman stood alongside the scene with her arms crossed and looked at them. "They're dead. The last thing they told me was that 'you should move on'."

"Oh, who are you?" Jonathon asked in a confused manner, noticing her frock resembled a waterfall cascading off her body.

"I'm Asami, Charlie's gorgeous older sister," she replied.

Chapter 8
The Funeral and Aftermath

The next morning the ceiling of the enormous cavern slowly became lighter. Jonathan sat at the window of his guest room looking out at the huge lake as the others slept. The water was still as glass, dead calm.

In the distance, a hovercraft appeared, slowly moving closer, its motor quiet as it glided and then paused above a white pebble beach and hovered onto the sand. A door opened, and a group of neatly dressed men unloaded two coffins. They laid several bouquets of flowers on top of the empty coffins and carried them towards the morgue next to the hospital.

Jonathan knew they were picking up Wally's and Tohru's bodies.

The propeller on the hovercraft began spinning, and it rose above the water and powered away, disappearing over the lake.

The phone rang and Jonathan reached over and answered it.

"Hi," the man's voice said. "I'm Wally's son, Eric."

Jonathan immediately sat up. "Oh, hi."

The other kids had heard the phone ring and came into Jonathan's room.

"The funeral is this afternoon at the church in the village," Eric said. "Yourself and all your friends are invited, and I was hoping you might be able to give a reading and join us for his wake in our place?"

Charlie's mother appeared, carrying some suits and black dresses. "I hope you will attend the service today."

"Of course, we will," Kim said. He looked slightly hungover from all the sake he'd drank the night before.

"Great," Akia said. "Charlie asked around and found some villagers who looked to be your size. They said you could borrow these for the service."

"Thank you," Yvonne said. "That's very kind."

Akia smiled. "I hope they are okay."

That afternoon, the small church overflowed with villagers. Those who didn't get seats, stood outside to show their respect. Eric greeted them, thanked them for honouring his father's life, and led Jonathan and his friends to the front of the church. Wally and Tohru's coffin rested on the altar and was covered in flowers. Organ pipes reverberated a slow mournful tune.

"Everybody seems to be looking at us," Cathy whispered to Sebastian as they took their places in a pew in the second row. Yvonne chose to sit with a group of aborigines further to the side of the church.

The minister, a young man dressed in robes, spoke kindly of Wally and Tohru. The congregation sang some hymns and Jonathan gave a reading and a plate was handed around and a collection made. They all sang another hymn, and then the eulogy was recited. Finally, the two coffins were lifted onto the shoulders of eight relatives and friends of Wally and Tohru and carried slowly down the aisle and out of the church.

Sebastian and Kim remained behind. It was a traditional Christian church with colourful stained-glass windows and a statue of Christ on the crucifix on the wall. They noticed a half-open door leading to a small room and peered inside to see a group of villagers counting the money from the collection.

"It looks like they keep detailed books," Kim whispered. He pointed at a long table covered with books, ledgers, and calculators.

The villagers were gleefully filling in all the figures in precise detail, and one of them glanced up to see Sebastian and Kim watching them.

"We love getting all the books to balance exactly," the man smiled.

"Does it require such major bookkeeping?" Kim asked.

"Yes! Of course!" he said, mildly annoyed. "We were sent from the island."

"Oh, okay," Kim said, realising he and Sebastian were intruding on them.

"Keep up the good accounting," Sebastian said with an uneasy smile.

The funeral procession meandered quietly through the village and up to the immaculately kept cemetery. A lot of the headstones had Japanese calligraphy on them. All the villagers who had passed on seemed to be buried in one cemetery.

"This view is so picturesque," Jonathan whispered to Cathy. She was smiling at a few Japanese students who were staring at them. Cathy waved and walked over to the group.

As the minister recited the last rites, Wally and Tohru's coffins were lowered into their respective graves, while family members threw some flowers onto the coffin and wiped the tears from their eyes.

Asami appeared next to Jonathan. "We met last night, and I was wondering if I could show you around our university."

"Yes, of course, I would be delighted," Jonathan whispered. It hadn't occurred to him that this village would have an actual university.

The burial service finished and all those present ambled away as the gravedigger shovelled dirt into the graves, which were next to each other. The Australian contingent, along with Sebastian, Kim, and Cathy, made their way to Wally's house where the wake was to be held.

Yvonne wandered off with the aborigines as they had their own traditional burial ceremonies planned, and the Japanese had their own wake for Tohru.

Asami and Jonathan strolled along towards the deserted university campus. Asami was extremely attractive and very fit looking. It occurred to him that for someone who was lost and unable to return home, he found himself in the presence of several attractive women, Cathy, Yvonne, and now Asami. Things could be worse, he thought.

"We closed the university today because of the funeral," she explained. "You know, if it wasn't for my grandfather's misguided patriotism, we wouldn't all be stuck somewhere way under the Northern Territory. I'm ready to get out of here. I would like to see the surface of the world I've read so much about. and seen it all on TV."

"So would I," Jonathan said with a laugh. "It's nice here, but I'm missing the real world. I mean the surface of the world, and we only got here yesterday."

Before long, they reached some modern buildings and Asami showed Jonathan a few of the small lecture theatres. They stopped in the library.

"This is certainly a comprehensive library," Jonathan said, reaching for a book in the science fiction section. "May I borrow this one?"

"Yes, of course. I'll just stamp it at the desk," Asami said, writing down the book title and Jonathan's name. She peered over at the cover. *Journey to the Centre of the Earth* by Jules Verne. She looked curiously at Jonathan. "I'm majoring in space exploration and water art installations here."

An interesting choice, Jonathan thought to himself, for someone who had never even seen the real sky.

They left the library and strolled into a large courtyard that was filled with plum trees in full bloom, the pink blossoms so sweet smelling. A mesh hung above the trees, and a fine rain sprinkled through it, dampening their formal clothes.

"Welcome to The Secret Garden," Asami said, as she led the way to a square water sculpture where a thin sheet of water cascaded off the sides. "This is the most secluded spot we have," she said proudly. "And it can only be used by the students."

"It looks like a double bed!" Jonathan smiled, looking at the sculpture.

"Yes, that's what the sculptor imagined, who was I," she replied proudly. A dense fog emerged from the overhead mesh. "And various climates encase this space." Soon the misty fog became so condensed that they could barely see each other.

"I suppose you don't get any change in the weather down here," Jonathan said. He couldn't see her at all now and heard only the sound of dripping water.

"Well, I actually study climate change also," Asami said. "And I created this installation to control the temperature in the garden."

A few minutes later the fog began to dissipate slightly revealing Asami through the mist.

"Do you know how we can get out of here?" Jonathan asked her.

"That's why I brought you here. I wanted to talk to you in strict privacy," Asami said. "I know how we can leave."

"How?" Jonathan asked.

"I've been thinking about it for a while, but after what happened with Wally and Tohru, now I know it's time to go. I can take you to Hawaii," Asami said. "I have a hovercraft that can take us there."

"Really?" Jonathan asked. "You know you might be leaving for good."

"Yes, I know. No one who has left has ever returned, including my dear aunt, many years ago," Asami said, gazing into Jonathon's eyes, "But I'm bored, every day is started, and nothing begins," she explained. For no apparent reason, they started undressing each other.

"I understand," Jonathon whispered, as a warm thick fog surrounded them, "It's a mood of diffuse restlessness, which contains the most absurd and paradoxical wish; the wish for desire…"

They climbed onto the double bed and pulled a sheet of water over themselves. "This is like linen," Jonathan said in a whisper.

"My name means 'beautiful linen', actually," Asami conveyed in a sensuous whisper, "and having designed this brilliant double bed as a water sculpture, I'm moist…"

"Well, I've never made love so deep in the earth's surface," Jonathan sighed.

On the outskirts of the village far below the sparkling stones, the *Anangu* tribesmen danced around a large fire. Yvonne sat with the aborigines, both exhausted and exhilarated by the traditional ceremony of mourning. She stared into the flames of the fire as the tribe burnt some of Wally's clothes.

The sound of the didgeridoo and the wood sticks clacking echoed out over the calm lake. She was sitting beside the eldest aborigine. He was too old to dance but enjoyed telling Yvonne his life stories.

"I was 16 years old when Japanese soldiers captured me," he said. He used a stick to draw a long snake in the sand. "And I thought they must be ancestral spirits because when we escaped along the side of Uluru, it opened up, and we went into the rock."

"Has that ever happened before?" Yvonne inquired.

"No, not in my lifetime," he said. "But a Dreamtime story told of a huge snake that was so big that the Pitjantjatjara and Yankunytjatjara people walked inside of it, not knowing it was a snake." He ran the stick down the middle of the snake. "And they never came out."

"Maybe this story was about the original aborigines who found the tunnel?" Yvonne suggested.

"Yes, I believe that is true." He pointed his stick at the mouth of the tunnel on the other side of the village. "Because when we slid down the long tunnel and came out here, there was nothing here but a tribe of aborigines who told us they had lived down here for as long as they could remember."

"But they were Anangu people?" she asked.

"Yes, and they were pleased to see us," the elder said, happily. "Because we gave them new ideas. And made their lives more interesting."

"Did you miss your life around Uluru?" Yvonne inquired.

"Yes, especially my wife who was pregnant. So I never got to see my baby because of the soldiers," he said, stabbing the snake with his stick in the sand.

"What's your name?" she asked.

"John Makepeace."

"Really?" Yvonne said in surprise. "Because 'my' name is Makepeace, Yvonne Makepeace. So maybe you are my great-grandfather!"

The old man was silent for a moment. A few other aborigines sitting nearby looked over at them.

"My wife must have had a boy then," the elder said looking into Yvonne's eyes.

"Do you remember that elder playing the didgeridoo on the television when you first went into the tunnel?" Yvonne asked.

"Do I? The tank smacked into it!" the elder laughed gruffly. "And do you know who that elder was?"

"Who?" she asked.

"My great-grandfather! I recognised the inscriptions on the didgeridoo," the elder said. "It said Makepeace!"

At this point, all the aborigines started laughing and resumed their dancing. Yvonne pondered the whole story, and then her mind drifted to the responsibility she felt towards the students. She was supposed to be their guide, but she was becoming too curious about this place. But how could she be their guide when she knew nothing more about this place than any of the students? She wondered.

Everything seemed pleasant enough here. They were treated almost as if they were honoured guests, but she realised they were all ignoring the obvious; they couldn't stay here. They had to get out and the sooner the better.

Chapter 9
Waterskiing Behind the Hovercraft

Kim's snoring didn't help Sebastian's hangover. He'd drank way too much at the funeral wake in honour of Wally. The sudden knocking on the door made him groan.

"Sebastian, are you asleep?" Jonathan whispered, peeking into the room.

"What?" Sebastian asked. "What time is it?"

"Six am, and I have a hovercraft," Jonathan whispered.

"What?" Kim interjected, also waking up.

"I made a new friend yesterday," Jonathan said proudly. "Her name is Asami, and she's Charlie's older sister. She's got the use of the hovercraft and is taking us on a tour of the lake. Now get up!" he said excitedly. "And then, if we decide to, we can take the hovercraft and go to Hawaii!"

Before long, the traditional Japanese breakfast ceremony was underway. Everyone shared in conversation as soft-boiled eggs and crispy tempura were passed around.

"How deep is this lake?" Jonathan inquired, scooping up some Maki-Zushi, rolled sushi, and spread seaweed.

"Very deep," Asami replied. "But as far as we know it's quite safe. No monsters," she assured, giving him a mild smirk, "at least not that I've seen."

Charlie bounded into the dining room and switched on the television. "There's something about you all on the morning news." They all turned to watch and saw the same reporter they'd seen earlier.

"Hopes are fading for the four Melbourne students and their guide who went missing under mysterious circumstances a few days ago in the Uluru-Kata Tjuta National Park. And in further developments, the parents of the Melbourne students have mounted their own search party in a desperate hope to find their missing children."

As they watched their parents climbing out of a convoy of land rovers outside Uluru, everyone looked at each other in shock. Sebastian's father appeared on the screen looking calm but concerned.

"I know that the rangers and Northern Territory police are doing their best," he said into the camera, as he looked up at the rock. "But we're also going to start searching. I flew here from Los Angeles. I want to find my son."

"There won't be room to move around Uluru," Yvonne responded.

The TV switched back to the reporter. "Rumours and gossip are rife throughout Australia after it was revealed that a bus load of Japanese tourists saw the missing kids after their bus hit a dingo on the road next to Uluru. Multiple tourists recognised photos of the missing students. They might have been the last people to see the students. I have the driver of the tour bus here who has agreed to talk about what happened. He is here again at Uluru with another tour group."

The reporter turned to the driver. "You claim a dingo ran out in front of your bus?"

"Yes. I swerved to miss it, but it changed direction, and I couldn't avoid it," he said. The camera followed him into the scrub next to the road. "And here is the dead dingo right here," the driver said, pointing to the ground. The camera panned down to see the bloodied dingo lying on its side.

Zara, the dingo pup, looked up at the TV and gave a mournful yelp.

"Oh, you are a poor little darling," Cathy cried in sympathy, picking up Zara and stroking her tenderly.

"And what about the students? Where were they?"

"On the side of the road. They were concerned about the dingo. That's the last I saw of them."

"So there we have it," the reporter said. "A classic Australian drama of four missing students and a dead dingo. And now to other news; bookkeepers in Brisbane have threatened to walk out…"

"Oh, switch it off!" Cathy demanded. "I can't see how they'll find the entrance to the tunnel if it's solid rock now."

"If only we could send a message to our parents somehow," Kim said, looking at Jonathan. They all turned to him.

"Well, don't look at me!" Jonathan protested. "My laptop has the GPS tracker, but I don't know what else to do. I've tried everything I can."

Sebastian balanced knee-deep in the lake's crystal-clear water, his feet strapped into the water skis, the tow rope in his hand. The rope was connected to the rear of the hovercraft. Asami sat in the driver's seat of the craft with everyone else on board and their backpacks.

"Okay!" Sebastian called. "I'm ready!"

Asami pushed the throttle forward and the hovercraft powered away. The tow rope tightened, and Sebastian allowed the rope to pull him out of the water as he found his balance on the water skis and began to glide across the surface of the lake.

Asami smiled at everyone and called out: "One of the redeeming features of life down here in this enormous cavern is we always have a great time!"

The dingo pup sat contentedly on the front of the hovercraft with her tiny ears blown back by the breeze from the speed of the craft.

The village was soon a dot on the horizon. Sebastian released the tow rope and slid into the water. Asami spun the hovercraft around and picked him up. After they all took turns on the water skis, Asami turned off the propeller, and they sat around the hovercraft as it floated listlessly on the flat, expansive lake.

"I guess you never realised there was such a huge body of water under the surface of Australia," Asami said. "It's perfectly safe."

She stood up, and Jonathan finally got a good look at the bikini she was wearing. It wasn't only how well the bikini defined her shapely body that caught his attention, it was the fact that it was made from a mirror-like material that reflected the light and continually glittered, and he wasn't the only one who noticed. Sebastian moved closer to Asami and tried to use her bikini top like a mirror. "I didn't realise my hair was so messed up."

She placed a hand on his forehead, pushed him away and then dived over the side of the craft. She bobbed up smiling. Then everyone dived in after her.

"How does your bathing suit look like that?" Sebastian asked. "That's so cool."

"I'm a conceptual artist," Asami replied.

He grinned. "So you study climate change and space exploration, and you're an artist. Is there anything you don't do?"

"Are you quite certain this water is safe?" Kim asked, treading water nervously. "I mean we can't even see the bottom of this lake…"

"Look, in all the time here, we've never had a problem," Asami reassured them, swimming further away from the hovercraft. Some dolphins emerged from the water in graceful unison. The pup started barking. Suddenly a huge blue whale broke the surface of the still water only metres away.

"Get out!" Kim yelled, thrashing around in terror. The whale slapped its tail against the surface, splashing them before disappearing.

"Asami! It 'is' dangerous!" Sebastian called out.

"Relax. It's friendly," she smiled, calmly paddling around.

"That's unreal," Sebastian responded in disbelief.

"The whale can sing," Asami said.

"Well, yes," Jonathan said. "Whales do sing."

"Not like the way you're thinking," she announced with laughter.

The blue whale emerged again, but this time it opened its enormous mouth and sang, *To Dream the Impossible Dream*... in a perfect male tenor voice. Several dolphins also emerged singing harmony. They all dipped back under the surface, leaving the group shocked.

"Now I've really seen everything!" Cathy said, swimming back to the hovercraft as Asami burst out laughing. Everyone clambered back on board, half fascinated, and half terrified by what they had just witnessed.

"There's nothing to be afraid of," She said as her mirror bikini dripped water. "We can get anything from Hawaii, and we ordered a whale and dolphins that can sing."

After this strange encounter, the conversation quickly turned into a heated argument.

"It's your fault Jonathan for going into the rock in the first place!" Cathy shouted.

"My fault?" Jonathan snapped. "You found the hole!"

"Look, it's no one's fault," Sebastian said. "The point is we're here, now!"

"You can talk!" Cathy yelled back at Sebastian. "You're the idiot who talked us out of climbing the rock."

"She's right Sebastian," Kim said. "If we had just gone with the normal tour, we wouldn't be in this mess to begin with."

"Well, it's not a mess," Asami quickly interjected. "It's a paradise."

"But we're stuck here," Cathy cried, cuddling the dingo pup. "And we can't contact our parents and they're worried about us!"

"Yeah," Jonathan agreed. "What sort of place is a paradise you can't leave?"

"We talked about this, Jonathan. You can leave," Asami said. "You can go to the island of Hawaii."

"But then what?" Cathy snapped. "You said no one ever comes back! Didn't you!"

"That's only a problem if you want to come back," Asami said and smiled.

"The issue is what happens after we get to the island," Jonathan said.

"Look, why don't we go there now?" Kim suggested, looking at everyone as they thought for a moment in silence. Zara began wagging her tail.

"Yeah! Why not?" Jonathan said.

"Are you sure it's safe?" Cathy asked Asami.

"Yes! It's safe!" she replied, avoiding eye contact. "Especially if you're a chartered accountant."

"A chartered accountant?" Jonathan laughed loudly.

"So how long will it take us to get to this island?" Sebastian asked, ignoring Asami's strange comment.

"A few hours at full speed," she replied.

"Okay then, let's go!" Jonathan said. Everyone agreed, but they went quiet with nervous tension.

Asami climbed into the driver's seat of the boat and turned on the ignition. The large propeller began whizzing around, and in a matter of seconds, the hovercraft was speeding across the dead-calm surface of the lake, headed towards the island of Hawaii. It wasn't long before the village vanished from sight behind them.

Chapter 10
Hawaii

After a couple of hours of speeding across the great lake, the cavern began to change, the ceiling seemed brighter almost as if it was glowing, and the lake now appeared like a vast ocean, As they continued, Jonathan drifted off, half-asleep, to the drone of the engine and the ride was long and monotonous with nothing to see but the endless blue waters, and it reminded Jonathan of a desert, a wet one.

He awoke sometime later when Sebastian shouted over the engine noise. "I can see an island."

"Yep. That's it, I guess," Asami replied.

It was massive and beautiful, covered in palm trees, hotels and villas and a ring of golden sand surrounding it.

"If it wasn't for the rock ceiling high above us, we could be in the South Pacific," Jonathan said.

As they got closer to the island, they could see people lying on the beaches and swimming by the shore and Yvonne leaned over the edge of the hovercraft and watched as sea turtles slid through the turquoise water.

"It looks like we're getting the official welcome," Asami noticed.

The hovercraft slowed as it approached the beach where a group of Polynesian women in grass skirts smiled a warm aloha and held colourful leis of fresh flowers.

As everyone stepped off the hovercraft onto the beach, the women placed the leis around their necks and a middle-aged man in a white suit held out his hand.

"Hello. Welcome to our island, I'm Stan," he smiled. "You must be Jonathan."

"Yes," Jonathan replied, slightly taken aback. "How did you know?"

"I've watched your story unfold on TV," Stan said. "You've all been on quite an adventure."

"Look over there," Kim whispered to the others. "There's an escalator on the beach!"

They all looked over and saw the strangest sight. Two escalators were going into the sand. On one side, people were descending onto the beach, disappearing under the surface, and on the other side, people were emerging from the sand.

Asami looked at the escalators. "That's weird. I don't know anything about that."

"Where does it go," Jonathan wondered.

When they started walking up the beach, the dingo pup yelped from the deck of the hovercraft. Cathy strolled back to pick her up, but before she could grab the pup, the dingo leapt off the hovercraft and scurried up the beach, disappearing down the escalator.

Cathy sprinted after Zara.

"Stop! You can't go there!" Stan yelled at Cathy, but she didn't stop.

She stepped onto the escalator and began running down after the pup.

"Zara! Here girl," Cathy called and grabbed the pup at the base of the escalator. "Got you!"

Jonathan bounded down the escalator joining Cathy. "Oh, good, you got her. Let's go back up," he said, breathlessly, stepping onto the ascending escalator.

As they went up, Jonathan looked over the edge of the escalator, and his eyes widened in disbelief.

"What's wrong?" Cathy asked, cradling Zara as she glanced over the edge. "Oh…"

Cathy grabbed her camera and snapped a photo as they reached the top and stepped off the escalator back onto the beach.

"I'm glad to see that you got your puppy back," Stan said, gesturing towards the nearby hotel. "We have a special luau prepared for you all. May we proceed?"

"Yes, of course," Jonathan said. "This dingo pup has a mind of its own,"

"What is a luau?" Cathy asked Sebastian under her breath.

"It's a party that can go on for weeks," he said, leading the group into the lobby of the hotel and into an elevator.

"I thought you might like to freshen up before dinner," Stan said. They took the elevator to the top floor and stepped inside a beautiful apartment.

"We've given you all the penthouse suite," Stan said. "Make yourselves at home, and I'll see you downstairs at eight." The elevator doors closed, leaving the six of them alone.

"Look at this!" Cathy said, showing them the photo, she took from the escalator. They all crowded around her and stared in amazement.

"It looks like escalators in a department store," Sebastian said. "Except it's endless."

"Connect your digital camera to my screen," Jonathan said, grabbing the laptop. Within seconds, they had the photograph displayed on the laptop screen.

"How can there be so many escalators?" Sebastian pondered aloud. "That must go down forty floors."

Jonathan tapped some keys on his laptop and some numbers appeared.

"Not forty floors… it goes down over four hundred and fifty floors below the beach," he announced.

"What sort of island is this?" Yvonne asked, glancing around the suite.

The penthouse was vast and luxurious with opulent furniture and upscale appliances. Four plush bedrooms opened off the large living area, and each one had magnificent white marble bathrooms with gold fittings and a panoramic view of the beach below.

"Hey, check this out," Jonathan called out, stepping into another room.

A large table with ten armchairs filled the middle of the room. There was a lectern, screens of various kinds, and a bar, and at one end was a huge television screen that covered the entire wall. Kim picked up the remote control and fumbled around with the buttons until it flickered on.

"It's my mother!" Jonathan said in surprise. The TV showed a close-up shot of Jonathan's mom at a press conference at an indoor site. Some of the student's parents were seated behind a long table cluttered with microphones and tape recorders.

"This is a special program coming live from Uluru-Kata Tjuta National Park," the compere said. "We're conducting a live press conference here with the missing student's parents. Any questions?"

"My question is directed to Professor Strong," a reporter said. "Now that you've witnessed the search in progress, are you satisfied that everything possible has been done?"

"Yes, it's been very thorough," Kim's father said.

"But I am told that one student, Sebastian, has his teacher's backpack?" the reporter asked.

"That's right," Sebastian's mom said, with an American accent, "And it contains various navigational instruments and compasses that the tour guide wanted to show his students on top of Uluru."

"And doesn't Jonathan's laptop show they are 'inside Uluru'?"

The police officer took the mic. "Well, this is only rumour and hearsay. The laptop can't be detected at all now."

Jonathan's mom took the mic. "It's not a rumour. This is true! The government is being secretive about this, tracking devices on my son's laptop shows this, they are somehow inside the rock, and we believe they are still there."

"Take it easy, ma'am," the police officer warned.

The reporters in the crowd began shouting out questions at the same time.

Jonathan's mom stood up. "Our children are inside the rock!" she repeated, banging her hand on the table. The other parents started nodding in support.

"Wow! Your mom doesn't muck around!" Yvonne said, looking at Jonathan.

The camera cut away from the press conference and Sebastian flicked off the TV and looked at Yvonne.

"So, Yvonne, do you think your elders will allow them to start drilling holes into Uluru in search of a tunnel?"

"As if…" Yvonne replied, rolling back her eyes. Everyone became quiet.

"What should we do?" Sebastian asked, strumming his fingers on the varnished wooden surface of the table.

"Well, let's think about this," Cathy said. "We're not dead… yet, and all of this seems real."

Kim looked at them. "I think we should all go down the escalator together and see what's there."

Asami looked at them. "I suspect once we go down there. We can't get out."

"But I did," Cathy said. "I went down, and I came back out."

"I know, but you only scratched the surface," Asami responded. "Jonathan said there must be four hundred and fifty floors down there."

"I agree with Kim," Sebastian interjected. "We should go down the escalator."

"Well, when and how?" Jonathan asked.

"Tomorrow," Sebastian said. "But let's go to this dinner tonight. We might learn something more."

"But we can't let them know what we're planning," Asami warned. "All of us in our village knew about the island, but we didn't know about the escalators. We all just thought this was an island called Hawaii."

Cathy nodded, hugging the dingo pup closer to her chest. "We don't want to bite the hand that feeds us."

Chapter 11
Kalua Pig from the Irnu

"Welcome to 'House of the Sun'," said Stan warmly as the students stepped out of the elevator and into the restaurant. "This is the crème de la crème of restaurants here in Hawaii," he said, smiling proudly.

"We've spent half the day water skiing, so we're quite hungry actually," Sebastian replied. "This place looks great," he said politely as waiters handed them all glasses of champagne.

The restaurant was crowded and noisy. A Tahitian rumba band played on stage, and Polynesian belly dancers were twisting and gyrating in their grass skirts as torches illuminated the central stage, giving the dance floor a bright reddish-yellow hue.

"This restaurant is designed around a volcanic crater," Stan explained, ducking quickly as a fire blower blew a blast of flames above the diners. "So it's quite a hot place," he laughed. "Anyway, help yourself to the buffet when you're ready."

They drifted away in different directions to enjoy the atmosphere and entertainment. The lighting was low and moody, and the long buffet table was covered with salads, appetisers, and entrees, as tall candles at either end of the buffet illuminated pineapple sculptures.

Sebastian did a double take as he spotted Jonathan seated in a private compartment with two Polynesians and a third woman joined them with a tray of food.

"You'll love this savoury Kalua pig," one woman said to Jonathan, as he grappled with tongs to place some on his plate. "It's roasted in an underground oven called an Irnu."

The four of them reclined comfortably into large colourful cushions around a bamboo table, as red, yellow, and orange lanterns cast light into the dimly lit compartment.

In a brighter area, Sebastian, Yvonne and Cathy were seated with some couples they had never met, and after some small talk, Sebastian began to subtly inquire about matters he and the others didn't understand. He had overheard people discussing that the escalators lead to different departments.

"Which department do you work in below?" he asked the man, casually avoiding eye contact with the conservatively dressed stranger.

"I'm just in filing and records," the man replied. "But after this holiday, I'll move up forty floors to auditing. What about you?"

Sebastian froze for a moment, since he was speaking blindly and didn't want to reveal he wasn't from the island. "Oh. I'm in cash flow," he replied nonchalantly.

"Cash flow?" the stranger asked quizzically.

Cathy glanced at Sebastian, picking up on his lie.

"Cash flow and financial advising," Cathy interjected.

"Ah… I see!" the stranger replied. "That is many floors below my department. Anyway, there are so many people working below," he continued. "And I like that everyone is dressed the same no matter the level of importance of your job."

"Yes, we are all important in our own way and that's reflected in our dress code," Sebastian said, hoping he was right, and he was relieved when the man solemnly nodded.

The three students glanced at each other and sipped on their glasses of champagne. The music picked up, and they glanced up at the fire dancer on the stage.

"Would you excuse us while we dance?" Sebastian asked, offering Yvonne a hand as they strolled onto the dance floor. Cathy also excused herself to the restroom but noticed Kim and Asami exploding around the dance floor performing flawless Latin dancing, a mix of Cha Cha, Samba and Rumba, so Cathy rushed over through other gyrating dancers and broke them up. "What the hell are you doing, everyone is looking at you!"

"But I'm a gifted Latin dancer," Asami replied breathlessly.

"We have to be low key," Cathy pleaded loudly over the music and drums. "Listen, Kim, you dumb idiot," Cathy said gripping Kim by the back of his neck, go to a quiet table with Asami and suck on Blue Hawaiian Cocktail; vodka, blue curacao, and milk out of a local coconut, or do ballroom dancing, as the two switched styles. "Sorry, Asami, I know you mean well," Cathy consoled her, and headed for the women's bathroom.

"This is such an exotic place," Yvonne said to Sebastian as they weaved their way around the crowded dance floor. "Where's Jonathan going?" she whispered, gesturing over his shoulder. He glanced around to see Jonathan entering the elevator with the three Polynesians in grass skirts, he had been sitting with.

"Looks like he's making the most of the Aloha Mai Tai greeting!" Sebastian laughed.

The women's restroom was the most luxurious bathroom Cathy had ever seen. As she walked in, two women were powdering their noses in front of a large mirror, lost in conversation.

"You mean you really got the promotion? Wow!" one woman said.

"Yeah! I've been working so hard in the auditing department, so it finally paid dividends," the second woman replied excitedly. "I take the train in a few days after my holiday finishes here."

"Congratulations! I'll leave you some of my mirror lipstick at the front desk."

"Really? Thank you so much! That's a first-class ticket!"

"What is your room number?"

"Room 230. Thanks so much. I can't wait to show it off on the ground floor station," the other woman replied. They both laughed and left the restroom, leaving Cathy wondering what they had been talking about. She'd never heard of mirror lipstick. And what train were they referring to?

After dinner and dancing, the six students all returned to the penthouse suite and sat around a large coffee table. Behind them, a wide window overlooked the sandy beach as they eagerly exchanged pieces of information they had gathered from the party.

"I found out that the ground floor beneath the escalators is a railway station," Cathy said, serving everyone coffee.

Kim looked at her in surprise. "Do you mean that there's a train four hundred and fifty flights down below this island?"

"I guess so," Cathy said.

"Well, Yvonne and I chatted with some of the other guests," Jonathan said, lowering his voice. "And it seems everyone at the party has some type of job in finance."

"I found out much the same thing," Cathy said glancing at Asami.

"Don't look at me!" Asami laughed. "I told you they were all a bunch of chartered accountants. It's been common knowledge for years around the village," she said.

"Yeah, but we didn't know what you really meant by that," Sebastian said.

"They dress like accountants," Kim chimed in.

"Speaking of which, look what I've got for you all." Jonathan stood up, and he walked into his room and returned with several fawn-coloured suits and dresses.

"How did you get these?" Kim asked, examining the outfits as Jonathan tried on a coat.

"It's not what you know, but whom," Jonathan replied proudly, as he also produced six smart fawn briefcases and satchels.

Sebastian smirked. "You got these from the Polynesian women, didn't you? We saw you get in the elevator with them."

Jonathan blushed. "I have no idea what you're talking about," he lied. "But, if we put those suits on in the morning and keep up a businesslike demeanour, I bet we can blend in and ride the elevator down to the train station."

"Stan said we can't ride the elevators," Yvonne said.

"Yeah," Jonathan said. "But if Stan doesn't recognise us, how will he know we're going?"

"Maybe below the island is some sort of giant, secret multinational organisation," Kim theorised.

Cathy jumped up. "What if the train could take us back to the surface?"

Jonathan shrugged. "Anything is possible."

"I guess it's feasible," Sebastian said.

"Well, I for one don't want to spend the rest of my life in the village," Asami said. "I'd rather keep going and find out what else there is."

"I agree," Yvonne said. "Even though I've already accepted that I'm probably going to lose my job as a tour guide," she sighed.

Sebastian and Jonathan looked out the large window, peering up at the cavern's ceiling hundreds of metres above them. The luminous rocks sparkled like stars, mimicking the night sky. On the beach below, they could see partygoers riding the escalators up and down, disappearing into or arriving from somewhere among the four hundred and fifty floors.

Jonathan looked at Sebastian. "No one will know we're just tourists. We can hop on the escalator, ride it down and catch the train, it must work."

Sebastian nodded. "Hey, we've got nothing to lose."

Kim nodded in agreement. "Let's fill in our breakfast menus for, say, 9:30. That way it won't look suspicious to Stan if he's keeping track of our activities."

"Guess we're going to work tomorrow," Cathy grinned, wondering if she'd be able to get herself a pair of mirror lipstick somewhere along the way.

Chapter 12
Going Down

Yvonne was the first person to wake up the next morning, and she walked into the main room and knocked quietly on the bedroom doors.

Everyone showered and put on their fawn suits and dresses, and packed their belongings into the briefcases and satchels, and since they planned to skip the hotel breakfast, they also added sandwiches and fruit from the hotel fridge.

"Okay, we all need to just stay calm and act natural," Jonathan instructed them before leaving the room. "Think like businesspeople, and stick to our plan," he said, pressing the button for the elevator.

The doors opened and a man in a luminous blue suit and matching cap smiled, assuming he was there to give them a tour around the island, their hearts skipped a collective beat. On closer inspection, they realised he was holding a spray can and polishing rag. He was just a friendly hotel janitor.

"Off to work early then?" he asked.

"Yep," Jonathan said, matching his cheerful tone. "Just another day on the grind," he said, leading the group into the elevator and pressing the button for the hotel lobby.

The doors closed, and they all stood in silence as the elevator began to descend. The door opened on the ground floor and the hotel lobby was empty except for another janitor who was manoeuvring a bulky floor cleaner, the machine's hum echoing through the vast space.

"Have a good day," Kim said to the janitor. The man returned the sentiment and continued polishing the floor. The group strolled confidently through the lobby and out the rotating doors, stepping onto the beach.

"Just one minute," Cathy said. She turned around and strolled briskly back into the lobby. The others looked around uneasily.

Cathy approached the long hotel counter, and the attendant greeted her with a smile. "I have a parcel to pick up, please," Cathy said confidently. "Room 230," she said, remembering the room number the woman in the bathroom had said.

"Yes, of course." The young man turned around and scanned the small compartments with his finger and located 230. He pulled out a small parcel and gave it to Cathy. She placed it in her satchel, slipping it beside Zara, but the dingo pup gave a small yelp, so Cathy coughed to try to cover the sound. The young man didn't seem to notice as he smiled, and Cathy turned around and walked back to meet the others.

Kim was gazing at the cavern ceiling as the colour started to lighten.

"Did you forget something?" Jonathan asked Cathy.

"I'll tell you later," Cathy whispered. "Let's go." There was a mix of nerves and anticipation as they left the hotel and strolled along the beach towards the escalator, forcing themselves to walk slowly, so they didn't draw attention to themselves. The beach was deserted except for a couple of cleaners in the distance who were raking the sand.

Once they reached the start of the escalator, they didn't hesitate, one by one, they stepped on and began descending and as they started to sink below the sand, artificial light illuminated their path. They held their breath, wondering if an alarm would sound, but nothing happened. It was surprisingly silent. Jonathan couldn't resist the temptation and took a quick glimpse over the side of the moving handrail.

"Seeing is believing!" he gasped. "It's amazing. I can't even see where the escalators end!"

Everyone else glanced over the side, whispering in amazement. Kim, who had a slight fear of heights, gripped the handrail tightly.

"So far so good," Jonathan said as they reached the end of the first escalator. They stepped onto a platform and back onto the next escalator. He fell silent as he spotted a few businessmen ascending the escalator next to them.

As they passed, Jonathan gave a polite nod, and the men returned the gesture and carried on with their conversation. They continued, each elevator going deeper into the earth, the artificial light became brighter as they descended. Occasionally, they passed sealed doors or shuttered windows. On one escalator, however, they began to hear the ambient murmurs of a crowd and the clatter of cutlery, like a cafeteria.

"This must be where everyone has breakfast before work," Cathy mentioned, as the escalator descended, passing a huge dining area where a few hundred people sat and ate.

The same scene went on for several floors, and they estimated they saw over a thousand people enjoying breakfast and the escalators became busier as workers stepped on and off at different levels.

Everyone was dressed the same, with clothes that matched identically. After a while, the floors transitioned into open workspaces with office partitions. Hundreds of people typed away at computer screens, the buzz of activity a blur of conversation that went on for about fifty floors and the art was amazing.

"Nothing seems to exist in isolation down here," Sebastian observed, "Everything seems entwined for some reason."

"Isn't that odd? As we go deeper, we see accountants going back in time. The computers have disappeared, now they are using calculators, and look, the art has become like Pop-Art, Minimalism, Photorealism..." Cathy observed, sneaking some photographs, as their journey down the escalators continued.

Soon the floors became more surreal, and the calculators began to disappear replaced by notebooks with people scribbling down numbers and comparing charts, and further away they could see large glass lifts going up and down.

"Maybe we could speed up our journey below in one of those lifts," Kim suggested. They all agreed, stepped off the escalator and strolled nonchalantly along to the large lift area. Jonathon pressed a button and a lift stopped opposite and the glass doors whizzed open, and they stepped inside and pressed 'ground floor'.

This was much faster as they descended and noticed more changes; they gazed at various people scratching figures onto papyrus, and they sailed past Impressionism, Post-Impressionism watching people working around Van Gogh masterpieces and musicians joined them. Sebastian suddenly pressed the stop button and the lift halted.

"We must stop to appreciate this," Sebastian demanded folding his arms in defiance. The lift doors opened, and they walked out into these offices and wandered around. No one seemed to notice them. They blended in. "If we do not stop to appreciate this beauty, listen to the best musicians, and witness the best art, how many other things are we missing out on?" he asked, almost pleading.

They had more time to absorb what they were seeing and then stepped back onto an escalator and continued down and realised they had reached the

Renaissance era and admired the frescoes and the fashion sense of the accountants and were joined by another person, so Cathy decided to make some conversation so no one would become suspicious.

"You're all accountants here?" Cathy enquired politely.

"We are not just accountants," the man snapped back as he shook his abacus. "We are also bureaucrats."

"Oh, what's your name?"

"It's Laud Melodrama."

"That's a funny name for a bureaucrat really," Cathy replied as the others became interested in the exchange.

"Not really. My parents here are all Melodramas, and we're very proud of our heritage. We go back hundreds of years here, blocking things, being difficult and generally making life unbearable for accountants," he said, smiling at the other students and pleased with his new audience.

They all turned around to look at some commotion unfolding further over where people were pushing and shoving each other.

"Ah," Melodrama said with an air of authority, "this is where I depart. It's why I came down here to sort out this scuffle between accountants and bureaucrats. It happens quite often. Good day." He covered his mouth as he laughed, then took his hand away revealing a sneer and then stepped off the escalator and briskly entered the fray separating the jostling groups.

Meanwhile, the students continued their descent, admiring the art. Kim, knowledgeable on these matters, became their guide, "The Renaissance era is possibly one of the most well-known, with Michelangelo, Leonardo da Vinci, and so on."

"Bureaucrats or accountants?" Yvonne enquired. Then they were surprised to see some most beautiful marble sculptures amongst the tables full of people working away.

"The eternal city," Kim pointed out, "Ah, The Madonna della *Pietà*, informally known as *La Pietà*, a marble sculpture of Jesus and Mary at Mount Golgotha representing the 'Sixth Sorrow'," Kim gasped in admiration of the masterpiece. "It means 'Pity' or 'Compassion', and represents Mary sorrowfully contemplating the dead body of her son, which she holds on her lap," he explained.

"I hope all these accountants appreciate their co-workers," Sebastian mentioned in passing.

"This era continued to focus on the individual human as its inspiration and took influence from the art and philosophy of the ancient Romans and Greeks," Kim explained, "the Renaissance can be seen as a cultural rebirth…"

A few floors further down they decided to again step off the escalator and chat with some accountants or bureaucrats, they were not sure. Nonetheless, one put his abacus, papyrus, quill, and ink well aside and looked at them all. "I had a dream last night; I was trapped in a large book, words and letters floated around me like water, and I tried to escape. I lay down on my back and tried to use my legs to open the book cover to escape but couldn't. I even tried to leave via the spine of the book, but I still couldn't…"

The students listened intently to the story, but he went silent. Finally, Kim continued his tour guiding. "Due to the Christian purpose behind Romanesque paintings, they often include mythological creatures like dragons and angels, and almost always appear in churches, and places like here apparently. At the most fundamental level, paintings of the Romanesque period serve the purpose of spreading the word of the bible and Christianity."

"Sorry," the bureaucrat apologised and continued, "finally, I tried pushing open the book cover with all my strength and suddenly it opened like a door, and all the words and letters, myself included, flooded out, releasing me."

The students looked at each other curiously. "Well, that's no worse than the dream we appear to be in," Sebastian muttered. "I suggest we move on," he said leading the way as the bureaucrat and others at his long ornate wooden table, returned to their work. The students walked back to the escalator. Down and down, they went, entering many crowded floors of classical antiquity. The floors became like classical stone buildings with the bureaucrats and accountants dressed in white robes and sandals, with more beautiful marble statues everywhere, almost like crowds.

"Ah, we seem to be in the Age of Enlightenment," Kim explained enthusiastically, "It ends with the decline of classical culture during late antiquity, a period overlapping with the Early Middle Ages. The glory that was Greece, and the grandeur that was Rome."

The next escalator they stepped onto made them stop in their moving tracks as they descended, it was a mosaic.

"There's no metal on this step tread surface," Sebastian announced in surprise. "It's made up of tiny terracotta tiles, pieces of glass, ceramics, and marble."

"And it works," Jonathon agreed in disbelief. "Oh and look at this floor," he continued as they gazed at the next level. Various mosaics stretched as far as the eye could see dotted with tables and benches with bureaucrats, many dressed like Roman guards, bossing around accountants working away patiently. Stepping onto this level they knelt down and ran their hands over the tiny rock and marble tiles of various colours combining to make a most beautiful large story inlaid into the floors and walls.

Kim immediately resumed his guided tour. "Pay attention, mosaics are symbols of wealth and status, blending art and home décor, Roman mosaics were commissioned to adorn and impress guests inside private homes and villas"

"I'm impressed," Yvonne said, placing her arm around Asami's shoulder to comfort and thank her. "Life is like a mosaic," she continued, "It's a journey comprised of thousands of smaller coloured tiles that make up your life. Every choice you make is a little tile in the mosaic."

Zara suddenly bounded away to one part of the floor and started scratching her paws on one area of small tiles. Cathy pursued, fearing they might lose her. But she stopped and rolled over, so Cathy picked her up, "Don't you dare leave us again Zara, or I will make a dingo lead." Then she noticed something strange, and on examining one mosaic it was a picture of a room, there were urns and windows and flowers and grapes, "but look at this," Cathy called over to the other students, "isn't that strange, it looks like a television, like that one we saw at the entrance to our journey," she said running her fingers over the surface, "that glass cube." Yvonne joined her quickly followed by the others. "The mosaic is so intricate, it almost appears three-dimensional," Cathy said, "and look at the screen," Jonathon reached the same spot and looked closely.

"There are people in the air with wings," he said, blinking at Cathy mysteriously. For a moment they gazed into each other's eyes, as Zara sniffed around inquisitively wagging her tail.

Yvonne became emotional, the recognition of this image in the mosaic made her homesick for their first entry into Uluru. She looked around at the crowds of people working at tables and benches and was jolted back into her role as the original guide.

"I'm still your guide," Yvonne announced defiantly. "We must move on, please."

"Yes, yes, let's not attract attention to ourselves," Jonathon agreed quickly, "and let's switch back to the elevators." They strolled casually back to the glass lifts and stepped on board a descending one.

Further down, they passed through the Egyptian layer, where they saw people chiselling numbers and hieroglyphics onto stone tablets. And then as the glass lift went deeper and deeper the large spaces became rougher and more rock-like.

"Well, we appear to be in pre-historic times, maybe four hundred thousand years ago," Jonathon surmised as they saw Neanderthals sitting around small fires in cave-like offices with drawings and paintings on the cave walls depicting buffaloes, horses, and other strange animals, with people holding clubs and spears.

Kim was quick to pick up on what Yvonne had noticed. "It's as if these bureaucrats and accountants are like the layers of rocks, metamorphic layers, and igneous rocks, and look, they're using small clay tokens to count and then tally sticks. Thousands of years of accountancy."

"Let's talk to them," Jonathon suggested eagerly. The lift stopped, and they walked out into the cave and approached a small group of Neanderthals counting piles of pebbles.

"Hi, there are a lot of these drawings of buffaloes and people with spears all over the walls, can't you do better than that, I mean only a few floors up we had the Renaissance with intricate paintings of angels and gods, no less," Jonathan observed, devoid of thinking.

The neanderthal was taken aback and looked offended as he scratched his prominent brow ridge above his eyes and the central part of his face protruded forward and was dominated by a very wide nose, which started to sniffle. A tear ran down from below his quite hairy eyebrow, and his lower lip began to quiver.

"Oh, my god! What have you said, Jonathan?" Cathy protested quickly, "you insensitive idiot."

"How was I supposed to know they speak English? I just imagined they grunted for chat," he replied defensively.

A few of the other Neanderthals stood up angrily as some of the women there in skimpy fur skirts began to openly weep.

"Let's get out of here," Yvonne suggested nervously as they backed away and then turned around and sprinted towards the lift treading carefully over boulders lined up almost in the shape of a newly invented horizontal abacus and started frantically prodding and jabbing the down buttons of the lift.

"You know Jonathan," Cathy angrily told him, "When people are dead, they don't realise it, others do however," she said, as a group of angry Neanderthals approached holding clubs, "and it's the same if you're stupid!"

Suddenly, a lift descended and stopped, and the glass doors opened, and the students bundled themselves inside and frantically poked at the close doors button.

The glass doors shut just as the group of Neanderthals reached the lift waving their clubs and bashing them on the lift doors angrily. The lift descended, and they went out of sight. The Neanderthals always found these glass lifts and escalators passing through their stone age caves incongruous and returned to their fireplaces scratching their heads and glancing at the cave paintings in a disappointed way.

The students breathed a collective sigh of relief that they had escaped, and realising they must be nearing the end of their journey, and no one had tried to stop them, the group started to feel more comfortable. They became increasingly relaxed, joking and laughing with each other. They returned to the escalators and trotted down the moving steps; sometimes pausing and peering over the handrail; Cathy took more pictures. At one point, they caught up to a couple of janitors polishing the moving handrails.

"Don't you get tired of cleaning escalators?" Jonathan asked them.

"Sick to death of it," the janitor smiled. "But it's a job." She was an Asian woman in her forties, and there was something about her that made Asami pause.

"Do you have nice sleeping quarters?" Asami asked with an empathetic smile.

"Oh, yes, not bad," the janitor replied, as a tear welled up in her eyes. "But not as good as where I came from." Asami grasped her hand and squeezed it gently.

Everyone noticed a connection between the two women. "What do you do in your free time?" Sebastian asked.

"See for yourself." the woman gestured as the escalator descended onto a floor with bowling alleys, swimming pools, tennis courts, and even an entire park with trees and birds chirping away, filled with janitors enjoying themselves.

"Let's take a break in this park," Cathy suggested. "I want to rest my legs and Zara probably needs to pee." They all agreed, and after Asami said goodbye to the janitors, they stepped off the escalator onto the park.

The park was beautiful, and various flower beds surrounded the perimeter and a jogging track cut through the middle. Yvonne opened her satchel and took out some sandwiches and drinks, and they all sat down on the park benches. Cathy carefully lifted the pup out of her satchel and put her on the lawn. She yelped, prancing around happily.

Asami looked back at the escalators with distant eyes.

"Are you okay?" Jonathan asked.

"That janitor is my Aunt Ichika," Asami whispered. "She left for this island from the village when I was eight years old and never returned. I don't think she recognised me."

"That's why you said people never return," Jonathan said.

"To think that all this time, she's been working here as a cleaner, and we never knew," Asami sighed.

Cathy picked up Zara and hugged her, sadly glancing back at the escalators.

"Well, we should reach the train station soon," Kim announced optimistically. "Maybe once we find out where it goes, we can come back and get her."

Asami smiled. "Yeah, I'd like that." A jogger rounded the running track and Jonathan's heart sank as he recognised the man.

"What do you think you're doing down here?" Stan asked their host from the previous evening, frowning, puffing, and sweating.

"We got a job here," Sebastian replied quickly. "And we start work today," he lied, shifting his feet uncomfortably.

"I haven't heard anything about this," Stan said. The group glanced back at each other, unsure what to say. Stan wiped the sweat from his brow. "That's the only job you'll get down here is as a janitor."

"Yep," Jonathan nodded. "That's fine. We love cleaning."

"All right then," Stan said suspiciously. "If you follow me, I'll take you to your new quarters, and you can begin training, and change out of those fawn suits."

The dingo pup suddenly jumped out of Cathy's arms and bounded across the park, disappearing into some bushes. Stan threw up his hands. "Well, go get that dog!" Stan ordered. "No dogs allowed!"

"It's not a dog, it's a dingo," Cathy snapped back, and then she and the others took the opportunity to get away from Stan, and they all darted after the dingo pup.

Asami glanced back across the park. "He's searching for us!"

Behind a thicket of trees, they heard a voice call out, "Come here!" So they peered around the trunk of the tree and saw Asami's aunt inside an elevator, holding the doors open. The group hurried towards the elevator just as Cathy found Zara.

Stan spotted them. "Stop!" he shouted. "I command you all to stop!" Stan started running across the park, waving his arms. Inside the elevator, everyone glanced around, breathlessly. Ichika pressed the button marked Station—Ground Floor, and the elevator descended before Stan reached them.

"Thank god for you!" Asami said, hugging her aunt. "I didn't think you recognised me, Aunt Ichika! We've missed you so much. Everyone in the village thought you were dead."

She laughed. "I recognised your smile and eyes. I assumed you're trying to get to the train?"

"We are," Sebastian replied.

Ichika nodded. "But how do you plan to get on the train when we reach the ground floor?"

"Good question," Sebastian whispered. Jonathan studied the various buttons on the control panel and pressed 'direct' so it wouldn't stop at any other levels on the way down.

"How long will it take to get there?" Jonathan asked.

"About ten minutes," Ichika replied. "It's a long way, thousands of years of evolution actually," They looked up at the numbers above the elevator door as they descended, past more caves and Neanderthals working away.

Meanwhile, Stan bolted back across the park, puffing, and panting as he started to run down the endless escalators.

Inside the elevator, everyone waited in silence. The dingo pup was sniffing around the briefcases and satchels. She stuck her head inside Cathy's satchel and took out a small parcel in her tiny jaws.

"Oh! I forgot about that!" Cathy remembered, grabbing the package from the pup, and unwrapping it. Inside was a small wooden box. Cathy opened the lid which revealed several lipsticks. She pulled the cap off one and stared at her reflection in the lipstick's silver surface.

"Mirror lipstick," Cathy mused.

"How did you get that?" Ichika gasped. "That's your first-class ticket!"

"I heard some women talking in the bathroom last night," Cathy grinned.

"You stole their package?" Yvonne whispered.

"I wasn't sure if it was actually a ticket or lipstick," Cathy shrugged.

"It's both!" Ichika said.

Cathy applied the lipstick, and her lips instantly became reflective, "When women wear this mirror lipstick, it's a first-class ticket onto the train," Ichika explained. "All the girls should put it on. And then you can bring the boys as your partner with you to board the train."

Meanwhile, Stan was making fast progress on the escalators. He had only a few floors to go and although he was becoming severely fatigued, he calculated he would be able to stop the students before they got on the train, save his job, and even get a promotion in the process.

"Come with us," Asami urged to her aunt.

"I can't," she said. "Not now, I have a husband I met here, a pleasant bureaucrat," she said proudly. "And I'm pregnant, and we're not sure if it will be an accountant or a bureaucrat."

Cathy handed Ichika some mirror lipsticks. "Have these, for when you're ready."

The lift continued its ascent but slowed dramatically, and they all stared out at the passing caves, except now the Neanderthals vanished and were replaced by skeletons scattered around rock benches.

"Wow, we must be really getting back in time," Kim concluded, winding down his eloquent guided tour.

"Oh, look at that!" They could all clearly see a skeleton holding a rusted supermarket trolly. "It must be terrible when you can't find your car in the supermarket car park," Kim remarked as that footnote in civilisation went out of site and the glass lift slowed to a standstill.

"Ah, good, the ground floor," Jonathon said, and the doors opened. Asami hugged Ichika goodbye, a tear dropping from her eye and wetting her mirrored lips. Everyone stepped out apprehensively, and when they saw no one waiting, they turned and ran along the corridor to the entrance of the station.

Stan appeared breathlessly at the top of the final escalator, but he never saw the students enter the station. Instead, he sprinted for the nearest elevator, holding a cramp in his side, but found only Ichika polishing the interior of the lift.

Frowning, he turned for the train station, running along the corridor towards the train, where he spotted the students in the distance.

"Wait!" Stan called out. "You are not permitted to move on!" but his voice started to fade as the stitch in his side took over, and he collapsed at the feet of the ticket collector and passed out from exhaustion.

Chapter 13
The Mirror Station

"This is amazing," Jonathan whispered. They all stood in awe, staring at their reflections on the station walls.

"Every inch is a mirror!" Yvonne said in amazement. "I've never seen anything like it."

Even the gleaming train in front of them was covered in a mirror surface. They all pondered their appearances, their well-tailored suits and briefcases making them look every bit the businessmen and women.

The station was huge. A few people at the other end of the mirrored platform were lifting suitcases onto the train and some station attendants in shiny silvery suits shuffled around preparing for the train to leave, and one approached them.

"You're cutting it a bit close!" The ticket collector said. He looked at the stunning mirror gloss on Cathy, Yvonne and Asami's lips. "This is the first-class carriage."

"Smile," Cathy said, snapping a photo of their mirror images reflected on the train exterior.

"Well, let's get on board," Jonathan said excitedly.

They strolled over the mirrored platform floor towards the train but couldn't see any doors or windows. Everything was a mirror. After a moment of confusion, part of the mirror on the train slid open.

A waiter in a white tuxedo was standing inside the carriage. "Bonjour," he said, his crisp French accent obvious. "My name is Marcel, and I will be looking after you all on this trip. Please enter. The train is about to leave."

"How long is this train trip?" Sebastian asked.

"How long? You don't know?" Marcel asked with a quizzical look. There was an awkward pause.

"How long… in hours and minutes," Cathy added quickly, "And seconds!"

"Oh. I see!" Marcel smiled. "The precise time is fifty-four hours and forty minutes exactly, madam, and thirty-five seconds."

A whistle was blown, the carriage door closed, and the train began to move very slowly and smoothly, as everyone gazed out the one-way windows, the mirror station disappeared and was replaced by a wall of shiny stainless-steel.

The first-class interior was decorated in various shades of white, and the grand lavish space was filled with large white sofas and matching armchairs with the chandeliers' crystals barely clinking.

"We made it," Cathy grinned, placing the dingo puppy on the pale shagpile carpet.

The students had the first-class carriage to themselves and after the remarkable journey to reach the station, allowed themselves to relax, collapsing in luxurious chairs as the train hummed along.

"When's lunch?" Sebastian called to Marcel waiting nearby at the ready. "We're famished!"

"Whenever you are ready, sir," Marcel said. "You can follow me to the dining carriage," which they did to the next carriage and looked around the five-star restaurant. A beautiful young waitress wearing traditional French lace passed them the menus.

"*Une jeune et belle serveuse,*" Marcel said with a smile. "I am sure your waitress will look after you or I might have to whack her bottom with a baguette," Marcel said, laughing away.

The waitress ignored him. "What can I get you?" The woman smiled at Jonathan, her white sequined apron glistening over her beautiful black dress.

"Are you Taylor Swift?" Jonathon asked out of the blue as everyone glared at him.

"No, no," she laughed, "I have dark hair for a start," she laughed in response as she adjusted her glittering tiara. "I was born in Montmartre, Paris, I promise you," she continued. "But people always say that… it is a compliment," she said politely in broken English.

"Let's see," Jonathan said, scanning the menu and adjusting his rimless glasses though distracted by her knee-high slender black boots covered in black sequins over her lacy stockings. "I'll have the cumin-dusted duck with a marmalade of girolles and papaya, please. And what is the carriage red?"

"Carriage red?" Sebastian asked in puzzlement. "Oh, I get it. Instead of a house red," he laughed.

"It's the medium-bodied Chateau Blanc Ledger," the waitress said. "A perfect partner for the exploration of the duck you have requested."

"Speaking of exploration," Jonathan said, as he placed a book on the table. "I've got a copy here of *Journey to the Centre of the Earth* by Jules Verne, which I've been speed reading. I wonder if our return to the surface will be as dangerous as their adventures."

"Of course not!" Marcel said abruptly. They all looked up at him in surprise, unaware he'd been listening.

"Will the train take us to the surface?" Yvonne asked hopefully.

"Oh, not the train," Marcel said. "You'll return to the surface by rocket!"

"Rocket?" Cathy gasped.

"You're wearing mirror lipstick!" Marcel said, glancing at Cathy's lips. "It's your passport for elite travel." They all ordered, glancing around at each other, very uncertain about this new stage of their journey.

"I don't know how I feel about rockets," Sebastian whispered.

Jonathan leaned in. "Well, according to this book by Jules Verne, some adventurers had an ancient map that showed the route to the centre of the earth. They followed it and returned on a raft that was propelled by an active volcano as they sped to the surface on a wooden raft."

"Surely their raft would burn?" Sebastian answered.

"But that's science fiction," Jonathan said. "It's just a book."

"Exactly," Sebastian replied. "And this is real, so a rocket of some sort makes sense."

"Seems a little far-fetched if you ask me," Cathy said, pouring a bowl of water for the dingo pup on the table. "Maybe we are still in a dream."

"Well, it might sound far-fetched to you," Asami said, breaking her silence. "But I've spent twenty years living in the village. This might feel like a dream for you, but I can assure you this is all real!"

Jonathan agreed. "And let's face it. If we hadn't escaped Stan, we'd be undergoing training as janitors, and we'd never be able to leave. I think we need to take all the chances we can get." Marcel returned with a bottle of red wine, uncorked, and poured it out in their glasses.

"Anyway, I think we should celebrate," Jonathan said. "Since it looks like we're going home."

The glasses clinked together, and they all smiled in nervous anticipation, and even though they still had hours to go, the idea of going home had never sounded so appealing. The waitress arrived with the French cuisine, and they ate happily, the celebration continuing into the night.

Finally, after chocolate, coffee, and a cognac everyone decided to head to bed. Marcel showed them to their first-class carriage and bid them goodnight. There were six rooms with queen-size beds and en-suite bathrooms.

After everyone went to their rooms, Jonathan stayed behind in the carriage. There was a television at the far end, and he decided to stay up a while longer and watch a classic French black-and-white movie, *The Hunchback of Notre Dame*.

After an hour, he was starting to drift off in the comfortable lounge chairs, when someone whispered in his ear.

"May I run your bath?" Jonathan sat up in surprise and spun around to see the French waitress standing behind him. "I insist." She was wearing a see-through nightie covered with transparent sequins.

"Oh, sure," Jonathan said blushing.

As the waitress walked off, he sipped the rest of his cognac and waited a few minutes before heading down the carriage to his compartment. As he entered, he could hear the tap running.

"*Mon doit de pied est coince dans l'evier*," the waitress whimpered.

He could tell she was in distress but didn't understand what she had said. He entered the bathroom and saw the waitress with her foot in the bathtub.

"Are you okay? I'm sorry, my French is limited to fries."

She giggled. "My toe is stuck in the bath plug hole," she whispered in a thick seductive French accent. "Can you pass me the soap crème?"

Jonathan handed her the soap and after a moment of trying to wriggle her foot out, she looked up at him. "Can you try pulling my poor toe out?"

"Okay," Jonathan whispered. He reached into the tub and gently tugged on her foot. On the third tug, her toe came out, but the force caused a domino reaction, and they both fell backwards, slipping into the bath and Jonathan's elbow knocked the tap causing the shower to cascade down on them.

"Time to wash off all that grime from the thousands of years of civilisation you have passed down through, *Tu es mieux que le bossu Notre Dame*! You're better than the hunchback of Notre Dame!" the waitress whispered with a smile.

"Is your toe okay?" Jonathan enquired.

She grinned. "It's more than okay, sir." She reached past him and grabbed a bottle of champagne from an ice bucket.

"*Je suis ton reve realise,*" she whispered. "*Voyage au centre de mon univers.*"

She leaned towards him, pressing her body against his.

"I have no idea what you said," Jonathan replied.

The waitress smiled. "I am your dream come true, your journey to the centre of my earth." This beautiful French waitress has been a sudden invasion into the love space of Jonathon who was still dealing with his romantic feelings for Cathy. He adjusted his rimless glasses and gazed at her beauty and after his cleansing followed her to his large bed.

The next morning Marcel knocked on every door and announced that breakfast was being served in the dining car. When Jonathan woke up, the waitress was gone, and for a moment, he fell back into bed unsure if he'd dreamed of their night together or if it was real.

But when he entered the dining carriage, she glanced up from across the room, paused taking an order and smiled at him. Jonathan blushed. It had been real. She really was a dream come true.

The day unfolded much like the day before, breakfast turning to lunch and dinner, their second day of celebrating, but this time when Jonathan went to bed, he was alone and left to excavate his dreams and memories on his own. The next morning Marcel announced that after breakfast the train would be arriving at the mirror station.

"The mirror station?" Sebastian asked. "I thought we just left the mirror station?"

"Maybe all the train stations are similar," Cathy wondered.

Occasionally they looked out the window, hoping to see if anything had changed, but the stainless-steel tube continued to whiz by. Just as Marcel served a second round of tea and coffee, the train began to slow down. Suddenly, the mirror station came into view.

"Oh, no," Yvonne whispered. "It's the exact same mirror station!"

Sebastian stood up to get a better look. "I think she's right."

"How do you know?" Jonathan asked.

"I recognise the elevator!" Sebastian said.

Kim shook his head as the train stopped. "We must have gone in a giant circle or something."

"Well, here you are," Marcel announced with a smile.

"Marcel, did we go in a circle?" Asami asked him. "Are we back where we started?"

"No, no!" Marcel responded. "This is a mirror image of the first mirror station. Just identical, that is all."

Everyone sighed with relief, grabbed their possessions, and stepped gingerly onto the mirror platform, as a few hundred people poured out of the other carriages.

"The first-class transit lounge is through there," Marcel said, pointing towards a door. "Have a wonderful journey back to the surface!"

The beautiful French waitress watched them from the carriage door and waved goodbye blowing a kiss to Jonathan. Everyone stepped onto a travelator that took them along to the departure lounge.

When they arrived at the end, a group of friendly people greeted them.

"Welcome, welcome! We are the rocket attendants. Welcome to the next step in your journey to the surface!"

Chapter 14
And We All Shine On

"Hello, my name is Valentina." The middle-aged woman welcomed in a Russian accent. She glanced down at their mirror lipstick. "I am your escort for this leg of your trip."

"How exactly does this work?" Jonathan asked.

"I'll explain everything if you'll just follow me," Valentina said, as she led the way down the hallway and through a bulky door. "This is the first-class cabin."

It was a spacious and modern compartment with a double row of large comfortable seats. Valentina handed each of them red suits and asked them to change. After they donned their new outfits, they sat down, and Valentina and her staff helped fasten their safety belts. Cathy tucked the dingo pup inside the seatbelt, so he was strapped to her lap.

Everyone was quiet with nervous anticipation. Jonathan glanced around a porthole window and watched in stunned surprise as a fish swam by, "Look!"

Sebastian leaned forward. "Are we in an ocean?"

"We are," Valentina nodded. "We're deep beneath the Pacific Ocean… very deep."

Kim glanced around the empty seats. "Are there more people coming?"

Valentina shook her head. "The economy class is full, but you all have first class to yourselves." She handed out scented wet hand cloths and headphones with tiny microphones attached. "Please put these on. We will be taking off shortly." They put their headphones on and discovered they could talk to each other.

"Greetings." A deep voice echoed through their earphones. "This is your captain speaking. We have begun the countdown and will soon be at the ignition stage. Please press the button on your seat labelled horizontally." Each of them pressed the button and the seats reclined, flattening out. The captain continued. "Have a pleasant journey back to the surface."

A deep rumble vibrated the compartment and slowly became louder. Everyone looked out the portholes as curious fish were swept away by a rush of smoky bubbles. The noise became so loud, they were certain it would have damaged their ears if they weren't wearing headphones. The bubbles outside turned yellow and red like the seawater was on fire.

Finally, there was a deafening blast and everyone's bodies compressed into their seats as the rocket shot upwards.

"I can hardly breathe! My lungs feel so compacted," Jonathan gasped. The bubbles began streaking past the windows, and the water went dark.

"Everyone okay?" Kim gasped, as they gave a nervous thumbs up, except for Yvonne who appeared to be unconscious.

"Yvonne! Are you okay?" Sebastian asked, clutching her sweaty hand. She began to blink and looked at Sebastian in a disoriented way.

"I think I passed out," she whispered.

"That's quite common when we blast off," the captain said, his voice echoing through their headphones.

"Oh, dear!" Yvonne muttered in embarrassment. "Can you hear us?"

"Yes," the captain said with a laugh. "If you look out your window, you'll see the surface in a moment."

"That was fast," Asami responded, looking around at the others. The seawater lightened, turning aqua, and suddenly, bright sunlight flooded the compartment. Everyone squinted against the glare, and after a moment of surprise, they broke into uproarious jubilation.

"We made it! We're back!'"

They all gazed out the portholes as the rocket burst through the surface of the ocean and into the sky. Sunshine beamed through the windows, warming their faces.

They peered out as clouds floated by. "Wow! What a scene!" Jonathan whooped loudly. "I wonder when we will land?"

"In three weeks," the captain announced.

"WHAT?" they all screamed.

"No!" Cathy shouted. "But I can see the surface of the earth right there!"

"You said we were going to the surface!" Yvonne shouted in panic.

"The surface of Mars," the captain clarified.

"Mars!"

Valentina looked at them from her seat further up the cabin. "You must calm down."

"But we were told we were returning to the surface!" Jonathan said.

"We never said the surface of Earth," the captain said. "We are returning home to Mars."

"But this is absurd!" Sebastian protested loudly. "We want to go home to Australia!"

"Turn this thing around now!" Jonathan screamed.

"Now listen," the captain said sympathetically. "That's impossible."

"Someone do something!" Cathy screamed, the veins in her forehead throbbing.

"I demand to speak to you now, captain!" Yvonne said. "In person!"

"Well, I'm afraid that's not possible right now," the captain said. "Once we're safely in orbit, you can float up here, and I'll talk to you."

Yvonne and Cathy began to cry.

Asami, on the other hand, was staring out the window in amazement. "Will you look at that? I can see Japan! It's beautiful."

Everyone went silent and gazed out the portholes in awe. Despite their shock, they couldn't deny that the view of Earth was breathtaking. Nothing could have prepared them for this experience.

"Australia..." Jonathan said under his breath. "Just look at Australia..."

"Would you like to watch some television?" Valentina asked. She unstrapped herself and turned a television on at the front of the cabin. "We get fantastic reception up here."

Everyone was too absorbed in the astonishing view of Earth to look at the television screen, except for Kim.

"Isn't that St Paul's Cathedral in Melbourne?" Kim asked, pointing at the screen. Everyone turned to the television.

Valentina turned up the volume, and they listened to the lyrics of a hymn, the singing of *The Lord's My Shepherd*. The images switched to shots of a congregation.

"Hey! Hold on! There's my family!" Cathy exclaimed in shock.

"And there's my mom and dad!" Sebastian mumbled in surprise. "Wait a second..."

Jonathan gasped. "They look like they're at a funeral."

"It's our funeral," Cathy whispered in horror.

The huge crowd of mourners at St Paul's Cathedral spilt out onto the street. There was a large contingent of students and as the television camera slowly panned around the cathedral, they could clearly see their friends, families, and relatives.

There was a sudden ringing sound, and everyone glanced around, confused. Jonathan looked down at his briefcase. "The cell phone!"

"Answer it!" Yvonne demanded.

Jonathan unstrapped himself and grabbed the cell from the briefcase.

"Yes!" His eyes widened. "Look at all these text messages!"

"We must be in range again," Kim said. "Read them!"

"What does it say?" Sebastian asked.

"It says the search party is looking for us," Jonathan read out aloud. "It's dated to last week when we went into Uluru. They're telling us to call home." He pressed a few buttons on the cell and connected it to the microphone on his headset.

There were over fifty missed calls and voicemails. He played one of the most recent voicemails and a man's voice echoed in all their headsets.

"It's the Uluru-Kata Tjuta National Park Ranger here, where are you guys? You're well overdue back here. Are you injured? Please return this call or call your parents."

"Jonathan, call someone NOW!" Sebastian shouted. "We might lose service soon."

"Okay," Jonathan said. "Who should I call?"

"ANYONE!" the others shouted.

"They think we're dead," Cathy cried.

"But this is Harrison's cell. It hasn't got any numbers I know. Hold on, I think I remember my brother's cell."

He typed in the numbers and pressed send. The call rang and rang, and everyone glanced at Jonathan with nervous anticipation. When it went to voicemail, everyone sighed in frustration.

"Text him!" Kim said.

On the television, the minister was conducting their funeral service and a few pews back sat Jonathan's family.

In the church, Jonathan's younger brother Philip glanced down at the text message.

"Turn off your cell, Philip," his dad whispered angrily.

"But Dad," Philip whispered back urgently.

"I'm not going to repeat myself."

"Look!" Philip whispered loudly, showing his dad the text message from Jonathan.

'We are alive. Not dead!'

"Someone's playing a prank on you," his dad said. "Turn your phone off for heaven's sake."

Philip turned his back on his father and quietly texted a return message.

"Where are you?"

"He replied!" Jonathan gasped. "He wants to know where we are."

"Don't waste time! Call him again!" Sebastian insisted urgently.

Jonathan pressed send again and the phone started to ring.

Philip's cell vibrated, and he glanced down at Jonathan's name. Was his brother really calling him? He answered it just as his mother snatched the phone from him.

"Didn't you hear what your father said?" his mother snapped.

"Just put it to your ear!" Philip urged. "It's Jonathan!"

His mother looked at Jonathan's name on the phone and slowly lifted it to her ear.

"It's me! It's me, Jonathan!"

His mother put her hand over her mouth in shock. She grabbed her husband.

"I've got Jonathan on the phone! It's his voice!" his mother screamed. "Johnny! It's Mom! Are you all right darling? Where are you?"

The other mourners were glaring at her.

Jonathan's father grabbed the cell. "It can't be. Who is this?"

"Dad!" Jonathan said. "It's me!"

"Jonathan?" he gasped. "We're at your funeral?"

"I know! We're watching it on TV!"

"Listen," his dad said. "Don't hang up. I'm going outside son, don't hang up." Jonathan grabbed his wife's hand and squeezed past Sebastian's family in the same pew. "I've got Jonathan on the phone; can you believe it?"

The minister looked up from the notes he was reading and watched them leave as whispers spread across the congregation.

Jonathon's father stepped outside the church but was immediately confronted by a disturbing scene of two huge demonstrations. On the one side were people demanding that holes be drilled into Uluru to find the cave and laptop, and on the other side a much larger demonstration, an angry crowd protesting this mad idea, and in the middle dozens of police, many mounted, trying to keep them apart.

The minister kept talking. "Jonathan had a vital sense of adventure and was always the first to put his hand up when it came to a challenge…"

Capsicum spray spurted all over the place, and splinter groups broke away and clashed as police horses reared up and galloped into the mayhem. "I can hardly hear you, it's so loud outside here!" Jonathan's father yelled into the mobile.

"Are you there, Mom? Dad?" Jonathan whispered.

"Tell them we're okay too," Cathy said in disbelief.

"Jonathan, are you there?" his dad asked loudly above the noisy demonstrators. "Are the others with you?"

"Yes!" Jonathan said excitedly. "They're all fine. You wouldn't believe what happened!"

"Well, where are you?" his father demanded.

"We're hundreds of kilometres above you, Dad!" Jonathan said. "Not in heaven, we're in a rocket… hello? Dad? Hullo…?"

"Jonathan! Hello? Can you hear me?" His father's voice cut off.

Jonathan looked at the phone in shock. "No!"

"What?" Cathy gasped.

"The phone died," Jonathan said. "It's out of power."

"Oh, no," Sebastian said. "Valentina, do you have a power cord?"

"It won't matter now. You'll be well out of range very soon. We're travelling at over 50,000 miles an hour," she announced, "Earth is far behind us. I'm sorry."

"But the television works," Asami noted.

"That's a much stronger signal," Valentina explained. "In fact, you can watch any TV station on earth."

Yvonne glared at her. "But all we want is to go back to Earth!"

Valentina smiled sympathetically. "I'm sorry. That's just not possible. I told you already."

For about an hour, the students watched their funeral service in St Paul's Cathedral. They couldn't decide whether to laugh or cry, or laugh and cry at the same time. On the one hand, Jonathan had told his dad they were all alive, yet their funeral continued, and it appeared that everyone still believed they were dead.

Asami continued gazing out the window at Earth.

"This is all my fault," Yvonne whispered. "I never should have agreed to be your guide."

Cathy held her hand. "It's not your fault."

"We talked you into entering the rock, Yvonne," Jonathan said. "It's not your fault at all."

Yvonne shook her head. "What sort of Aboriginal guide leads you from the red centre of the earth to the red planet?"

At one point, the camera cut to the demonstration outside the cathedral. A group of students were holding up placards and demanding holes be drilled into Uluru in search of the tunnel.

"I hope no one else goes in there," Kim said.

"At least we have a view," Asami said.

"My god, it's full of stars!" Jonathan said, quoting Frank Poole, the science fiction astronaut in 2001.

"Your funeral is finished," Valentina said, looking at the television as a congregation filed out of St Paul's Cathedral. "Now you can ascend to heaven."

She laughed and switched off the seatbelt sign.

Chapter 15
"... L'amore Che Muove L'universo E L'altre Stelle ..."

"The love that moves the universe and the other stars," the captain announced, his voice echoing through their headphones. The students released their seatbelts, lifted out of their chairs and began floating.

"Wow!" Yvonne exclaimed, drifting into a somersault. "I can't believe this feeling!"

"So this is weightlessness!" Sebastian said in excitement. "I wouldn't exchange this for anything." He gracefully pushed off the side of the first-class cabin and sailed to the other end.

"This is complete freedom," Jonathan said, floating through a series of gymnastic movements, moving in unison with Cathy. With each passing day, he was becoming more and more attracted to Cathy and, other than his perfect fling with the French waitress, he wondered what weightless sex would be like.

It seemed all their worries and concerns were forgotten as the students and the dingo pup gleefully floated through zero gravity. Yvonne made her way towards the captain's cabin.

"May I speak to you now?" Yvonne asked, reaching for the door.

"Of course!" the captain said. The hatch slid aside, and Yvonne floated through into the spacious cockpit. The large windows showed an infinite view of the solar system.

"'The love that moves the universe.' Where is that quote from?" Yvonne asked.

"Ah yes, it's one of my favourites. It's the last line of Dante's *Divine Comedy*," the captain smiled. "Would you like a cup of coffee?"

"Oh. Yes, thanks. Anyway, my name is Yvonne. I am their guide."

"You should call me Yuri," the captain said, pressing some buttons on a console, the coffee filling into a sealed cup. He released the cup, and it floated into the air towards Yvonne as she managed to catch it and took a sip.

"Delicious. This weightlessness is quite tricky," Yvonne said, starting to float upside down. Yuri, a handsome middle-aged cosmonaut, released his seatbelt and began floating around the cabin.

Yvonne began to feel dizzy and then sleepy. Her eyes closed, and she went into a deep sleep as she drifted upside down. Yuri smiled and floated over to her.

Inside the first-class cabin, the others drifted around, enjoying their newly found freedom. After ten minutes or so, Sebastian and Jonathan looked around.

"Where's Yvonne?" Sebastian asked.

Jonathan looked at the cabin. "I think she went to talk to the captain."

At that moment, the hatch slid aside, and Cathy's red space suit came drifting through. Sebastian, Kim, and Jonathan glanced at each other.

Yvonne's naked body then floated through into the first-class cabin, relaxed and serenely beautiful. Her long curly hair drifted in all directions.

"What happened?" Sebastian said angrily. "Yvonne? Yvonne? Wake up!"

"Where am I?" Yvonne muttered, her speech slightly slurred. Her eyes opened lazily, and she half smiled.

"What have you done to her?" Jonathan demanded.

"Why? Nothing," Yuri said.

"Yeah, I bet," Sebastian said as he and Cathy helped Yvonne back into her red space suit. They all returned to their chairs and fastened their seat belts as Yvonne slowly woke up.

"How do you feel?" Jonathan asked her.

"Groggy," she reassured him.

"What happened?" they all asked.

"Don't know… something was in that coffee."

"Yeah, the bastard drugged you."

"I don't remember anything," Yvonne said.

A few hours passed, and they occupied themselves by reading all the text messages on the mobile phone and listening to the backlog of voicemails.

Eventually, Valentina floated in and announced that dinner was about to be served and invited them to the glass-dining cabin. As they strapped themselves into the chairs, Jonathan marvelled at the three-hundred-and-sixty-degree panoramic view of the stars glittering in the solar system. "The Earth and moon are so close," Cathy observed.

Captain Yuri joined them at the head of the table, and everyone turned silent. "What's wrong? You are all very fortunate," Yuri said with a smile. "This is the best restaurant in the universe."

"Yeah, we're just not used to our friends being drugged and raped in space," Jonathan replied angrily.

"No harm done. Right, Yvonne?" Yuri chastised as Valentina smirked and Yvonne frowned at him.

"Well, we certainly can't complain about the view!" Kim said, easing the tension. "I guess you get used to it."

"I have paradigm shifts actually," Yuri explained. "The paradox of time and space is always beguiling… red?" He held up a bottle of red wine and squirted some into a long-stemmed glass with a nozzle on top.

"Let me taste it first," Jonathan said. "You know, like they do at the best restaurants in the universe."

"Oh, sure," Yuri said with a laugh.

Jonathan tasted it and looked around. "Hmm, Hesperian Epoch, 3 billion years BC…"

"Very good Jonathan," Yuri replied. "I see you all will be wonderful company on this trip."

"Maybe not as wonderful as you would like." Cathy glared at him.

"Bon appetite!" Valentina announced, floating in with a pile of eight glass plates filled with steak and chips and crisp salads. She sat at the other end of the glass table as they clipped their plates down.

"This steak is perfect," Kim said. "So what do all the passengers in economy class eat?"

"Mainly fast food that is stored and heated," Valentina explained disdainfully. "Since we have a few hundred passengers there, I'm a five-star chef, so I only cook for first-class guests."

"Valentina informs me that your family and everyone think you are all dead," Yuri said. "You just watched your funeral on television?"

"We did," Jonathan nodded.

"Do you want to watch the news?" Valentina asked, glancing at her watch, and pressing a couple of buttons. A large television screen slid down from the ceiling, and Valentina turned on the seven o'clock news.

"Controversy continues to follow the disappearance of the four Melbourne students and their Aboriginal guide," the reporter announced. "The parent of one of the missing children has claimed his son called him during their funeral service at St Paul's Cathedral this afternoon and said that all five of the missing individuals were alive."

"This is the text message we received," Jonathan's father said to the camera, showing his phone.

'WE ARE ALIVE, NOT DEAD.'

"And then he rang us and said they were all right. But then the call dropped out."

"Is it true that it has been revealed that Jonathan's laptop has been traced to somewhere in the Pacific Ocean going up into the sky?" the reporter asked.

"Yes, it has," Jonathan's dad replied. "And they said the tracking chip in the cell phone reveals the same thing!"

"So do you think this means your son is going to heaven?" another reporter inquired.

"Don't be stupid," Johnathan's mother snapped. "If my son and his friends were dead and were ascending to heaven it would be above Uluru if that is where they perished! And they probably wouldn't be taking their digital devices with them!"

Yuri glared at the students. "You're not really chartered accountants, are you?"

Valentina looked at Cathy's mirrored lipstick. "How did you get on this flight?"

"I stole the mirror lipstick," Cathy whispered.

"Yes, but we had to escape that island!" Sebastian explained. "Or we'd end up as cleaners for the rest of our lives. We're students, not janitors! You must understand."

"No, I don't," Yuri responded, putting down his knife and fork. "It's one thing to take a tram trip for a few stops without paying your fare, but this trip is about two hundred million kilometres."

"Well, it looks like you'd better turn this thing around and drop us home then," Cathy said.

"No, can do," Yuri said. "We're stuck with each other until we reach Mars."

"Then what?" Jonathan chimed in. "Will the Martians do experiments on us or is that only what you do?" he responded with a sneer.

Yuri and Valentina burst out laughing. "It's nothing like that," Yuri said.

The frank exchange cleared the tense atmosphere, and everyone relaxed and continued eating their meals and sipping on red wine. All except Yvonne, who wouldn't even take a sip.

After dinner, Yuri floated back to his cockpit and Valentina showed the students their sleeping quarters. As soon as she left, Yvonne called the students together before they retired for the evening. "I want to say that I have absolutely no respect for Yuri after what he did to me. I can't just leap out the window and parachute home. I'll just have to put up with him. We all will, not that he will care."

"Whatever you do, don't drink the coffee in the morning," Kim said.

The dingo pup floated over and began licking Sebastian on the face, but this propelled the pup into a tailspin and Cathy had to grab the confused pup to stop her from rotating out of control. Jonathan, in turn, grabbed hold of Cathy to slow her down, and they tumbled together for a few moments drifting above the others. He wished he could guide her right into his berth, but they both needed more time to sort out their feelings for each other.

Chapter 16
The Computer Is the Thing

This must be a dream, Cathy thought to herself as she floated into the first-class cabin's bathroom holding Zara. 'How can my inner consciousness be so detached from reality?' she wondered.

The shower was a watertight cubicle made of glass. The view was incredible, with the window looking out on the never-ending expanse of space, and she struggled to comprehend how many stars existed in the universe. Once inside, jets of warm water spurted from different directions as the face washer and soap drifted around, and she tumbled gracefully around nude.

"This is more like a cosmic washing machine than a shower," Cathy whispered out loud to Zara. After she'd rinsed, she pressed a button that vacuumed the water away. Warm air blasted around them from all angles and Zara shook herself spraying the water off her clean coat, and in seconds, they were completely dry. Cathy felt as if she was the cleanest being in outer space. She also couldn't help wondering what it would be like to take a shower with Jonathan. She smiled to herself at the thought.

There was an exclusive gymnasium available to the mirror lipstick travellers in first class. Like the shower, the window of the gym overlooked the vast universe. Sebastian and Kim worked out on the stationary bicycles bolted to the floor. They had strapped themselves onto the seats to keep from lifting. With the view of space, working out had never been more enjoyable. Barbells were tethered to the floor by thick rubber cords that provided resistance. But they also had to strap their feet to the floor to keep from floating into handstands as they gripped them. Droplets of sweat drifted.

Jonathan, Cathy and Asami spent most of their time in the astronomy compartment. Asami enjoyed using the powerful telescopes to peer out the windows into the vastness of space. Jonathan whiled away the days pottering around on his laptop computer. Yvonne spent more time in her locked berth than the others.

After a week of travel, the group had settled into their daily routines. Earth was a dot on the cosmic horizon, and the red planet was growing marginally larger. Everyone had become accustomed to the total freedom of weightlessness. Gravity was a distant memory.

Cathy, Yvonne, and Asami were having morning tea one day midway through their trip when Sebastian and Kim decided to float in and visit Jonathan to see how his work was going. When they entered the astronomy cabin, Jonathan excitedly motioned to them.

"Are you alright?" Sebastian asked Jonathan. "What's up?"

"Shh," Jonathan insisted. "I need to focus. Give me a second." His laptop's webcam was aimed at him.

"Isn't that your dad?" Kim asked, noticing Jonathan's father on the screen.

"Yeah," Jonathan said.

"Jonathan is that you?" his father asked. His face occasionally faded in and out.

"Oh, my God," Sebastian gasped, waving into the camera. "You did it!"

"Hi, boys!"

Jonathan grinned. "Dad, if we lose connection, I'll try again this time tomorrow. Okay?"

"How did you do this?" Kim asked.

"Basically, this laptop has a mini satellite and after days of fiddling around. I managed to hook into the television satellites above Earth," Jonathan explained.

"The same television programs that this rocket gets, you mean?" Kim asked.

"Exactly," Jonathan said. "Except I plugged in my little webcam here and sent back an image! And I managed to zero it in on my dad's laptop."

"So couldn't any other TV stations pick up this image?" Sebastian asked.

"Well, that's what we were afraid of when we first tried to make contact," Jonathan's dad interrupted. "So we don't know, yet."

"But don't we want everyone to know we're alive?" Kim gasped.

"We don't think it's a good idea to stay online too long," Jonathan said quickly. "No one believed my dad when my text went through at our funeral. They still think we're all dead. And we don't know if a TV station or a government agency could tap into this."

"Or NASA," Jonathan's dad interjected.

"But does it really matter?" Sebastian inquired.

"Hold on," Jonathan's dad said, looking around.

Suddenly, the screen went blank. Jonathan pressed exit and slammed down his laptop cover in frustration. "No!" Jonathan cursed as he wiped his perspiring brow and put his head in his hands in despair. They all remained silent for a while.

Sebastian looked at the other two.

"Let's not tell the others," he suggested. "We don't want to create unnecessary expectations… or panic."

"I agree," Kim said, nodding. He patted Jonathan on the back. "Don't be too upset. You did something amazing here, and you and your dad said you'll try again tomorrow, same time."

Jonathan nodded. "Yeah, you're right."

They floated back to the dining cabin and changed their conversation as they joined the girls at morning tea. Cathy immediately suspected something was up.

"What's going on?" she asked.

"What do you mean?" Kim asked.

"You guys look weird," Cathy said.

"No, we don't!" Sebastian replied.

"Yes, you do!" Cathy snapped back. "You're hiding something."

"No, we're not," Jonathan said quickly.

"We're not stupid," Cathy snapped. "We know what you're doing."

Asami shrugged her shoulders. "Sorry, boys, I already told them Jonathan has been trying to make satellite contact with his dad."

"And I did it," Jonathan grinned.

"It worked?" Yvonne exclaimed, jumping up.

Sebastian looked quickly at her. "But you can't say anything. It must be a secret."

Yvonne rolled her eyes. "Of course not."

"We lost the connection," Jonathan explained. "But I saw him. I saw my dad! We're going to try again tomorrow."

Later that evening, after dinner, Sebastian floated around with Yuri and Valentina and pointed at the television.

"I've found a good current affairs program about us," Sebastian said.

The program, called Abduction or Seduction, gave a brief history of each student. It concentrated on Harrison's cell phone and Jonathan's laptop computer and how these machines had been tracked, first inside Uluru and then into the upper atmosphere.

However, they were not expecting the next thing the reporter said. "This program has received information through an intermediary that suggests Jonathan's father has made contact with him via the sophisticated laptop computer Jonathan has with him."

"Absolute nonsense," a government spokesman said, rejecting the theory.

"So that's what you've been up to in the astronomy cabin, is it?" Yuri said, looking at Jonathan. "It must be some laptop you have!"

Jonathan was unsure if Yuri was angry.

Yuri continued. "We've been travelling between Mars and Earth for thousands of years, and we've done so undetected!"

The students looked at each other in silence.

"Do you mean this rocket is from Mars?" Sebastian asked incredulously.

Yuri and Valentina laughed loudly.

"Of course!" Yuri replied, still laughing. "Do you think this is some enterprise from Earth?"

"Are you a Martian then?" Cathy asked casually. The dingo pup's ear pricked up, and she growled.

"No!" Yuri replied. "Valentina! Pour me a vodka, and one for our guests!"

Valentina could hardly contain herself; she was laughing so hard. She opened a panel and squirted several vodkas and began handing them around to the mystified students.

"I was born and bred in Kazakhstan," Yuri explained. "I graduated as a cosmonaut at the *TsNIMASH* Space Research Centre, and I did various spacewalks for the hammer and sickle brigade. The first dog in space was ours, yours is the first dingo."

"Yuri, use plain English!" Valentina interjected, throwing back a vodka in one gulp.

"I met my fellow astronaut Valentina here, and we got married," Yuri explained.

"We drifted apart years ago," Valentina quickly reassured everyone. "But we still have a working relationship."

"Then, on one mission, our craft appeared to just blow up: 'KA-BOOM!'" Yuri shouted. "But, in fact, we were headhunted by people on Mars... Their money and conditions were a lot better; you know."

"So we've been doing the Mars to Earth return leg ever since. We just love it," Valentina smiled.

Sebastian looked concerned. "So why hasn't NASA or some other space agency detected this rocket on their radar?"

"Impossible!" Yuri replied firmly. "Mars has an advanced civilisation. These crafts have all sorts of radar shields and detection blocks."

Valentina nodded. "When we arrive at Earth, we do so by night, and if anything, we just resemble a meteorite."

"So how is my laptop working?" Jonathan asked.

"That's a very good question!" Yuri said, gulping down his vodka and spinning the empty glass across to Valentina for a refill. "It's a mystery. I'm just the bus driver here!"

"I'm homesick," Yvonne whispered, gazing out the window at the crystal-clear universe. "I'm sorry..."

"Why?" Yuri asked, taken aback.

"I'm descended from the Pitjantjatjara and Yankunytjatjara people, the Anangu tribe," Yvonne said. "We are desert people, and we respect the stars and the universe. I was born in a shelter at the base of Uluru-Kata, that rock. We had such fun dancing around the fire at night. We used to lie down and watch the stars above us. The ancestor spirits were with us all the time with their myths and legends. We own the universe, not you."

"Yvonne? You're starting to cry," Cathy whispered, floating towards her, her tear drops adrift.

They all hated seeing Yvonne sad, but they couldn't deny how beautiful and articulate she was even when she was upset.

Chapter 17
Deimos and Phobos

Fear (*Deimos*) and terror (*Phobos*) were what everyone felt as they waited twenty-four hours to try and make video contact again. The astronomy cabin was crowded as they all floated around watching Jonathan fiddling with his laptop.

"So much pressure!" Jonathan said with sweat from his forehead hovering as he tapped away on his keyboard. The lid was open, and the satellite dish pointed at Earth and the screen changed colour and flickered around until suddenly his father appeared.

"Yes! It worked!" Jonathan's father said in a delighted tone.

"Okay then," Jonathan said quickly, but nervously. "We're all fine, and we will land on Mars in a week and…"

"And do what you're told!" Jonathan's mother suddenly shouted as her face filled the screen before it went blank again.

"So is that it? The search for intelligent life?" Yuri said with a laugh. Everyone drifted in silence for a moment and watched Yuri and Valentina float into another cabin.

"Oh well, I guess we should follow orders, Jonathan," Sebastian said.

"What now?" Asami inquired after the students were alone again.

"I'll keep trying to make contact," Jonathan replied. "When my mother demanded, 'Do what you're told', it was a code, a game we played when I grew up. It means I should do the opposite."

"But why are we going to Mars?" Asami asked, obviously frustrated by their situation. "I wanted to see the surface of Earth!"

"Possibly it's just wild luck that's put us here," Jonathan suggested. As they continued to theorise, Jonathan started to feel more special as if he and the others had some extraordinary 'otherworldly' calling. Maybe they had been singled out by greater power or force to fulfil a specified mission.

"Or bad luck," Yvonne said.

Nonetheless, as the red planet drew closer and their arrival date nearer, both excitement and trepidation began to manifest. Fortunately, Yuri was helpful, answering every question they posed. The students just hoped Yuri was telling the truth, that they truly would be greeted respectfully and treated honourably as special guests, and not as criminals who snuck aboard a Martian rocket. If they had prisons on the red planet, he hoped they would never see the inside of one.

"What are those two small planets orbiting Mars?" Kim asked Yuri as he floated back in.

"The larger one is called *Deimos* and the other one is *Phobos*," Yuri explained in his usual straightforward manner. "They are artificial planets, which the people of Mars put into orbit in 1878 when astronomers from Earth were becoming sticky beaks…"

"What do they do?" Sebastian inquired.

"Not much. Mainly security… they're like battleships really. They circle around the equator of Mars."

"But when I study the surface of Mars through this telescope, it just seems like a red desert with some rocks and canals," Kim observed.

"That's the roof you're looking at. Not only does it hide entire cities, but it acts as insulation," Yuri continued. "Mars has gone through global warming like Earth but on an enormous scale. It used to have a pleasant balmy atmosphere during its 'Noachian era', was green and lush, but severe climate heat baked it, so it turned red."

"What are the people like on Mars?" Cathy asked Yuri.

"Basically, just like you and me," he answered, shrugging his shoulders.

"Since the Martians are an ancient civilisation, wouldn't they have another name for their planet other than Mars?" Jonathan asked.

"That name was created by the Romans who named it after their terrible god of war," Kim informed them all.

Yuri laughed. "Good point, but Mars was what they have always called their planet. Many centuries ago, they visited the Romans for research, pointed skyward at their home, and told them they were from the red planet Mars."

"Sure, sure, that makes sense," Cathy replied sarcastically.

"And I'm certain before they left for home, the Martians ordered takeaways, maybe pizza," Yuri added with a smile, "It's only hearsay."

The curious students canvassed every topic under the sun and on the final night before arriving at their destination a special dinner was prepared by Valentina to celebrate their journey and their friendship.

"Since you claim these people on Mars are an advanced civilisation, can they travel through time?" Sebastian asked Yuri as the captain was about to propose a toast.

"Yes, certainly, of course!" Yuri responded enthusiastically as the glasses clinked together. "In fact, I have travelled in time on a few occasions."

"What year did you go to?" Kim inquired.

"This year. That's all I know," he answered coolly.

"What do you mean by that?" Sebastian asked.

"Well, I can only speak of my experience and others who I've compared notes with," Yuri explained. "You see, when you time travel, your mind thinks you are still in your own time."

"How do you time travel?" Jonathan inquired.

"It's like what has been commonly theorised already on Earth, you go through a 'wormhole' in space. You go in at one time and come out at another! Time tunnels are parallel realities."

"So has this journey been in a time tunnel?" Jonathan inquired.

"No, because you made video contact with your father, I don't think we have moved out of normal time," Yuri replied glancing at Yvonne, who looked away. "When we arrive on Mars tomorrow, it will be much the same as when I last left it… at least, I hope so."

Late in the evening after everyone had floated off to bed, Jonathan stayed up for a while longer and wrote in his diary.

My three-week journey has been amazing. Even in my wildest imagination, I never dreamed I would travel in space, let alone to Mars. We discussed 'time travel' with Yuri, and it occurred to me that maybe my journey on the mirror train with my beautiful French waitress was time travel, but I didn't realise it. I keep recalling her saying, 'Voyage au centre de mon univers'.

"Oh, that's incredible," Asami exclaimed in a whisper as she opened her eyes to see the surface of Mars filling the entire window of their compartment.

Jonathan sat up and felt slightly disappointed as he realised that she wasn't referring to their recent lovemaking on her double bed water installation inside Earth.

The surface of Mars was mainly red with orange patches here and there. It certainly didn't look like a habitable planet.

After morning showers and a final breakfast, they all adjourned to the cockpit at the invitation of Yuri and sat in a row of seats behind the pilot. "There might be a small amount of turbulence since we're going through some giant sandstorms," he warned. Within minutes, the surface loomed closer and the wind howled angrily around them, blasting the craft with red sand.

"That's some welcome," Sebastian shouted.

"Hold on! We're going to crash!" Jonathan said in alarm. The sandstorm continued to engulf them as the rocket hurtled towards the planet.

"Relax!" Yuri said calmly and suddenly the bright redness disappeared as the rocket slammed through the surface of Mars, the rugged red landscape seemingly no denser than a cloud.

The dingo pup had her paws over her eyes and then peeked through two quivering paws to see an enormous valley with a city in the distance.

"We made it," Yuri announced proudly. "We're below the surface and up ahead you can see the airport."

"Wow! It's just like what you said, a roof over an entire sprawling city!" Cathy exclaimed in admiration.

"Yes, incredible. The civilisations here took hold and evolved along these enormous canals over millions of years," Yuri explained, gesturing widely across the expansive cockpit window. "And when global warming began, they simply roofed over the canals."

"There are mountains and trees, and the sun looks beautiful," Cathy exclaimed as she grabbed her camera and snapped a photo of the panoramic spectacle.

"Well, the reddish ceiling filters out a lot of the heat and also gives a permanent sunset effect during daylight hours," Yuri explained. "My favourite colour is red!"

"I'm feeling a gravitational pull," Jonathan observed.

"Well, it's about half that of Earth's," Valentina said. "You'll need to watch that spring in your step, kids, or you might bounce into the roof!"

"What happens after we land?" Jonathan asked.

"I have a de-briefing on this flight, and then I prepare for my next one."

"We won't see you again?" Yvonne said, brightening up.

"Oh, don't look so happy," Yuri said with a laugh.

As they closed in on the airport, they could see rockets and spaceships scattered about and a few flying saucers hovering nearby. The landing wheels on their rocket opened and moments later they touched down and then taxied along the runway. "I hardly even noticed the actual landing," Jonathan said in surprise. "I guess you have advanced landing gears."

"Yes, and these are the clothes you are to wear," Valentina said handing them piles of clothes. "I hope you like the fashions."

They adjourned to their compartments and gathered their briefcases as the rocket finally came to a standstill. A door opened revealing a luminous red stretch limousine with a middle-aged gentleman in a conservative dark suit and tie standing next to it. The students descended a short escalator onto the tarmac.

"Welcome. I'm Cecil Snodgrass, your chauffeur and butler," he said with a crisp London accent in a friendly manner.

"That's a funny name for a Martian," Jonathan replied.

Cecil at first looked surprised and then hurt. His bottom lip began to quiver, and the corners of his mouth arced down as tears began to well in his eyes. "Jonathan! What have you said?' Cathy angrily exclaimed.

"I'm terribly sorry, Cecil. I didn't mean any offence," Jonathan replied apologetically.

"We're not Martians, sir," Cecil replied, trying to regain his composure. "We are just like you people." He whipped out a crisply pressed hanky from his top pocket, dabbed his nose and wiped away some tears. "Of course, you are!" Cathy interceded, even more sorrowfully. "We're all the same really."

"Yes, we are, madam," Cecil replied, tucking away his hanky. "But maybe we are slightly more 'advanced'."

"Absolutely!" Cathy said to back up Jonathan and calm the drama. "We all know that!" She turned to Jonathan, "It was only three weeks ago you insulted that poor neanderthal," Cathy whispered angrily, "Do you just travel through time and space upsetting everyone you meet, you idiot."

"May we go then?" Cecil enquired. He opened the door of the limousine and stood stiffly as everyone clambered in.

Before long, the stretch limousine was speeding down a highway with the students seated three and three, opposite each other admiring their new clothes in the spacious limousine with tinted windows.

"Everything seems the same as it is on Earth," Sebastian noted, "except for those flying saucers hovering around and even the cars look the same."

"Do you think this is some sort of metaphor for our first venture into Uluru?" Yvonne asked innocently, sending everyone into a deep train of thought, only to be broken by Cathy.

"Excuse me, Cecil," Cathy said tapping on the glass partition that separated them from the chauffeur. "I noticed some *Daleks* remonstrating with people over there. Are they dangerous?"

"Goodness gracious no, madam," Cecil replied, glancing into the rearview mirror, "They're giving parking fines. We have robots here for that sort of trivial work and the local senate decided to adopt their design from the *Dr. Who* TV series… terribly popular here."

A Dalek was in the process of placing a parking ticket on the windshield of a car parked illegally and other cars were being hastily moved as more Daleks approached shrieking, 'Exterminate!'

"One of the benefits of being advanced and observing Earth so closely is that we can adopt any of their ideas we like," Cecil replied proudly.

The stretch limousine turned off the freeway and sped along tree-lined suburban streets with large houses, as normal everyday people went about their daily lives and, other than the permanent red sunset effect over the entire city, everything seemed very Earth-like.

"It's hard to believe we're on Mars," Yvonne concluded, wondering aloud. "What sort of guide have I turned out to be?" noticing as they drove along, the large houses morphed into opulent mansions.

"I guess you have only wealthy people here on Mars?" Cathy enquired.

"Mostly," Cecil replied curtly, "others are elsewhere," he said in a slightly superior way. A tall wrought iron gate swung open, and the limousine cruised along a winding drive through spectacular gardens and pulled up outside an imposing palace.

Chapter 18
Friendly Joviality

"This is your accommodation," Cecil announced, opening the limousine door. They all stepped out and looked around in awe. "At your disposal, you have fifteen servants, three chefs, twelve gardeners, and, as you know, I'm your butler."

"We won't forget that," Cathy reassured, "Thank you so much." The students couldn't quite believe the gardens and the palace, with its magnificent French Baroque architecture.

Kim quickly took over as their knowledgeable guide, "This looks like *The Palace of Versailles*," he advised excitedly as they walked over white crushed gravel and strolled through the front door into the atrium and then climbed the wide staircase to the second floor. Cecil showed them to their luxurious bedrooms and invited them to change into the clothes they had been supplied with and look around the mansion. After a considerable time getting changed, they gathered.

"It all seems a bit too good to be true," Jonathan observed, adjusting his rimless glasses, and looking out his window at the expansive gardens below, "Versailles was the centre of power for Frances pre-revolutionary ruling class, the material embodiment of absolute monarchy that reigned over France until the Revolution from 1788," Kim continued as they strolled past a large room and paused to admire a billiards table in the games room and then ambled down the staircase chatting away.

"And, in a clearing in the garden, I noticed a sundial," Jonathan mentioned, "I wonder how that would work since there is no real sunrise or sunset here?" Sebastian pondered as they reached Cecil.

"Lunch will be served shortly," He announced.

They all assembled in the opulent banquet room, "I can hardly breathe in this jacket," Jonathan said in breeches, short trouser-like garments, and doublets, tight-fitting jackets, covered by a jerkin and over that a cape, as the girls agreed, all dressed in their newly acquired French fashions from the early 1700's, with voluminous embroidered gowns in the style à la française, gold, and silver threading everywhere and silk stockings, and all sat around a long formal dining table with servants standing nearby.

"Well, I can hardly breathe in this bodice either," Cathy complained to Jonathan, "and we had no time to set our feathered hair over our foreheads properly, or adjust our linen coifs with these fiddly lace trims."

"But we all look grand and historically accurate," Kim concluded as he tore a baguette apart, admiring the table settings, all strictly symmetrical, with several candlesticks flickering, and place settings spaced evenly around the table, glittering glasses, and silverware, lined up at the same distance from the edge of the table, admiring the large dining room, which was like the *Hall of Mirrors* with various paintings that depicted the glorious history of Louis XIV, "These works demonstrate that the French could rival the Venetian monopoly on mirror manufacturing," Kim explained with his encyclopaedic memory and knowledge of everything.

"Ah good, our dinner guest has arrived on time," Cecil said, looking out the window as a Volkswagen convertible sped up the drive and screeched to a halt on the gravel. A shaggy-haired gentleman wearing a cardigan stepped out and shuffled towards the mansion.

"May I introduce Albert Einstein?" Cecil announced as everyone stood up in surprise when Einstein appeared at the door with a smile and a nod.

"To what do we deserve this unusual honour?" Jonathan inquired in his politest manner as he tried to remember what year Einstein had died, at least on Earth.

"DNA," Einstein replied quickly. "When I died in 1955, my ashes were scattered, except for my brain! My neurologist sold part of it to a Mars agent, and they brought it back here and reconstructed me in entirety!"

"Oh. Can they do that?" Kim asked.

"Yes, of course. This is a very advanced civilisation." Einstein gestured towards the window.

"That suburb over there has thousands of reconstructed humans from Earth, they've recreated heaps of big-time humans up here: Bell, Edison, Ford,

Shakespeare, Lennon, Da Vinci, Wright Brothers, obviously," he smiled at his attentive student audience, "big wigs who lived in the past and whose deeds exerted a significant impact on other people's lives and consciousness, Napoleon, Galileo, a dear friend of mine, Darwin, Jesus, it was only a few weeks ago my best friend Archimedes told me spaghetti was invented by the Greeks and stolen by the Romans. This is typical of people who fed Christians to the lions."

"I hope they only reconstruct people who made positive contributions to civilisation," Cathy chimed in adjusting her hair slightly tangled in her glittering tiara.

"Oh, don't count on that. It's a very wide collection; Dadaists, Cubists, Freudians, dictators, rock stars, the works!"

"Dictators?" Sebastian replied in shock.

"Yes, of course! One of the most popular TV programs here is *Big Brother* with a house containing Mao, Hitler, Mussolini, Stalin, Pol Pot, that ilk," Einstein explained avidly.

"Who was voted out first?" Jonathan asked.

"Voting? There is no voting! It's a 'dictatorship'! That's the whole point!" Einstein responded, scratching his head. "It's the longest-running program on TV here, another idea they stole from Earth and produced properly. You know, they then all formed a debating club… God, it's a bloodbath on good days."

My neighbour, Aldous Huxley, and I attended one of these debates, and he had the opinion that the greater part of the population is not very intelligent, dreads responsibility, and desires nothing better than to be told what to do…"

Cecil cleared his throat. "May I suggest we sit down for lunch?"

Albert continued, "… Provided the rulers do not interfere with their material comforts and cherished beliefs, they are perfectly happy to let themselves be ruled, he told me."

"The art of seeing, Albert, we have your favourite dish, Rheinische Sauerbraten!" Cecil interrupted.

Everyone sat down with Einstein at the head of the table. "Yes, good, beef roast stewed with wine. Thank you, Snodgrass!" Einstein said as waiters busied themselves, pouring drinks and placing napkins on everyone's laps and one around the dingo pup's neck as she chewed on a fossil.

"What on Mars will we talk about?" Jonathan whispered to the others as he looked at Einstein, "Here is the man who said, 'Only two things are infinite, the universe and human stupidity, and I'm not sure about the universe.'"

The waiters passed around Badener Schneckensuepple, a snail chowder flowered with herbs. After a moment of silence, Jonathan looked at Einstein.

"So what's life on Mars like?" Jonathan asked him.

"Good question," Einstein said. "Well, recently, NASA landed that six-wheeled rover on the Meridian Planum to collect samples, and the Mars people asked me what they should do about it." Einstein wiped chowder from his bushy moustache. "So I said, 'Look, give them something to analyse!' So they scattered a whole lot of dark red powder around the machine and the rover scooped it up, analysed it, and sent the results back to Earth."

"What did they find?" Cathy asked curiously.

"Coca Cola powder!" Einstein replied, laughing heartily. "You see, we play these little games with NASA, it's harmless fun really!"

"Who do you mostly hang out here with, Mr Einstein?" Yvonne ventured to ask as Albert gazed at her incredible indigenous beauty.

"Good question. Up in the foothills, there is a cave where Aristotle, Socrates, Aristophanes, Pythagoras and Pericles meet in darkness with Plato, mostly reconstructed earthlings, or intelligent look-alikes anyway, and I go to help them re-work Plato's *The Allegory of the Cave*. In *Republic*, it is a place where people are chained and cannot move, and are only able to view shadows on the wall of the cave, representing the physical world and the ignorance of its inhabitants."

"Why do you meet in darkness," Kim asked.

"Well, we decided the shadows confuse the symbolic narrative," Albert replied as Haupt perse, the main course, was served with Spannferkel, spit-roasted baby pig, Bulletten, meatballs, and Soeier, pickled eggs, as the students described their journey to Einstein.

"Ah yes, I've heard about that place, they're all from here."

"All those chartered accountants and bureaucrats we came across below the underground island named Hawaii are from Mars?" Jonathan asked in disbelief.

"Yes," Einstein nodded. "The Martians built all the tunnels long ago. Their original purpose was to create secure tourism on Earth for Martians. They had to find a place to get all the paperwork done and run the tourism leg for Mars, sometimes one pays most for the things one gets for nothing," Einstein replied, "And this advanced computer you say Jonathan has… can I see it?"

"Yes, of course," Jonathan replied. "I'll be happy to show it to you after lunch."

"Yes, good! Oh! And Schwartzwalder kirsch torte!" Einstein said happily as Cecil served the desert, Black Forest cake. "My favourite with Bavarian vanilla crème!"

"May I suggest you all adjourn to the nursery for your Bluemchenkaffee?" Cecil asked after they'd finished their desserts.

"Ah! Small flower coffee is the best coffee, Snodgrass," Einstein replied as he stood up and brushed the Black Forest cake crumbs off his red cardigan. "That was a delicious lunch. Thank you."

Everyone strolled out to the large glass-encased nursery near the sundial and took a seat on the patio where exotic plants and statues surrounded them. The waiters poured coffee and passed around mints while the students lounged comfortably in their green surroundings.

"Do you miss life on Earth, Albert?" Sebastian asked, sipping on his coffee.

"Yes and no. You see, life is very good here, and I've already had a fun life from 1879 to 1955, so this new life is really the icing on the cake," Einstein said. "But yes, I guess if there is an after-life, this must be it."

"But it's not exactly heaven, is it?" Sebastian asked. "I mean you've proved by being here that you're not in heaven and therefore there might not be a God."

Einstein stroked his chin thoughtfully, dropped a lump of sugar into his coffee and stirred it. "Hmmm... what really interests me is whether God had any choice in the creation of the world."

"So do you think the people from here created the world millions of years ago?" Sebastian asked.

"No, they are advanced, but not 'that' advanced. I think Mars is just another cog in the cosmos," Einstein responded.

"Do you dream ever?" Sebastian continued.

"Oh, yes, I do, and I remember them also. In fact, recently I had a 'zenith dream', Einstein revealed.

"What is that?" Sebastian asked as everyone leaned forward.

"Well, Zenith implies a pioneering spirit, say a natural born leader, highly focused and achievement orientated. And you, Yvonne, appeared in it, this is before I even met you." Einstein said as everyone looked at Yvonne. "It was like déjà vu. It was so clear that I decided to have it analysed, so I visited my friend Sigmund Freud, who lives down the road."

"Wow, me?" Yvonne said blushing.

"Yes, so Sigmund told me to lie down on his very comfortable couch and describe it."

"What happened?" Yvonne asked.

"Well, I fell asleep, so I never got to tell him."

"So what was this dream? Please tell me," Yvonne insisted.

"I ascended a black mosaic escalator and met you in the prime minister's office, in twenty years' time, that was it."

"So your dream indicates we are alive in twenty years' time?" Kim chimed in.

"Possibly, but it was only a dream," Albert replied.

"Well, I miss life on Earth," Yvonne said, taking the think tank by surprise. They all looked at her and thought for a moment in time.

'God, she's beautiful', Sebastian thought to himself, 'maybe it's her lips or her graceful features, or just the way she keeps bringing us back to basics on earth', as he gazed at her.

"What do you miss most?" Albert asked, as he too secretly admired Yvonne's beauty.

"My family," Yvonne said sadly. "I miss my family right now. How about you?"

"You mean my 'theory of relatives'?" Einstein asked with a glint in his eyes, placing his cup on the saucer, and studying the coffee granules.

"Well, yes," she said thoughtfully.

"That is an interesting question," Albert replied with a nod of approval. "When I was on Earth, I only saw them at Christmas, and they gave me presents. One Christmas I got seventeen pocket calculators, they remembered I had failed mathematics at school."

At that moment, Jonathan entered the nursery holding his laptop and placed it on the table.

"Well, here it is," Jonathan announced proudly, turning it on.

"What's so special about it?" Einstein asked.

"For one thing, the lid of the laptop acts as a solar and satellite dish," Jonathan explained, breathing on his rimless glasses, and polishing them, "but most importantly, I can make video contact with Earth, and it can't be blocked by this so-called advanced civilisation here on Mars."

"That's amazing!" Einstein exclaimed, "This means our cover will be blown here! This is sure to have major ramifications!"

"Who for?" Jonathan wondered aloud.

"Heavens! Earth, Mars, the universe, time, matter, energy, everything, holy cow!" Einstein said, throwing up his arms in excitement.

"Should I try to make contact?" Jonathan asked tersely, looking at the others.

"Of course! There shouldn't be any secrets in our universe!" Albert answered loudly.

"Well, I don't know, Jonathan. You know what your father said," Cathy reminded him.

"Bugger it then," Jonathan said, tapping on the connect key.

The screen showed the satellite was searching, and it began to flicker with different colours and patterns making blips, beeps, babble, and twaddle sounds as everyone looked on with intense interest.

"What's with all this babble and twaddle noise?" Albert inquired.

"Well, my laptop is trying to find a suitable dish on Earth," Jonathan explained. "And it could zero in on anyone."

"There are millions of satellite dishes," Kim explained, so it might link up with one anywhere."

Chapter 19
Flying Cups and Saucers

Back on Earth, a newsroom was quiet. Reporters ambled around watering the plants and filling in crosswords, many using crayons. The phone rang on the editor-in-chief's vacant desk. One of the reporters answered it.

"Yes, what?" he demanded.

"It's Studio 3 here, and we're getting some interference with our satellite cross to Canberra for an interview. We've got some guy coming through who claims to be Einstein."

The reporter rolled up his eyes but decided to record it anyway.

"We're talking to Albert Einstein," the reporter said to the camera. He swivelled around and faced the large screen. "So, Mr Einstein, have you broken any chalk on your blackboard recently?"

"Have I what? Oh! Chalk! Yes, all the time," Einstein said. "But I have something of vital importance to say."

"What, that you discovered the mathematical formula for stronger chalk?" The reporter said, guffawing away.

"What? Will you shut up and listen, you numbskull? I am talking from the planet Mars!" Einstein replied angrily.

"Is that a school?" The reporter chortled.

Einstein looked around at the students in exasperation. "What will I do with this idiot, Jonathan?"

Sebastian and Jonathan stood up and walked behind Einstein, and they all peered into the webcam lens.

"Hello?" Jonathan said. "We're telecasting from Mars here. Is there someone normal there we can speak to?"

"'The most terrifying fact about the universe is not that it is hostile but that it is indifferent and however vast the darkness. We must supply our own light'" Albert mentioned. "My friend Stanley Kubrik told me this, he runs a great local cinema down the road."

The makeup lady in Studio 3 looked more closely at the TV monitor. "Isn't that two of the missing students from Uluru?" she gasped.

"Yes, we're the students who disappeared in Uluru-Kata Tjuta National Park," Jonathan exclaimed as Cathy, Yvonne and Kim joined them. "It's true. We're speaking from Mars."

A buzz erupted around the studio.

"We're alive and well!" Cathy said to the webcam, holding Zara, as the group stood behind Albert and put their arms around each other.

"Yes! And I'm Albert Einstein, speaking to you live from Mars!" Suddenly the screen went blank.

"Bummer!" Jonathan sighed. "We've lost contact."

"But now they know we're alive!" Cathy announced jubilantly.

Jonathan tapped a few more keys but the screen was black.

"Well, we can try again later," Albert suggested. "Although that may be too late." glancing up as the group followed his gaze. A flying saucer with a flashing red light was hovering over the mansion.

"Do you think it traced the source of our video contact?" Jonathan asked.

Albert nodded, and they watched in shock and awe as the flying saucer hovered lower and landed near the sundial that strangely spun around and melted. A door opened and unfolded down onto the ground, revealing a short escalator. A man in a suit descended and strolled over to their table.

"They made contact with Earth, sir," Cecil said to the man.

Yes, I know," he said looking at Albert. "We need to talk."

Everyone sat down and looked at this visitor. He was handsome and intelligent in his demeanour and showed no animosity towards them or what they had just achieved.

"My name is Walter. I'm from the senate, which is the governing body here," he explained calmly. "We're an advanced civilisation here on Mars, and I'm afraid we don't want Earth finding out about us."

"Why not, Walter?" Einstein inquired. "We could be celestial neighbours living in peace and harmony."

"Harmony?" Walter replied in surprise. "Earth doesn't know the first thing about harmony. Not a clue about amiability either."

"Isn't that the pot calling the kettle red?" Albert protested.

"Are you going to have us sent to the guillotine," Cathy added, as she looked at her long fingernails.

Snodgrass became upset again and tears welled up in his eyes. "Look! We're not like that," he replied with a quivering voice.

"Not at all," Walter said. "But we're sending you back to Earth for work experience."

"Work experience?" Jonathan exclaimed in surprise. "Why do we need…"

"Shut up, Jonathan!" Cathy said angrily. She wanted to go back to Earth more than anything. "Don't argue!"

"Now, if you could gather your belongings, we'll leave shortly," Walter said.

Everyone couldn't believe their luck and jumped to their feet. Jonathan started to pick up his laptop, but Walter put his hand on it. "We keep the computer," he said firmly.

"But it's mine," Jonathan said. "I want."

"Just shut up!" Cathy demanded, grabbing Jonathan by the arm, and pulling him along with her.

"That is good! I need the latest laptop, anyway!" Albert said eagerly.

"Wrong again," Walter said without hesitation. "You're going with them, Einstein."

"Ah, down to Earth, I like the idea!" Albert replied raising his bushy eyebrows.

Within minutes, they had collected their briefcases and satchels and were strolling towards the flying saucer, the dingo pup scampering along beside them, with Albert neatly arranging his shaggy hair.

"Amazing!" Sebastian whispered to Jonathan. "Whoever thought we would get to ride in a flying saucer!"

"After you," Walter said.

They all stepped onto the short escalator and rode it up into the flying saucer. The door closed behind them, and the saucer made a loud humming noise as it lifted into the sky and then whooshed off sideways.

The students, dingo pup, and Einstein sat down on comfortable chairs inside the craft, nervous and excited. The only other person on board was Walter, and he stood in the middle of the ship, operating a control panel.

"Imagine what our parents will think when we land in Melbourne in a flying saucer!" Jonathan whispered.

"I can't believe we're finally going home!" Yvonne cried in relief.

"I'm taking you to the airport. You'll take the rocket back to Earth," Walter informed them. "You should put this science fiction nonsense out of your head."

"Oh well, first-class rocket travel was great!" Jonathan said.

"Fifth class this time," Walter replied.

"Will there be food?" Kim asked.

"Not much," Walter sighed. "Just scraps."

"Oh…" Kim sighed, glancing at the others.

After some time, the flying saucer came to a standstill, hovered and then slowly descended to the airport tarmac, and the door opened.

"Out!" Walter ordered.

A large windowless, bus-like vehicle stood in front of them. The door zipped aside and some men in suits gestured for them to enter. They were bundled inside, and the door slammed shut, locking them in darkness with many others.

"What is going on here?" Yvonne protested, "Our brief holiday to the red centre cut short?"

"We don't know," an unfamiliar voice in the dark replied.

The vehicle jolted forward, and they all stood in silence for about five minutes until it suddenly stopped. Then the door swung open, revealing a passageway and a few more men.

"Come on!" One yelled. "Get out! Walk up that corridor!"

The students disembarked with the others on the bus and as they followed the men, they entered a large door and joined a queue of hundreds of people and found themselves in a large compartment with no seats and only a couple of small windows.

"The lipstick!" Asami urgently whispered to Cathy. "Have you got the mirror lipstick?"

"Oh! Yes! Hold the pup," Cathy whispered, as she frantically searched through her satchel. "Ah! Got it!" she said, quickly applying it to her lips and then handing it to Asami and Yvonne. "Hurry!"

The other girls hurriedly put the lipstick on, and the group pushed their way through the crowded compartment to a man guarding a back door.

"Here! Look!" Cathy said forcefully, as she and the others pouted their lips out at the guard.

"At what?" the guard inquired.

"Our lipstick! It's like a mirror!" Cathy said impatiently.

"I can see myself in your lips," the guard replied arrogantly and with a shrug. "So?"

"So we should be in first class!" Cathy answered angrily.

"I don't see the connection," the guard said. "Surely if you want to be in first class, you should have a first-class ticket. No wonder you're being sent to Earth."

"Oh…" Cathy said, suddenly feeling foolish. "I guess so." As they retreated sheepishly into the crowded compartment, and then the door shut closed.

After a while, they could feel the rocket taxi onto the runway. Some other passengers in fifth class crowded around the few portholes and confirmed that the rocket was preparing to take off.

The engines fired up and suddenly there was an enormous surge of energy as the rocket was launched. Without seat belts or even seats, all the passengers were thrown into the air, slamming into the roof of the compartment.

As everyone groaned and cried out, Jonathan managed to force his way to a porthole and peered out. "Well, we're in the air and about to pass through the ceiling," he said, staring at the roof that covered the enormous canal where the civilisation of Mars lived.

The rocket surged through a hole in the ceiling and into outer space.

Gradually the pull of gravity diminished, and the hundreds of passengers started to float around, bumping into each other.

The students, Einstein, and the dingo pop managed to float towards each other and formed a huddle. They stayed like this for what felt like days, and everyone could only despair about it all.

Three times a day, a hatch would open, and packets of fast food and bottles of water would come drifting through. No one knew how long it would go on for, but the students estimated three weeks since this was the length of their trip from Earth to Mars.

"We are about to enter a wormhole so there will be some turbulence," came an announcement over the speaker.

"My god! That's Yuri's voice!" Yvonne whispered.

"A wormhole?" Albert uttered in amazement. "We must be going to travel in time!"

Suddenly there was a loud roar, and the rocket began to vibrate violently. Kim and Asami were close to a porthole and peered out at the universe.

"The stars are all long streaks!" Kim described to the others. "We must be going faster than light! Wow! Look at the colours!"

"Hold on to each other tighter!" Jonathan called out.

"This is terrible, my vision is blurring!" Yvonne moaned.

The noise became louder and the vibrating worse. All the passengers started to lose consciousness and soon the compartment was full of bodies floating around limply and aimlessly.

Chapter 20
Down to Earth

When Sebastian opened his eyes, Yvonne was gazing at him with a smile. "We're almost back on Earth."

Jonathan peered out the porthole and out into space. They were passing the moon, and it was massive, sandy grey and beautiful. "It's a full moon!"

Everywhere in the compartment people began to regain consciousness.

"I've had the time of my life!" Albert exclaimed, but this wasn't the case for everyone.

All the students were fine, but some of the other passengers had died in the wormhole, their bodies pushed through the food hatch along with half-eaten meals.

"Time to eject the rubbish and dead humans," Yuri announced, as a large door opened, and all the humans and rubbish were sucked out. "They will drift to earth, burn up on re-entry and look like a human meteorite shower and be cremated at the same time," Yuri concluded, "Rest in peace."

"What time in history do you think we've travelled to?" Sebastian asked Albert.

"History?" Einstein replied. "We might have gone to the future! Who knows?" he replied holding on to the other students.

After a couple of hours, the moon faded into the distance and Earth, the blue planet, loomed large. Outside the portholes, a stream of fire burst from the rocket as it started to vibrate again.

"We must be entering the earth's atmosphere," Jonathan said, peering out the window again. "And it looks like we're heading for the Pacific Ocean."

'Bip, bip… bip, bip…' came the sound from the mobile phone.

"Christ! The cell phone!" Jonathan remembered, fumbling through his briefcase. He found it and tapped the text message button.

'WE SAW YOU WITH EINSTEIN ON TV', a text message conveyed with a surprised emoji.

"We must have coverage!" Jonathan shouted, showing the message to the others. "There's a second message!"

"Call them!" Cathy ordered, but before Jonathan could dial any numbers the phone started to ring.

Jonathan answered quickly. "Hello?"

"Where are you now?" The voice was unfamiliar. "Are you all well?"

Suddenly, there was a crash, and everyone was thrown around the compartment. Outside the porthole, water appeared, and Jonathan realised the rocket had collided with the Pacific Ocean. Gravity returned, and the passengers collapsed in a tangled heap on the floor.

The phone went dead, and Jonathan glanced at the screen. "We lost service." He checked the second text message.

'R U BEING HELD HOSTAGE?' the text read.

"They must think we've been kidnapped or something," Cathy said. "Oh well, at least we made brief contact."

"But how can that be if we've travelled in time?" Kim asked Albert.

"That is a good question!" Einstein replied. "Maybe the cell phone doesn't know this!"

After about an hour, the rocket came to a standstill. There was a lot of moaning and groaning from injured people, but it was completely dark, and no one knew what was happening.

The compartment door opened, and people in suits ordered everyone out.

They were all herded down a long dimly lit corridor and through another door and entered a railway station. The station was plain and drab and resembled nothing like the gleaming mirror station.

The train had several carriages, and the passengers were instructed to get on board. The carriages were dimly lit, uncomfortable, and crowded. Everyone stood in confused silence as the train pulled out of the station and headed into a tunnel.

After a while, the students made small talk with some of the other passengers and learned they were all from Mars, and a theme quickly became apparent. All the passengers had misdemeanours on their records, and Jonathan was slowly putting it together.

"Work experience on Earth is 'punishment'," he whispered to the others.

"I had a run-in with a Dalek," one passenger explained to Sebastian. "Just a simple parking infringement."

"This is like convict transportation, really," Sebastian suggested.

"Worse! It could be the final solution!" Einstein said.

"Really?" Cathy whispered. "They wouldn't go to this much trouble to kill us, would they?"

"Well, maybe they don't have the death penalty on Mars," Jonathan hoped. "They are an advanced civilisation, after all."

No one knew how long the train trip would go on for. It certainly wasn't as fast as the mirror train, and there wasn't any food either. Jonathan wistfully recalled his wonderful train journey with *une jeune et belle serveuse*, the beautiful French waitress. This trip sucked in comparison, he thought to himself.

Eventually, they decided to look at what food they had in their briefcases and satchels. They still had the canned food from Mr Harrison's backpack, mainly *Camp Pie*, and thankfully, this kept them going.

After a couple of days, the train began to slow down and arrived at an underground station made of stone and polished granite.

All the passengers were ordered off the train, and they congregated on the station platform. They were handed clothes that looked like loincloths, short kilts and sandals made of rope.

"Oh, my god, I'm so pleased to change out of these seventeenth-century French fashions," Cathy announced as they loosened and removed their tight corsets, "we can breathe again!"

"Jonathan," Sebastian whispered. "Hide the phone."

He managed to smuggle the phone under his belt, and Cathy secured the dingo pup under her loincloth dress. Then all their discarded clothes were collected by the guards and placed into sacks on the train.

Finally, a guard addressed the passengers, "We have arrived at your destination for work experience," he said in a gruff bossy voice. "You will now be fed, and then you have a one-day walk ahead of you before you start work."

Some more guards emerged from a door with plates of food and placed them along a wooden table. It was a combination of bread and salad. Flasks of beer made from barley grain were also plonked on the table and everyone began eating and drinking.

"I hope you enjoy this cuisine," the guard said. "Because you'll be eating it for the next twenty years."

"I hope he's joking," Sebastian said.

"I can't survive on this," Kim agreed.

"We're not going to be stuck here for twenty years, are we?" Cathy whispered in a panic, grabbing Jonathan's hand.

"I hope not," he said, but he had no idea of what was going on, although Einstein seemed to be figuring out something.

Albert studied the writing on the wall and attempted to decipher it. "Unless I'm mistaken, those hieroglyphics on the stone wall are ancient Egyptian."

"Really?" Asami asked. "That would fit in with these ugly loincloths we have to wear."

"Well, there is more," Albert continued. "I think those hieroglyphic ideograms and pictograms are Egyptian for 'Cairo Underground Railway Station'!"

The students looked at each other in silence. Soon enough, the next step in their journey began as the guards ordered them to start marching.

Reluctantly, all the passengers entered a long stone corridor. It was dank and only lit by sporadic electric lights hanging from the roof. The air was hot and stuffy, and the hiking was uphill and relentless.

Occasionally, they came across a series of stone steps and the guards allowed everyone to rest. It was particularly hard on the passengers from Mars because they had grown up with a lighter pull of gravity, so walking on Earth made them breathless.

After about six hours of marching, they reached a heavy metal door. One guard tapped in some numbers on a small control panel and the door slowly opened. Everyone was ushered through the metal door, and the guards laughed and wished everyone good luck and then slammed the heavy metal door shut behind them.

A group of new guards dressed in long white robes appeared. They were carrying flaming torches that illuminated the anger on their face. These guards didn't speak English but yelled and swore at them in Egyptian.

The marching continued, and the group became more spread out as some became too tired to continue. The five students were young and fit and set the pace at the front. The dingo pup scampered along happily, and even Einstein kept up with them.

"It's mind over matter," Albert joked, explaining his physical prowess.

However, after a while, the walls of the tunnel began to change in appearance. The corridors became lined with Aswan pink granite and the floor became more polished.

"Wow!" Asami exclaimed, stopping momentarily to admire an unfinished painting on the wall.

"This looks like a pharaoh." Kim touched it and looked at his finger. "It's still wet. It must be a work in progress."

"The hieroglyphics suggest it's King Khufu!" Albert explained in excitement.

"Who's he?" Jonathan asked.

"Second king of the Fourth Dynasty, builder of the Great Pyramid in Giza," Kim quickly explained, but he was cut short.

'Bip, bip… bip, bip… bip, bip…' came the familiar sound of the cell phone. One of the guards looked around furiously and screamed something they couldn't understand.

"Turn it off, Jonathon!" Sebastian whispered urgently. He began to whistle loudly to cover the noise. Jonathan fumbled beneath the loincloth, reaching for the cell to silence it. One of the guards pushed him forward to keep him walking.

A few yards on, Jonathan pulled out the cell again and secretly looked at the text message.

'R U IN CAIRO?'

"Hey, Sebastian!" Jonathan whispered. "The text asked if we're in Cairo!"

"When you get a chance, reply yes," Sebastian said in hushed excitement. "But just act natural and keep walking."

Further on, Cathy strolled in front of one of the guards and gently lifted her loincloth and lowered her underpants. The guard stopped and stared, causing the necessary distraction for Jonathan to pull out the phone again.

'Yes!' he quickly texted back.

When the text didn't send, he glanced at the 'NO NETWORK COVERAGE' in the corner of the screen.

"It won't go through!" Jonathan whispered to Sebastian.

The corridor suddenly opened into a large unfinished tomb. Craftsmen were working on various parts, with painters and stonemasons going about their daily work. They paid no attention to the crowd of people filing through.

"Book of the Dead," Albert said solemnly to the others, "Is the term used to describe a text used in funerals and will be placed in his tomb!"

"What?" Yvonne whispered, breaking a long silence.

"I believe we are inside the construction site of the tomb of King Khufu!" Albert whispered before the guard ordered them to keep walking.

"What exactly are you getting at?" Yvonne asked Albert quietly.

"We are inside a pyramid!" Einstein said loudly, his voice echoing around the chamber. "That will one day in the future contain a dead King Khufu, mummified."

"Did you hear that?" Yvonne asked the others.

Before they could comprehend that they had time travelled far into the past, a guard shoved them to keep walking.

After an hour of weaving through a maze, they literally saw light at the end of the tunnel and a minute later, they walked out into direct sunlight.

"It's the Giza Plateau!" Einstein proclaimed. "And that must be Cairo over there," he said, pointing to a large settlement of mud brick houses with thatched roofs. "We are very far back in the past, indeed."

"Do you believe this?" Jonathan exclaimed. "We just came out of a half-finished pyramid!"

"Yes! This is Cheops!" Albert explained. "The Great Pyramid of Khufu under construction. It's amazing!"

"So we've travelled to what time?" Sebastian asked as the rest of the passengers began emerging from the pyramid bedraggled and tired.

"It was completed around 2570 BC," Albert answered. "So I guess it's now 2555 BC. You see, these pyramids take nearly fifty years to build, and this one is the biggest!"

"So you think there's another twenty years of work needed on this baby?" Jonathan asked.

"Yes! And, what is worse, I think this is our work experience!" Albert said.

"They want us to build the pyramid?" Cathy gasped.

The guards pushed them towards a huge ramp that had dozens of stone blocks being pulled on sledges by slaves.

It was definitely a construction site in progress and even though it was late afternoon, and a perfect red sunset was forming over the river Nile, one shift was finishing and another one was about to begin.

"You lot! Get over here and push this block of stone!" a slave yelled at them. "We're off to dinner then bed!"

"Oh, so you can speak English?" Sebastian asked as he began pushing a two-ton block.

"Yes! Of course! Most of the slaves here speak English!" he replied, sauntering off. Sebastian wanted to keep talking but a guard came over holding a whip. The others got the message and began their work experience on Earth.

Chapter 21
Egypt

Blood, sweat, and sand became the epitome of their experience working on the Great Pyramid of Khufu. The sun finally set, and it was marginally cooler, but their Za, or work gang, had only managed to move the two-ton block about a centimetre up the steep ramp. Asami had never experienced direct sunlight before, and she sat down exhausted and dehydrated.

"Work you lazy sod, work!" One of the guards barked at Asami.

"Will you not be so rude?" Cathy snapped back. It was the wrong thing to say.

The guard stormed over, grabbed Asami by the arm, and leaned her over the block of stone. He lifted her loincloth dress and whipped her sweating backside. The others protested, but it made no difference. Asami was left in tears caressing her red welts.

They resumed work, pulling and pushing the block slowly up the ramp along with fifty other work gangs. It was painstakingly slow, gruelling labour. Occasionally, they exchanged some idle chatter.

"I've done some calculations in my head," Albert said breathlessly. "And I estimate it will take 2,300,000 blocks to build this pyramid."

"King Khufu must have an enormous ego!" Sebastian replied. "Why would a pharaoh want such a monumental tomb?"

"Well, you see everyone here believes the pharaoh maintains order in the universe," Albert explained.

"And so they bring in slaves from other planets?" Jonathan asked.

"Well, maybe the local Egyptians are too lazy!" Albert concluded.

A guard marched over to them. "STOP! Stop work!" He shouted. "You will be shown to your quarters now. Go away, shoo!" He waved his arms urging them to move away as another shift took over.

A young Egyptian woman approached them with a warm smile. "My name is Lucinda, please come with me," she said with a welcoming voice. Exhausted and bruised, they followed her down the long ramp. After a fifteen-minute walk, they reached a large village of mud brick houses near the base of the pyramid that housed the slaves.

"The shock of the first shift is the worst," Lucinda explained sympathetically, showing them to a house with four rooms. Each room had a wooden bed with a mangy straw mattress on it. Clay urns of water were scattered around.

Everyone eagerly drank the water and washed the blood and sand off their aching bodies.

"This is much harder than working out new theories," Albert lamented sorrowfully. The dingo pup sat on his lap, panting, exhausted from watching them toil.

Lucinda gave Sebastian a small container of olive oil, which he gently applied to Asami's backside as she lay face down, fatigued and humiliated from the beating. Jonathan gazed out the window at the pyramid, staring at the moon and the stars in the sky. It looked like a postcard, but no view of an Egyptian pyramid would ever impress him again, he thought.

After everyone had rested, they sat on the floor around a low wooden table talking to Lucinda. "I am a local citizen, but I speak English because I learned it from slaves like yourself who have arrived from Mars," she explained.

"Oh! You know we're from Mars?" Sebastian asked.

"Yes, of course," Lucinda said. "This has been going on for as long as I can remember. It's the worst-kept secret in Egypt. We're not supposed to talk about it, but I do. I'm fascinated by it."

"Well, we're not from Mars, actually," Yvonne said proudly. "We're originally from Earth, the twenty-first century AD. We travelled to Mars against our will and then came back in a time tunnel."

"Oh! That's different!" Lucinda replied, her eyes widening with admiration.

"When's dinner?" Jonathan asked. "We're famished after all that work experience building the king's cemetery."

"I've got lots of friends who work as servants for the king," Lucinda said quietly. "Why don't I take you to the palace and you can eat there?"

"Really? Is it safe?" Asami asked.

"Yes, just don't speak until I say so," Lucinda cautioned.

They all stood up and followed her into the warm Cairo night, walking along lanes and fields and past camels and carts. Half an hour later, they reached some small houses located next to a sizeable palace. Lucinda knocked on the door and spoke to a friend. They went inside the house and changed into long clean white robes that the king's servants wore.

"You'll have to brush your shaggy hair," Lucinda told Albert.

"But I haven't brushed my hair since 1930!" Einstein protested. But after thinking about it, he agreed and when he finished, he'd lost his famed wild-man appearance.

They walked to the main gate of the palace and strolled in without any problems, the guards assuming they were servants.

"Security is really slack in Egypt," Lucinda mentioned in passing.

Jonathon liked her Egyptian accent as well as her curvaceous form and wondered if he could get to know her better.

Before long, they reached the luxurious servant quarters. "Being a servant to the king is about the best job you can get on Earth," Lucinda explained, and introduced them to some of her friends, and they sat down around a long wooden table.

It was nearly midnight and the king's chefs were preparing Suhur, the midnight meal which consisted of various fish dishes. Lucinda told them that a freshly netted catch from the Nile had just been delivered.

"Poisson a la Grecque, baked fish, is delicious, but the Tagin samak bi-l-firik fish casserole with the hulled grain is excellent," Lucinda boasted.

The best wines in all civilisation were poured from gold-plated flasks and Fatush, home-style bread salad, was served. Everyone sat around discussing the theories of who exactly thought up the original idea of a pyramid.

Lucinda looked around at them. "Well, one rumour that's been doing the rounds for a few centuries says that the Martian civilisation actually colonised Earth thousands of years ago, and they dug all these tunnels everywhere."

"You mean like the one that ends here at the pyramid?" Cathy asked as she tore apart some Fatush.

"Yes," Lucinda said, glancing at Kim. "But there's one to The Great Wall, also."

"Really?" Kim asked. "I come from China, and I know our dynasties go back a long way."

"Apparently, this has been used as an underground trade route between our two dynasties for generations," Lucinda continued.

"And we've heard of other tunnels under the Incan Empire in South America and another site in England called Stonehenge," a friend of Lucinda's chimed in. A plate of savoury figs, leeks and dates was passed around.

"Why would an advanced civilisation from Mars want to build all these monuments?" Lucinda wondered aloud.

"Martian tourism," Jonathan answered.

"And all these tunnels lead to some huge underground place where thousands of people gather with papyrus scrolls, and quills and abacuses and do the accounting for these projects, a bureaucratic paradise," Asami whispered in a conspiratorial tone.

Suddenly, a man wearing a red flowing gown appeared and looked at these new different women.

"What's happening?" Asami whispered.

"Oh, my god," Lucinda whispered. "It's the king's advisor, he's been told to get a virgin for King Khufu!" Lucinda replied, trying to keep a low profile.

"Can he do that?" Asami replied.

"Of course he can, he's the king, the *pharaoh*, the most powerful man on Earth!" Lucinda replied as the man stopped and looked closely at Cathy and began touching her hair. Within seconds, he snapped his fingers and another couple of soldiers arrived and grabbed her.

"But I'm not a virgin!" Cathy yelled in protest as she was dragged out of the room.

"This is an outrage!" Jonathan shouted as he leapt up, but Lucinda grabbed his arm and held him in place.

"I'm so sorry!" Lucinda pleaded apologetically to Jonathan and the others, who sat silently in shock. "What a terrible misfortune," she lamented. "But apparently he's gentle."

The dinner continued in a somewhat subdued manner as the students glanced nervously at each other. About fifteen minutes later, Cathy strolled in again and sat down with a stunned expression.

"That was strange," she said with a blank face. "I was taken into this amazing gold bedroom chamber. My robe was pulled off, and I was thrown onto the king's enormous bed where he was waiting for me. It was very fast and impersonal. Then he rolled over and went to sleep. My robe was handed back to me, and I was escorted back here."

"What does King Khufu look like?" Albert enquired ingenuously.

"He's young and terribly good-looking," Cathy replied. "I was going to try to fight him off, but I knew it would be useless, and I might end up dead… And he had so much charisma, my King Khufu," she said wistfully.

"And what is going to happen to us?" Sebastian asked as he glanced at Lucinda.

When she didn't reply, Lucinda's friend spoke up. "Well, you will be worked to death and then buried."

"Do we get buried alongside Cathy's new boyfriend?" Sebastian wondered aloud.

"Don't be silly," Lucinda scolded. "Slaves are buried outside the pyramid in unmarked graves."

"Hmmm…" Albert said, scratching his brushed hair, "that returns us to the original problem, how can we get out of this work experience?"

Feteer Bel Asaag—pastry with ground lamb—was served along with Egyptian marinade and whole butter fried chicken. As the students ate, they discussed their dilemma with Albert.

"I noticed when we passed those hieroglyphics in the tunnel before the burial chamber that the mobile phone worked briefly," Jonathan said. "Lucinda, can we go back to that place tomorrow?"

"I guess so," she replied tentatively. "If you wear these white robes and I go with you, no one will notice."

"Great. Well, let's try it," Jonathan said eagerly.

"And, if we can't make contact, we'll just go back to work and get flogged to death!" Sebastian concluded as he gulped down more fine wine.

Eventually, the delicious Egyptian feast was consumed, and Lucinda took them all back to their quarters at the base of the enormous pyramid.

It was a beautiful warm evening, and she dropped behind to chat with Jonathan.

"I don't have a boyfriend, Jonathon," she mentioned. "And you're from the twenty-first century AD, you know what I mean?"

"I think I do," Jonathon said, though he didn't know what the future had to do with getting laid in ancient Egypt. "Is there somewhere we can go to be alone?"

Lucinda led Jonathan down to the banks of the river Nile, and they sat in the moon shade of some palm and olive trees. Lucinda had beautiful Middle Eastern eyes and a sensuous darkly tanned body, and they kissed passionately as the mirror-like Nile flowed gently by.

"I've never made love to an Australian," Lucinda whispered into Jonathon's ear, "In fact, I have never even 'heard' of Australia."

She opened her long white robe to reveal her naked body underneath gleaming from the moonlight reflected off the Nile. Lucinda groaned with pleasure as they made love.

Chapter 22
The Great Pyramid of Khufu

Jonathon woke up as Zara the dingo jumped on him and began licking his face and wagging her tail as she pranced about on his chest.

"What are you doing here?' Jonathon asked as he sat up on the banks of the Nile and saw the sunrise over the uncompleted Great Pyramid. Lucinda slept serenely next to him. He shook her gently, admiring her beautiful body.

"We must go," Jonathon said as he picked up the pup and followed Lucinda. Before long, they arrived back at the mud brick house where everyone was waiting impatiently.

'Oh, here they are!' Cathy said angrily. "God, it's lucky we have Zara, she went off and found you both! What a clever little pup, you are," Cathy said molly-coddling the dingo while glaring at Jonathon.

The Giza Plateau was a veritable hive of activity as thousands of locals and slaves worked on the pyramid and went about their daily lives.

The students strolled along in their flowing white robes and looked a class higher than mere slaves. They passed the huge ramp where the granite blocks that had arrived by barge along the Nile from Aswan were being schlepped ever so slowly towards their resting place on the pyramid Cheops. Further over were the completed pyramids of Khafre, Chephren, and the smaller Menkaure, Mycerinus.

Eventually, they reached the entrance of Cheops and a guard nodded and gestured for them to enter without a second glance. Lucinda lit a couple of torches which gave off an eerie light that flickered about as they made their way along the corridors lined with polished granite.

"Try sending a text message again," Sebastian suggested to Jonathan who took out the phone, tapped a short note and pressed send. It showed 'No Network Coverage' again.

They walked down one corridor after another, and it was only thanks to the excellent memory of Albert that they took the correct turns and bends in the labyrinth and myriad of tunnels and eventually located the impressive main tomb where King Khufu would be laid to rest.

"If you had played your cards better last night with King Khufu," Sebastian whispered to Cathy. "You could be buried here next to him one day."

'Yeah sure, thanks," Cathy replied sarcastically. "He was better than you in bed!"

The same artists and various stonemasons were still working away diligently and paid scant attention to them as they strolled through the chamber and entered another tunnel.

After a while, they came across the same location they had stopped at the previous day where Albert had deciphered the hieroglyphics.

"This is it!" Albert announced. Cathy took the dingo pup out from under her robe and placed her on the granite floor. There were no guards to worry them, so Jonathan took out the mobile phone and tapped in a new message, 'WE ARE INSIDE CHEOPS'.

Jonathan showed the message to Sebastian who nodded in approval. Jonathan then pressed send.

"It worked!" he hooted, excitedly.

"This means that somehow there is network coverage right here!" Kim said.

Suddenly the mobile phone sounded, bip, bip… bip, bip… and Jonathan read the text message immediately.

"Are you safe? They want to know if we are safe!" Jonathan said as he showed the mobile screen around.

"Okay. Now try and ring them!" Sebastian suggested.

"Where's Zara? I just put her down a moment ago," Cathy said as she searched around urgently.

Jonathan, meanwhile, tapped in a number and pressed the call button. There were a few beeps and then a familiar voice.

"Is that you Jonathan?" a female voice asked incredulously.

"Yes, yes! It's me. We're inside the Great Pyramid of Khufu!' Jonathan said loudly.

"I don't believe it!" Albert said, looking further down the corridor.

"What? That this mobile phone works?" Sebastian asked.

"No! I just saw your pup emerge from that wall!" Albert exclaimed as the dingo pup danced around.

Kim quickly went to the place and put his hand into the solid granite stone. "It's a hole again!" he yelled. "Hurry everyone. Let's go through it!"

With that, Kim walked into the wall and vanished. Yvonne, Cathy, Sebastian, and Jonathan followed with haste.

``Now I've seen everything!" Albert said nonplussed as the students disappeared leaving Albert, Asami and Lucinda puzzled.

"Come with me," Albert commanded as he grabbed Arsami and Lucinda's hands, and they walked through the solid granite wall.

"How did we do that?" Lucinda asked in amazement.

Einstein picked up a piece of chalk-like plaster from the ground and started furiously scribbling some complex formula on the wall.

"You see, '$E=mc2$.' It's my most famous equation, but what does it really mean? Energy equals mass, times the speed of light squared, and so on. My equation says that energy, mass and matter are interchangeable; they are different forms of the same thing." He explained enthusiastically as he scratched a three-by-three grid, "Would you like a game of noughts and crosses?"

Cathy rushed back to them. "Would you stop it? We must get out of here. I'm sure we're in the present time. We might be free!" she said urgently.

On the other side of the wall, they all found themselves in an identical tunnel except it was much more worn down. The granite wall was old and unpolished, and they could hear voices echoing down the corridor and growing louder.

"...If you follow me here, we'll soon reach the amazing tomb of King Khufu!" a voice reverberated along the tunnel. A group of Japanese tourists, with cameras dangling around their necks, rounded the nearby bend of the corridor with a guide. They stopped in their tracks and looked at the students and Albert standing there.

One Japanese tourist whispered to the other, "I'm sure I've seen those students somewhere else."

"Follow me," Yvonne instructed the students still as their guide, and with the addition of Lucinda and Albert, walked along the tunnel following the 'Exit' signs, and they all stepped outside into brilliant sunshine and squinted as they looked around to see the enormous, polluted metropolis of Cairo with endless apartments and busy traffic as far as the eye could see.

Lucinda gazed in disbelief bordering on horror, "What the hell have they done to my suburb!"

In another direction, they could see the Sphinx and other pyramids scattered around the Giza Plateau, and then they slowly turned around to look at the Great Pyramid of Khufu from which they'd just emerged. It had a pinnacle and seemed to be complete.

"Oh, look, I can see the block we moved," Asami said pointing at one. "My god I understand the surface of Earth."

"There's something infinitesimal about this pyramid," Jonathan said as he took Cathy aside, and they hugged in relief. The air felt thick and hot and seemed to waver, and in the distance, like a mirage, Uluru appeared and rippled, the bending or reflection of light passing through layers of hot air having different temperatures, and then faded and vanished. "My god, we're back in 'present-day Egypt'," Jonathan gasped.

"It's not a dream," Yvonne said proudly, as their guide, "I told you so!"

Enjoying their perceived freedom, they all walked over amongst tourists and wandering camels and sat down in a café next to an air-conditioner.

"Ah, Jonathon, here's your phone back," Albert said returning it to him.

A large helicopter flew over the pyramid and landed nearby blowing sand everywhere with an American flag fluttering. As the rotors stopped, the door on the side slid open and a soldier with mirrored sunglasses waved at them.

"Are you the Aussies who disappeared at Uluru?" He called out to them.

"Yes! We are!" Sebastian called back. "How did you know?"

"I just rang the Oval Office and alerted them," Albert said casually. "I'm an American citizen, don't forget."

"But so I am, and from Los Angeles, no less," Sebastian protested.

"But I have a higher IQ," Albert replied, as they all stepped outside.

The soldier walked down the small staircase and marched straight over to the assembled students, brushed them aside, saluted, and grabbed Albert's hand. "It is such an honour and pleasure to meet you, Mr Einstein." And then looked deeply into the eyes of Yvonne, "You are some tour guide, Makepeace." The compliment caused silence but that was broken by the helicopter rotors beginning to turn again. "Listen up," he said urgently, "we are under orders to fly you to the Cairo airport where an aeroplane is waiting to fly you back to

Melbourne, Australia, so please climb on board." He ushered the group towards the helicopter. "I will brief you once we take off."

Cathy unzipped her backpack and took out her camera. "Okay, photo opportunity here, stand next to the chopper with the pyramid in the background, now… smile!" The shutter clicked and the group began to climb into the helicopter.

"Lucinda, do you want to move to Australia?" Jonathan asked with a smile.

"Hmmm…" Lucinda pondered momentarily. "It's all very confusing. I have gone forward by a few thousand years, and I guess I can't go back. Okay, why not? I am with you," and she glanced at Sebastian, "More adventure."

They all sat down in the helicopter, fastened their seat belts, the door slid shut and the rotors started spinning loudly. They took off as Cathy snapped more shots out the window.

A senior soldier addressed them. "Righty oh, here's your brief, this whole adventure of yours is now completely top secret, and you're not allowed to tell anyone about it, at all. Do you understand?"

They all nodded except for Albert.

"What about me?" Albert asked, ruffling his long hair. "I died seventy years ago; won't people start asking questions?"

"Good point," the soldier answered. "You'll need to be incognito from now on in America."

"America? Why can't I go to Australia with my new friends, and I can be more incognito there?" Albert asked. "If I got a neat haircut no one would recognise me anyway."

"Great thinking Albert," Jonathan replied enthusiastically. "You can live at our place. We have a Granny flat out the back that has been empty for years, it's very comfortable."

"Hmmm…" Albert thought aloud. "A Granny flat in Australia sounds good to me, and I accept it with thanks."

Modern-day Cairo was a sight to behold for Lucinda as she gazed down in awe, having never flown anywhere, and in no time, the helicopter landed next to a large Qantas aeroplane on the Cairo airport tarmac, and they boarded it. They were the only passengers and were upgraded to first class and drinks and meals were served as they jetted back to Melbourne, Australia.

A hostess approached their seats with a bundle of clothes. "Here, you can change out of your sweaty loincloths into these smart present-day fashions." In minutes, everyone changed and returned to their first-class seats wearing smart jeans, singlets, and sandshoes.

"Look at my jeans! They have gaping holes in the knees and are ripped at other places," Lucinda lamented looking down. "They're worse than the rags the poorest slaves wear."

"There's nothing worse than people from four thousand years ago criticising Australian fashion sense," Cathy joked as they all admired Yvonne's stunning frock covered in indigenous art, and they returned to their seats and partied on merrily.

"This is much better service than we got on our Mars to Egypt leg," Sebastian joked to Lucinda, but she was elsewhere in her thoughts, with earphones on and watching a movie Cathy had set up for her, "You'll love this film, *War of the Worlds*, it's a long flight down under," Cathy had quipped, and then there's *Casablanca*, Albert will no doubt join you for that, and finally *Barbie*, that's about all the briefing you'll need. Oh, then our movie," Cathy added proudly. "The hostess has told me about the latest '*Hollywood App*'".

"All you do is download all your photos and videos from your holiday," the hostess explained, "and after a few hours, with the help of 'AI', they are turned into a Hollywood blockbuster, and you can watch the film before arriving home," she smiled handing Cathy a stick, "It's been very popular recently."

When the students were tearfully reunited with their families, no questions were asked, "It was all a big fuss over nothing," Jonathan explained, and like cosmic magic, all stories in the media archives vanished and were replaced by sporting news.

Chapter 23
Friend and Flyer

Friends and family did notice, however, a certain strange aura emanating from them all; an energy formed from their achievement of time travel, adventure and spiritual power through extreme mental and emotional focus, and this power increased their natural abilities in their following lifetimes.

Yvonne returned to Alice Springs, now an extremely experienced guide. She stood as an Independent in the seat of Namatjira, an electoral division of the Legislative Assembly in the Northern Territory and soon became Lord Mayor of Alice Springs. She had an instinct for opening the right doors and was incredibly popular, while Asami flew to Tokyo, to seek out ancestors and with her sights set on being a modern artist, specialising in weather and water installations.

It wasn't plain sailing for all of them. Cathy discovered she was pregnant, and the father was a pharaoh, no less. Nine months later she gave birth to a baby boy they named Alexander. The fact that he had olive skin and an Egyptian look about him was never discussed by anyone, and soon after, with the baby in her arms, she married Jonathan in a private ceremony, which they all attended.

It was a wonderful reunion, and Albert had the pleasure of walking Cathy down the aisle, with Sebastian as the Best Man, Yvonne, Lucinda, and Zara, merrily wagging her tail, were bridesmaids.

Cathy looked gorgeous in her fawn-coloured wedding dress standing opposite Jonathan, equally handsome in his fawn-coloured tuxedo with a red bow tie. The exchange of rings was intriguing, as Lucinda giggled and confided with Yvonne.

"Did you know that Cathy managed to pinch that beautiful gold ring from the dresser of King Khufu after he went to sleep?" Lucinda whispered as Cathy presented the ring to Jonathan. "She cleverly wrapped it in one of the King's beautifully embroidered handkerchiefs and smuggled it out."

"Really?" Yvonne replied in surprise, "Yes, indeed, and they arranged to get the DNA from the mummified King Khufu, you know, Egyptian antiquity authorities claimed they had, and it matched the DNA of their new-born son, Alexander."

"I now pronounce you man and wife!" the priest announced jubilantly, as Jonathan and Cathy embraced and kissed. A few years later, the happily married couple had their own babies, a girl, Stacy, and a boy, Chips.

Lucinda and Sebastian soon became an item and decided to move in together in Melbourne and bought a nice house on the banks of the Yarra River that reminded them of the Nile River, "I might be a few thousand years older, but my boyfriend from LA has an open mind," Lucinda joked many times.

Once Lucinda mastered writing English, rather than Egyptian hieroglyphics, she soon became a very popular university lecturer in Egyptian history, and many of her students, Egyptian archaeologists, and Professors of Antiquities regularly commented that her grasp of detail was so good it seemed like she must have lived there back then, which always made Lucinda laugh, *If only they knew*, she would think to herself.

Albert happily moved into his luxurious Granny flat behind Jonathan and Cathy's house, and it had a studio next door with large blackboards everywhere for him to scribble his latest formulas and equations on.

Kim, with his Taiwanese, tough, wire-like frame, became a 'Human Statue'; a living statue attraction as a street performer, with his ability to stand motionless and occasionally come to life with comic or startling effect. He met and married another human statue, and everyone attended their wedding ceremony which went for ten long hours, and they had several children who would never keep still and became philosophers. The others occasionally came across Kim at various locations in Sydney completely covered in paint, often silver or gold, or their favourite, a smart suit and hat in mosaic tiles.

The years zoomed by as Cathy's son, Alexander, grew up to become a handsome young man studying Egyptian history, leadership and ornithology at university. Twenty years passed like a day and amazing advances were made in technology all around the world, but not without drama and conflict.

Chapter 24
Busted Wings

The green and yellow Melbourne tram rumbled along the tree-lined Flemington Road, passing the enormous safari park that adjoined the Melbourne Zoo where elephants, giraffes, and other ruminant mammals grazed contentedly on the extensive brush, oblivious to the bumper-to-bumper traffic on the other side of the high cyclone fence.

Schoolchildren jostled with each other inside the tram to get the best view of the wildlife, and Jonathan, now forty, grabbed his phone to call his wife.

"Hey, Cathy, I'm here on the tram," as he eased his briefcase under his seat. Jonathan always considered the wildlife enclosure next to the Melbourne Zoo to be a welcome distraction for city commuters, and it was much better than the cement wall that used to circle the old Melbourne Zoo.

Outside, a turbulent disturbance caused the children in the tram to run over to the windows. "Hold on one second," Jonathan said. "Sorry dear, but two flyers seem to be fighting. I hate it when this happens. Oh, dear, and this one is bad."

It was. High above the safari park, two flyers were locked in a vicious air battle. The passengers in the tram craned their necks and oohed and aahed as the aerial fight unfolded.

Way up in the sky above the morning traffic, the twenty-year-old Alexander tightened the shoulder straps of his winged backpack, screaming at Sandy as she careered towards him in another attempt to tear off his wings. They kicked and scratched at each other as their wings flapped and interlocked, sending them plummeting towards the earth. They managed to separate at the last second and shot back into the air.

"You'll kill us both!" Alexander shouted as Sandy tore at his left wing.

Far below, inside the tram, Jonathan could hardly bear to watch as he squinted to make out the faces of the two aerial fighters. "I'm afraid this one could end in tragedy," Jonathan whispered into his mobile. "The way they're going at each other makes me think they must be seasoned flyers," Jonathan said, watching the battle. "Oh, and the Friend Corporation called earlier and it's arriving at noon today. My car will be serviced by then so I should be there. Will you be home?" He enquired sensing Cathy was annoyed, "And please honey, try to be positive. These Friends can be rather fun, you know."

"Fun? 'Fun'? Well, I'm not talking to your stupid bloody Friend!" Cathy screamed and hung up. Jonathan pursed his lips as the tram screeched to a standstill while the driver leapt out to look up into the sky and witness the final moments of the fight.

The two flyers had separated, but there were huge tears in their wide wings. Then Sandy baulked, circled, and swooped on Alexander again, this time ripping a large hole in his right wing.

"Take that!" Sandra smirked as Alexander, her boyfriend, dropped out of the sky like the coyote in *The Roadrunner*. She watched his descent with glee as she hovered, "And keep your so-called Friend away from Team Providence!"

Sandra Sequeira was originally from Ipanema Beach High School in Rio de Janeiro, a former gold medal soccer player and now a scholarship sportswoman at university, and majoring in ornithology, where she met Alexander in class, dropped football and took up flying, and soon became captain of Team Providence guarding her team pride like an eagle, her surname meaning 'dry place'.

Sandra understood everything about lift, thrust, drag and gravity, the main components of flight, and was so beautiful with her Brazilian features, intricately woven dark brown dreadlocks, and olive skin that she was offered lucrative modelling jobs all the time but rather than modelling, she enjoyed flying in a bikini to confuse her rivals, as well as her handsome boyfriend.

Alexander looked down at the safari park some two hundred metres below. His wings were shredded and as he lost control, started spinning, plummeting downwards, and reached for his emergency parachute.

The crowd in the tram, and in the traffic below, drew their collective breath as the injured flyer spiralled towards the ground, desperately pulling on his emergency cord, before it billowed out, and slowed him slightly, but the earth raced up towards Alexander. He spotted a herd of hippos beside a pond in the safari park and aimed for the water, the sunlight reflecting off the still surface like a mirror.

"I think he's going to land in that small lake," Jonathan said to the old lady seated next to him inside the tram.

"I hope so," she replied in a quivering gossipy voice. "But it could still be a fate worse than death."

Alexander landed in the deepest part of the lake, the cold water splashing around him, and he sank instantly, the muddy water blinding him, so he instinctively unzipped the pouch around his stomach, grabbing his repellent spray as three crocodiles slithered into the lake, and there was a momentary silence from the onlookers.

Alexander exploded to the surface. The crowd cheered but then went silent again.

Even if the safari park helicopter was thrown into action immediately, it was unlikely they could save Alexander. More people crowded up against the cyclone fence to view this spectacle, the chaos disrupting the quiet Melbourne autumn morning.

"Good luck!" one commuter called out. Alexander gave him a cursory glance. He had heard of quite a few incidents where people had either fallen into the safari enclosure from flying mishaps or had been silly enough to scale the high wire fence and attempt to feed the wildlife. No one ever escaped alive.

Jonathan viewed the encounter silently from within the safe confines of the tram. Alexander paid no attention to the onlookers as he trod water, searching for the crocodiles, but they had gone underwater, and he knew they would probably attack soon.

He paddled quietly towards the edge of the pond. Baboons scampered around the fence line, hoping to get peanuts from the crowd, seagulls, cranes, and birds settled on the shore as Alexander grasped his repellent spray tightly, his index finger poised on the nozzle.

A hungry crocodile broke the surface, its jaws opening wide. Alexander sprayed the repellent into its eyes and the crocodile lurched backwards in pain. The crowd gasped, the noise of the altercation sending the birdlife into the air in a flurry of panic. Another crocodile surfaced and Alexander turned quickly and sprayed away. The baboons screeched in excitement.

"You can make it, flyer!" an onlooker yelled, "Swim, swim!"

Alexander paddled faster; then his feet scraped the muddy bottom of the pond; and able to stand now, he glanced around in a panic, wondering where the third crocodile had gone. He would need to make a dash for the fence, maybe even clamber up a nearby tree.

Suddenly, the third crocodile surfaced, its sharp teeth gleaming in the sunlight, so he sprayed the repellent into its mouth, sending the crocodile into an agonising retreat, as the onlookers cheered, and Alexander unglued his feet from the mud and stepped onto dry land.

"Go! RUN! Faster!" The crowd shouted in encouragement.

Alexander sprinted towards the gate some fifty metres away where a zookeeper opened it waving his arms and yelling. "Over here, this way!"

The crowd urged him on. Alexander glanced back over his mangled wings and realised there were no ferocious animals chasing him, the crocodiles had retreated under the water, an elephant nearby wasn't even watching, two giraffes continued munching on leaves, and the hippos ignored the whole drama completely. Alexander feared a lion would spring from nowhere and maul him to death. The gate was only metres away.

He had survived and was about to be safe, turned around and raised his clenched fist in victory, and the crowd erupted in cheers. It was a happy ending.

"Well done," the zookeeper said in a relieved voice, as Alexander triumphantly stepped through the gate onto the footpath alongside Flemington Road and was more than pleased to hear the gate clang shut behind him.

Chapter 25
The New Friend

It was noon when Jonathan swung into his driveway, his red Holden Uluru humming to a standstill beside the delivery truck with the words 'Friend Corporation' written on the side. He stepped out, waving at the delivery people.

"Right on time," Jonathan said cheerfully. "Do you want to bring it in?"

They lifted a large square container out of the truck and carried it up the drive. Jonathan went ahead and prepared what he would say to Cathy.

"Are you home, dear?"

Cathy stepped into the hallway and gave Jonathan a long penetrating look. She was as attractive now as she'd been twenty years ago, and she still maintained her figure by watching her diet and doing hot yoga three times a week. "I'm here all right. Are you quite sure you want to bring your TV Friend inside? How about you forget the idea and buy a cute little puppy instead?"

"Come on honey," Jonathan pleaded. "Don't be like that."

It was an awkward situation, but Jonathan wanted his fun, and after all, it was the money he was spending.

He liked to think that he hadn't aged much at all in the twenty years since he and Cathy had married. Except now he wore suits every day instead of T-shirts. Admittedly, there were some wrinkles on the outer corners of his eyes, and his blond hair was not as thick as it once had been, and he was increasingly aware of his slightly receding hairline, but when he wore sunglasses and a baseball cap, he knew he still looked twenty-five.

The two delivery men paused with the large container. "Where do you want it, sir? In this corner?"

"That will be fine," Jonathan sat down on the sofa and watched the men unpack it revealing a medium-sized television. There were no cords, no dials, no buttons, no switches, not even an antenna, just a normal-looking, everyday television set. The only markings were some small letterings along the top that read: 'Television Friend'.

"Okay," Jonathan said. "Switch on, Friend." The television flickered on, and a beautiful thirty-year-old woman appeared on the screen.

"Good afternoon, Jonathan," the Friend said politely. "Hello, Cathy. How are you all? Thank you for inviting me into your house."

"That's all right, anytime," Jonathan said. "I hope you enjoy your stay here. Would you fix up the delivery people?" Jonathan asked, testing his newly found power.

"Certainly, Jonathan. That will be all. Thank you, gentlemen. I've transferred your delivery payment into your corporation's bank account. Have an enjoyable day." With that, the delivery people strolled out the front door whistling.

At that moment the back door flung open, and Alexander burst in, his clothes sopping wet, and he plonked his mangled backpack and torn wings on the kitchen floor.

"You'll never guess what happened to me!" Alexander said, slightly distracted by the TV Friend filling the corner of the living room.

"Oh, dear, you poor thing," Cathy said, hugging her son. "Did you have a malfunction and crashed?"

Jonathan stared at his son, shocked. "That was YOU? I saw the whole thing… I thought I recognised the flying language." He stood up and examined the broken wings. "You're lucky to be alive. What happened? Was it a skyway robbery?"

"No, no, worse than that," Alexander said sorrowfully. "It was Sandy! There's no end to what she'll do to keep Team Providence on top. I just can't understand it. I'm still furious."

"Sit down and gather yourself," Cathy said sympathetically, "Tell me what happened."

It was all too much for Jonathan. "Friend!" He commanded. "Pour me a stiff drink." Instantly the small bar in the corner of the living room lit up and a block of ice dropped into a glass with a spray of brandy. Jonathan grabbed it and took a mouthful as Alexander momentarily forgot his self-pity and looked at the TV in the corner.

"So you're here now," he said to the Friend. "Try not to get on the wrong side of mom," he advised.

"Not me, Alexander," the Friend replied reassuringly. "Your mother and I will get on fine."

Cathy stared deeply into the TV. She was almost lost for words. "Friend! Would you mind switching to colourful scenes of a fish aquarium with soothing music?" she snapped.

Instantly the beautiful thirty-year-old woman disappeared from the screen and was replaced by an aquarium with colourful tropical fish swimming around. Classical music played in the background. Alexander smiled as he grabbed his father's drink and took a gulp.

"No, it certainly wasn't a malfunction with my wings," Alexander said. "I was flying along, minding my own business when suddenly Sandy swooped down on me out of the blue. I mean, Team Providence won't put up with this sort of thing. She's lucky I don't report her to the Sky Patrol, that's if they haven't already decided to take their own action." His voice quivered slightly as he thought about the fight.

Jonathan and Cathy listened in horror as their eldest son recounted every scratch, tear, and terrible moment of his shocking encounter.

The doorbell rang and Jonathan glanced over at the Friend. "Who could that be, Friend?"

The aquarium scenes disappeared, and the beautiful woman appeared on the television. "That would be a member of the Sky Patrol at the front door, Jonathan. It's probably for Alexander."

Alexander hurried to the door and opened it. A gentleman in an aviation suit was holding a briefcase. The miniature feathered wings on his shoulders proved the TVF correct.

"Good afternoon. You must be Alexander. I'm from the Sky Patrol, and I would like to speak to you."

"Yes, yes, come in. As you can see, I'm still recovering from my ordeal."

"Why don't you get changed into dry clothes, and we can have a chat, maybe at your Team Providence headquarters," the sky patrolman said firmly. Alexander hesitated for a moment. A scowl clouded over his face, and then he shrugged his shoulders.

Chapter 26
The Headquarters of Team Providence

Alexander and the sky patrolman settled into the bright blue patrol car as it hummed along the freeway towards the vast wetlands below the West Gate Bridge. Tall towers loomed in front of them, their tops resembling huge birdhouses in the sky. Looking up at them, they could see numerous flyers arriving and leaving the structures.

After parking in an underground car park, Alexander and the sky patrolman strolled into a glass elevator and ascended one of the towers, rising two hundred metres.

"Well, here we are," Alexander said, as the glass elevator glided to a standstill. The doors slid open revealing a large sign that read: 'Welcome to the headquarters of TEAM PROVIDENCE'. He turned to the patrolman. "Where would you like to conduct the interview? The briefing room has a nice view."

They turned down a passageway and entered another large room with a floor-to-ceiling window and sat down at a table surrounded by chairs. The sky patrolman placed his briefcase on the table and opened it. Inside was a monitor and various papers and documents. He placed a small stick into the slot and switched it on. The monitor flickered to life and a video started to play, showing Alexander and Sandy in aerial combat.

"Now Alexander, this is a record of your altercation above the Melbourne Zoo Wildlife Reserve taken by a sky patrolman in the vicinity. It quite clearly shows that you were set upon by the other flyer and you really spent most of the fight trying to defend yourself," the patrolman said as he shuffled other documents on the table.

Alexander watched the replay and then gazed out the window at a formation of Team Providence flyers preparing to take off. There were six of them in the training session, and Alexander recognised his team. They adjusted their backpacks and exercised their wide wings. One of them turned around and looked at Alexander through the window. She gave a quick, quizzical expression, smiled and then turned away.

Altogether, in exact formation, the six flyers started flapping their wings and leapt off the edge. They flew into the distance, past the other towers, and over the West Gate Bridge.

The sky patrolman continued. "We're primarily concerned why flyers like Team Providence can get themselves into such a ludicrous situation. You're right at the top of the pecking order in competition, both in speed and formation flying, yet at the same time you can expose our down-to-earth citizens with such a vicious aerial fight," he said scratching his head. Alexander gazed out the window watching his team.

The sky patrolman studied his monitor and continued talking. "I mean, really, this team member of yours could have quite easily finished you off. What would have happened to you if you had landed on a pile of crocodile eggs for example? The mother crocodile would not have thought twice about tearing you apart, limb by limb." The patrolman became irritated as Alexander continued watching his team go through their formations high over Williamstown. "Alexander, are you listening to me?"

He looked back at the monitor and watched himself fall into the pond with a big splash. He wondered where Sandy was now and how damaged were her wings. From the other end of the briefing room, he heard children and looked over to see a group of schoolchildren on a guided tour of the Team Providence headquarters.

"When will we be allowed to fly?" one child asked.

"When you learn to behave yourselves," the public relations manager said with a laugh. "No seriously, I'm sure you could fly as well as the rest of us, if not better, but you must remember that these backpacks with wings were only invented twenty years ago, no one predicted it at all. These wings have become bigger than the invention of the steam engine, the automobile, or even the bicycle," she explained. "But they can be dangerous, oh yes, very dangerous."

Alexander watched the guided tour leave and then turned to the sky patrolman. "You're not going to confiscate Sandy's wings, are you?"

"Oh, no, there's no risk of that… Unless you want me to."

"Well, it hardly matters. Now that the other teams know that our feathers have been ruffled, they'll never let us forget it." His voice wavered off as he wondered about Sandy's whereabouts.

The sky patrolman studied him suspiciously. "Exactly why did this fight occur?" Alexander glanced away. "You don't have an answer?" the sky patrolman asked. Alexander didn't respond. He gazed out the large window again, watching his team flying.

"All right then," the patrolman muttered. "I'll put 'don't know' in my report. But the video of this aerial battle will go into our files. Is that fair?"

"Sounds fair to me." Alexander shrugged.

He noticed that a seventh flyer had joined Team Providence, but they were too far away for Alexander to tell if it was Sandy. The sky patrolman closed his briefcase and Alexander went to the storeroom to pick up another winged backpack, so he could join his team in their training session.

The frumpy old store manager smiled at Alexander from behind the counter and pushed a piece of paper towards him.

"Here's your death certificate. Would you sign it please?" she laughed.

At the top of the form were the words 'Flight Insurance' written in big letters. Alexander signed it and the manager placed a new winged backpack on the counter. "And try not to feed this one to the crocodiles dear… or to Sandy," she said laughing.

Alexander smiled and slipped the new backpack onto his shoulders. He strolled down the passageway towards the entrance to the take-off platform. The large glass door slid open, and he stepped out onto the platform.

A fresh sea breeze swept his hair back and elevated his wide wings as Alexander began his relaxation exercises. He held his breath for six seconds, exhaled and then repeated the exercise ten times. He waved his wings up and down and adjusted the straps around his shoulders to make them more comfortable.

Alexander looked out beyond the towers at the West Gate Bridge and then back down at the wetlands two hundred metres below. It had only been a few hours since he had nearly plummeted to a painful end, but it wasn't long before the wonderful anticipation of freedom overcame him. He spread his wings and prepared to jump. The tingling sensation in his toes was always there at the beginning of a flight and this flight was certainly no exception.

He leaned forward and jumped. The fresh breeze made the take-off even more exhilarating. He set his sights on Team Providence, still going through their formation training a thousand metres away high above the West Gate Bridge.

Chapter 27
The West Gate Bridge Discussion

Jonathan's favourite armchair was set up directly opposite his Television Friend. He sat down and sighed comfortably.

"The wind will remain at between ten and fifteen knots for the remainder of the day with bright sunshine," the beautiful woman on the screen replied to Jonathan's rather pointless question. "So the washing can go on the line instead of in the tumble dryer, Jonathan."

"Thank you, friend," Jonathan said as Cathy looked on. She was holding a basket of Alexander's dirty clothes.

"Friend, would you switch on the washing machine?" Cathy asked, and headed towards the laundry. "And I suppose you couldn't hang out the washing when it's done?" she asked sarcastically.

"Sorry, I can't help you there," the Friend beamed back.

"What's on my agenda this afternoon, Friend?" Jonathan asked. He felt he should make the most of his new acquisition, but he should also keep testing it for any design faults.

"Well, Jonathan, you've got a business meeting this afternoon at 4:00 pm in Williamstown and then the rest of your day is free," she said.

That was fine with Jonathan. It meant he could see how Team Providence training was going on his way to the meeting.

"Okay, Friend, you can switch off now, and I'll see you when I get home for dinner," Jonathan said.

"Have a good afternoon," replied the Friend before disappearing from the screen.

Jonathan said goodbye to Cathy and was soon in his Holden Uluru humming down the freeway towards the West Gate Bridge. High up in the distance he could see various flyers going through their formations. He tried to make out Alexander's team, but they all looked a bit the same from the ground.

As he drove up the rise of the bridge, he switched on his favourite computer-composed swing music, a current hit at the time, and it blared loudly from the speakers as Jonathan scanned the sky in search of the flyers.

Suddenly, Team Providence swooped down in formation past his car. He slowed down, pressed a button, and his sunroof slid open and tooted his horn. Alexander dropped back from the pack and flew along above the car. Jonathan slowed to twenty kilometres an hour and Alexander glided closer and grabbed the roof racks of the Holden Uluru.

"How are your new wings?" Jonathan yelled out of the open sunroof.

"Fine. Thanks, Dad!" Alexander grinned, enjoying the rendezvous the two had perfected over the years.

"And what about Sandy?" Jonathan asked, turning down the music. "Have you talked to her yet?"

"Well, yes," Alexander replied. "We spent a bit of time treading air up there while we all exchanged some home truths." The car reached the top of the bridge and Alexander continued. "I'm afraid Sandy isn't very pleased about the Friend you had installed today. She mentioned our neighbours, the Joneses, and the rest of the team laughed at me."

"I see," Jonathan said. He had forgotten about the next-door neighbours. He hadn't seen them for a couple of weeks.

"Well, the laughter turned to sneers you know," Alexander said, holding onto the roof racks as the car started going down the far side of the West Gate Bridge.

"Okay then," Jonathan responded, giving Alexander an annoyed look. "But I've got my own life to lead, the same as you, and nothing bad has really been proven about these Friends."

"Right," Alexander said, releasing his grip on the roof racks and quickening the pace of his wings. "I'll see you at dinner."

Abruptly, Alexander soared up into the sky and Jonathan closed his sunroof, turned up the music, and continued his drive towards Williamstown.

Through his rearview mirror and sky-vision mirror, Jonathan watched Alexander fly up behind his team and join them in their formation training high above the bridge over the lower Yarra River.

Chapter 28
Homework

Chips Day, Jonathan's spritely twelve-year-old son, parked his bicycle outside the back door and pressed the lock button on his handlebars, clamps emerging instantly from the bicycle frame making it unrideable to anyone who might consider stealing it.

He stepped inside the back door, lugging his school bag and papier mâché replica of the planet Mars and dumped them on the kitchen floor. He was about to get a glass of lemon cordial when he spotted the TV Friend in the corner of the living room.

"What a wonderful thing," he said out loud, sitting down on the couch opposite the Friend. Chips glanced down the passageway to make sure nobody was there. He looked at the TV and gave his first command.

"Turn on Friend and speak to me," he said cheerfully.

The Friend sparked to life and the beautiful thirty-year-old woman appeared on the screen.

"Hello," she said. "You must be Chips. Did you have a good time at school today?"

"Same as usual, Friend. Where is everyone?" he asked.

"Your father is at a meeting, your mother is in her study upstairs, and Alexander is training with Team Providence." Chips smirked. He had heard at school during morning recess about Alexander and Sandy's fight that morning.

"Right then. Let's get down to business," Chips said, knowing full well its capabilities since the Jones' next door had one. He held up a piece of paper in front of it.

"This is my handwriting, can you write an essay on the imperfections of modern technology please, in my handwriting."

"Shouldn't you do it yourself to improve your English?" The Friend asked, "Your mathematics and physics are excellent…"

"What do you expect if you have Albert Einstein as your tutor?" Chips snapped back. "Let me speak to Hal."

"Who?" the Friend responded quizzically.

"Hal! HAL 9000, Space Odyssey."

The friend vanished and was replaced by a large red light with a silver circle around it.

"How are you Chips?" Hal asked in a soft, calm voice and a conversational manner.

"I don't want the friend to wreck Team Providence or my parents' marriage, for that matter," Chips demanded firmly and perceptively.

"I know I've made some very poor decisions recently," Hal replied in a slightly hurt voice, "but I give you my complete assurance that everything will be back to normal," as a tear rolled over the red light that resembled the pupil of an eye.

"Oh, spare me," Chips said throwing up his hands in despair. "Go away and give me my Friend."

The beautiful woman reappeared wiping a tear away from her cheek. "Of course, Master Chips, I can do your English homework for you."

The computer in the living room bookshelf lit up and, after a few seconds of tapping and whizzing, a sheet of paper came sliding out and Chips snatched it from the machine and studied it. Sure enough, it was written in his handwriting and quite definitely creative, and it even had a few words crossed out and corrected and the content was excellent, so Chips knew his teacher would pass him.

"Very good, my Friend," Chips muttered with a sly glance.

Cathy burst into the room holding a tablecloth, her face red with anger.

"Turn off, friend, 'now'!" She screamed at the television. It immediately went blank and silent. She glared at Chips. "I knew this would be the first thing you would do!" as Chips sank mournfully into the couch, trying to hide the essay under his sweater.

"I knew that once your father had a Friend installed it would cause trouble," Cathy shouted. "And it's trouble for you Chips!" Cathy said, trembling with rage. "Now go to your room and work on your planet Mars this minute, you silly boy."

Chips obediently picked up his papier mâché planet Mars and skulked off upstairs to his bedroom. Cathy, meanwhile, stared angrily at the Friend then flung the tablecloth into the air as it billowed out and wavered down covering the television entirely.

"As far as I'm concerned, Friend, you're nothing more than a table when I'm around," she said. "And I want you out of my sight and out of my mind. I'm not going to allow you and Jonathan to turn us into the Joneses next door. I don't care how good you are." She turned around and stormed off into the kitchen.

Chips sat with his feet up on his desk, juggling his papier mâché replica of the planet Mars. He had achieved a good variation of red over its surface and added craters and mountains. He tossed it in the air and caught it again. He carefully opened the little trap door on its surface and peered into the tunnel and considered his planet Mars to be much more realistic than the Saturn and Neptune planets that had been completed by some of his classmates, and he imagined how all the planets in his astronomy class would look hanging together from the ceiling. Maybe his father, Jonathan, would have a few ideas to offer over dinner. More than likely, Chips thought to himself, dinner table conversation would focus on the controversy of the friend's entry into the Day household.

He would be hard-pushed to prolong any discussion on the dunking of Alexander into the wildlife pond, after all, Alexander was a master at turning around unpleasant situations to suit himself, and anyway, Chips didn't want to hinder the confidence of Team Providence. He was, however, rather pleased that his father had put the Friend in the living room.

Chips continued to spin his papier mâché planet and caress the texture of its surface, and his thoughts were light years away when the doorbell rang. He jumped up from his desk and raced downstairs, along the hallway still juggling his planet Mars and flung open the front door and stared at Sandy. Her wings were folded down, and she was smiling.

"Hello, Chips, how are you?" Sandy asked, unstrapping her backpack and wings.

"What are you doing here?" Chips asked.

"Your mother invited me for dinner," she said. "Can I come in?"

Chips was startled. He knew Sandy well and thought of her as one of the best flyers he'd ever set eyes on, but he was also slightly confused about her fight with Alexander earlier in the day.

"Sure, come in. Where's Alexander?" Chips asked, quickly searching the sky.

"He'll be here shortly," she said. "He had to make a few modifications to his new wings at the Team Providence headquarters." She followed Chips down the hallway and glanced at the sheet over the television. "I see you've got a new table."

From the kitchen, Cathy heard this and laughed. "Yes, a very expensive table. Just what we all needed." She gave Cathy a hug and kiss. "Now Chips, would you be a good fellow and go and go finish your homework… what's left of it."

Chips ran off spinning his planet excitedly. With Sandy at the dinner table, the aerial combat would be back on the agenda, and he'd have a reason to poke fun at Alexander. As he entered his room, he could hear his mother and Sandy clinking teacups as they chatted away about current developments.

Feeling elated, Chips closed his door, switched on his favourite Planets symphony, and busied himself by working on his Mars creation and hoping the time until dinner would pass quickly.

Chapter 29
The Dinner Table Conversation

The Day family and their guest Sandy sat in silence around the dining room table in readiness for the vegetarian meal prepared by Cathy.

Annoyed by the silence, Chips broke the ice, "Should we invite the Friend to say grace?"

There was a mixed response to his dinner table joke. Alexander, who had just arrived home was surprised to find Sandy there and wanted to make her feel at ease, so he laughed.

"Chips, be a good fellow and go down to the cellar and fetch a bottle of white wine, maybe a 2046 Sauvignon Blanc," Jonathan said.

Chips leapt from his seat and headed out the dining room door. The others began eating and chatting about the events of the day. No one really wanted to mention the actual aerial combat between Sandy and Alexander, but Cathy was waiting for her opportunity to tackle Jonathan over the installation of the Television Friend, and it hadn't been lost on Jonathan that the Friend was now covered by a tablecloth.

"How was your formation training today, Sandy?" Jonathan asked. "I saw some of it, and it looked good. When is your next competition?"

"Not for a few weeks," Sandy said. "And the next one isn't that important, anyway, it will give us time to smooth over any ruffled feathers," giving a sideways glance at Alexander.

"My feathers are not ruffled!" Alexander snapped defensively. "Rather they're torn to shreds and in the trash. Anyway, my new ones are better."

Chips returned to the dinner table holding a bottle of wine and gave the corkscrew to Jonathan. "You know something," Chips said. "After I climbed down the spiral staircase into the cellar, I could swear I heard a tapping noise. Do you think there is something wrong with the freezer down there?"

"Probably," Cathy replied. "You should have a look at it, Jonathan, instead of wasting your time and money on your Friends." Her voice trailed off as she exchanged glances with Sandy. Everyone fell silent.

Jonathan wasn't about to be drawn into another argument about his prized possession, and so he decided that the less said, the better, but Sandy seemed to think otherwise.

"Did you know the Friend Corporation Flyers all have TV Friends?" Sandy said calmly.

"Is that right?" Jonathan asked.

"Yeah," Sandy said. "They're second last on the ladder. And only six months ago half their team had a mass nervous breakdown."

Cathy glared at Jonathan. "Let's hope our Friend doesn't affect Team Providence."

Jonathan rolled his eyes. "That's not going to happen."

Sandy put down her knife and fork. "Even though these Friends can be very informative. and helpful in many ways, the research shows that they have a detrimental effect on members of a family that possesses one," she said in her lovely lilting and strong Brazilian cadence.

"That's what I heard too," Cathy said. "They may not affect the actual owner, in this case, you Jonathan."

Alexander spoke up. "The reality of the matter is that the Friend is here." He looked through the arch into the living room. "And the Friend can't do too much harm in the short term. I mean, look at it!"

Jonathan stood up from the dinner table and walked into the next room. He grabbed the corner of the tablecloth and ripped it off the square set.

"Switch on Friend and give us your opinion," Jonathan said.

"Really, Jonathan!" Cathy snapped in annoyance.

The Friend flickered on, and the beautiful woman appeared with a smile. Cathy and Sandra remained silent. Alexander and Chips looked on.

"Thank you for bringing me into your dinner table conversation," the Friend said politely. "Most families I know who have a Television Friend have drawn a huge amount of satisfaction from it. After all, television in the old days was a one-way affair, and there was never any real interaction between the couch potato and the box in the corner, but now, with Friends like myself, you can count on me as an actual friend; intelligent, helpful and above all, a companion," she concluded happily.

"Quite so," Jonathan said, nodding approvingly. He walked back to the table to resume dinner. "And Friend, would you mind playing some pleasant dinnertime music for us all?"

"Certainly Jonathan," she replied, immediately switching to scenes of a huge orchestra playing *The Planets* by Gustav Holst, *Mars, the Bringer of War*, and seemed to dissipate any acrimony over the two main issues of the day.

Alexander decided to direct the family conversation around the astronomy project Chips was working on. Everyone had an opinion about the papier mâché planet. Jonathan suggested that a light could be located inside the tunnel under the small trap door so that when it was opened a ray of light would beam out, and then the conversation switched to the real planet Mars and the current debate over the tourist trips to the red planet. They were not only excessively expensive but also incredibly boring.

"I mean, who wants to spend three months in a spacecraft to reach a holiday destination that is absolutely devoid of any vegetation?" Alexander pondered, causing Cathy and Jonathon to glance at each other.

The subject matter led to Jonathan commenting on his itinerary the following day. "I've got a business meeting in Sydney tomorrow, so I'll be away for the whole day."

"Will that meeting be in the Old Sydney Tower?" Sandy asked, harking back to Team Providence, "because I hear Team Rocks will be training there with the Rainbow Lorikeets."

"As a matter of fact, it will." He replied as he poured himself another red, "so I'll be able to watch some of their flapping."

Chapter 30
Old Sydney Town

Jonathan strolled along the platform of Flinders Street station in search of carriage 10 of the internationally admired *Extremely Fast Train*, known as the EFT. As usual, he had timed his arrival at the platform only minutes before the EFT departed.

Jonathan tapped his plastic ticket on the armrest of his window seat and placed his briefcase on the empty seat next to him. Without even the smallest of shudders, the platform vanished as the EFT zoomed through the outskirts of Melbourne running so smoothly that it felt like it was stationary, and the world was moving outside. Jonathan flipped through the morning newspaper and sipped on his glass of freshly squeezed orange juice as the terrain outside became mountainous and the EFT glided silently through the numerous tunnels of the snow-capped Mount Bulla, Beauty, and Feathertop.

Jonathan found himself listening to the conversation of the elderly couple seated on the other side of the aisle. "The Snowy River won't come into sight for some minutes," Jonathan explained to the elderly pair. "And when it does it will only be in sight for about ten seconds."

"Thank you very much," the gentleman said courteously. "And will the train slow down there at all?"

"I'm afraid not," Jonathan answered. "The only time it slows down, or even sometimes stops, is on the seabed leg between King Island and the mainland, in Bass Straight."

The elderly couple were obviously familiar with this sightseeing spectacle as they had boarded the EFT in Hobart early that morning and had breakfast with the whales. The train line crossed Tasmania passing the picturesque Derwent River and continued through Cradle Mountain in central Tasmania and went into a tunnel underwater at Circular Head, along the seabed in Bass Strait, where the scenery became as spectacular as the journey through the mountains.

The elderly couple enthusiastically explained to Jonathan that during the seabed leg of the train journey, where it quite often slowed to a stop, the passengers had time to get a close-up view of a school of whales that showed interest in the train.

"As a matter of fact," the gentleman recounted with deepening fascination. "A marine specialist in our carriage told us that the school of whales by the windows probably had the same interest in us as we had in them!"

Jonathan was very familiar with this subterranean treat and had had breakfast with the whales on many occasions during business trips to and from Hobart.

"There's the Snowy River now," Jonathan said as the elderly couple turned around and gazed out the window. Soon, it was out of sight as the EFT sped through tunnel after tunnel on its fast journey through the Snowy Mountains as the elderly woman compared the blue and green mountain ranges to the coral under the water. At the far end of the train carriage, the glass door whizzed open.

Jonathan smiled as he saw his tenant, Albert, shuffle down the aisle towards him. Albert had accepted Jonathan's invitation to join him on a train trip to Sydney to watch Team Providence and the Rainbow Lorikeets training. Albert greeted Jonathan with a wave and sat down beside him.

"I heard from Cathy that you are the new owner of a Television Friend," Albert said, going straight to the point, as always.

"Yes, I like it very much," Jonathan replied.

Albert lifted an eyebrow. "I take it from what Cathy told me that the Friend is somewhat controversial in your home."

Jonathan hesitated. "That's true."

"She is not alone. There have been some well-publicised complaints," Albert said, glancing out the window as he took out a stack of papers.

"What's all this?" Jonathan asked. "I thought you were going to just enjoy watching the training session today."

"It's just a short report on the most recent research into your new Friend, that I obtained from the library carriage," Albert continued proudly. "I still say you should keep her."

Jonathan didn't need to read the report because Albert talked about it non-stop for the remainder of the journey to Sydney. His main conclusion was that when a Friend did become faulty, the household usually didn't suffer any more than it did with any other electronic breakdown, and Albert certainly considered it unlikely that such a state-of-the-art appliance from the Friend Corporation could do any harm at all. Albert was an astute judge of modern technology, Jonathan thought to himself, and his feeling for the good and the bad of a new piece of hardware could never be underestimated.

The EFT sped silently along the Goulburn Valley as Albert continued to reassure Jonathan. The elderly lady on the other side of the aisle had been listening to their conversation. She took the opportunity to lean over and get Jonathan's attention.

"Our local council in Hobart had the Friends banned completely!" she said in a gossip-like whisper.

"Is that so?" Jonathan replied.

"Yes, it is. And the suburb is a lot happier!" she said emphatically.

Jonathan stared out the window of the EFT as the countryside transitioned into suburbia and soon they were speeding through the outskirts of Sydney, and then, suddenly, the train was enveloped by the steel frame of the Sydney Harbour Bridge as it slowed down for the arrival at Circular Quay.

Jonathan shook hands with the elderly couple he had been chatting with as he and Albert made their way to the door of their carriage. With barely the smallest vibration, the station slid into view and stopped as the doors parted, and the two long-time friends stepped out onto the platform that overlooked Circular Quay with the Opera House crouched proudly in the background.

A taxi hummed up alongside them and stopped and Jonathan leaned down and spoke to the driver, "Can you take us to the Old Sydney Tower please?" He handed over his plastic card and stepped inside the back seat with Albert, the taxi pulled out and was soon speeding through the tunnels under the city.

"Up here on business this time?" the Indian driver inquired.

"No, not this time," Jonathan responded. "We're going to watch some of your flyers training from the tower, the Lorikeets."

The driver glanced a frown at them in his rearview mirror as the brightly lit tunnel veered left, and the taxi pulled up beside several elevators. Jonathan and Albert stepped out and strolled over to one of the elevators marked 'Old Sydney Tower'.

Albert pressed the button for the observation deck and the elevator whisked them upwards at great speed, their stomachs dropping as they shot quickly up the tower. Abruptly, the lift came to a standstill; the door opened; and they walked out onto the open-air observation deck and sat down in the sunshine.

Through the forest of towers and buildings that dwarfed the Old Sydney Tower, the wildlife reserves and native pastures surrounding the Opera House were clearly discernible and parts of the Harbour Bridge could be picked out among the tall cityscape making the view breathtaking.

Through the glass partition of the observation deck, the flyers of Team Rocks spread their collective wings in preparation for a leap into formation training. Their headquarters occupied the entire second level of the Old Sydney Tower, and although it was surrounded by so many taller structures that it made flying hazardous, the convenience of being in central Sydney far outweighed the pitfalls.

Jonathan tapped on the glass partition and attracted the attention of Myia, one of the top Rocks, who was always happy to chat with a parent of an opposition flyer. She was completing her final stretches and smiled at him.

"How are you, Jonathan?" she called out. "We're flying with the Rainbow Lorikeets on this outing." She spread her emerald-coloured wings to their full expanse. The team began to make up a line along the edge of the take-off platform. "How's my friend Alexander?" Myia enquired, "Is he 'lonely'?" she asked with a lop-sided smile.

"Lonely? Why lonely?" Albert interrupted defensively.

Myia pressed her hands against the glass partition and momentarily feigned claustrophobic panic like a mime artist in a glass cube.

"I can't talk back to you," she grinned, "must fly."

Myia, a lovely Greek name meaning 'fly', turned away and the eight flyers leaned forward and in exact formation leapt off the edge of the platform with their wings fully expanded they flew away in the direction of the harbour.

Jonathan peered into the telescope on the observation deck and followed the formation of Team Rocks as they soared and dived in intricate patterns amidst the various towers and buildings of Sydney. The spectacle was made all the better by the power of the telescope which caused the flyers to look like they were about to crash into the numerous vertical structures at any moment. They veered off for the pastures surrounding the Opera House and glided to a hover then gracefully landed amongst the native bush and fauna.

The entire area was filled with a variety of Australian bush life, from emus to wallabies and the sanctuary continued right up to the native flowers that brushed against the windows of the huge Opera House, the bush on one side of the giant white sculpture-like building and the harbour on the other.

Jonathan gazed silently through the telescope as the group of flyers huddled together in conversation, he wondered if Albert had noticed how Myia had said, 'I can't talk 'back' to you,' instead of, 'I can't talk to you.'

"Hey, the Lorikeets are coming in." Albert pointed skyward.

Jonathan scanned the view high above the Opera House and located the colourful team of Rainbow Lorikeets winging their way down in a rather scattered formation.

Silhouetted against the bright white exterior of the Opera House, their green wings and gleaming yellows, blues, and reds around their necks and chests gave the team a vast aesthetic advantage over most of their winged counterparts. They tumbled onto a clearing and strolled over to Team Rocks waiting nearby.

Jonathan couldn't stop thinking about his short conversation with Myia. She held the same position in Team Rocks as Sandy held in Team Providence. Certainly, without Sandy, Providence wouldn't be at the top of the national pecking order, and in Rocks' case, if they didn't have Myia, they wouldn't be the top New South Wales flyers, either. Jonathan watched Myia through the telescope as she chatted away to one of the Rainbow Lorikeet flyers, and then she looked back at the Old Sydney Tower.

The Lorikeets were based at the Minyon Falls in Whian Whian near Nimbin, North Coast of New South Wales and were a popular team. They built their headquarters like enormous bird nests in tall dense eucalyptus in the rainforests there, which captured the imagination of all the flyers around Australia and the world, but Team Rocks saw them as a mediocre team to train with, and they certainly drew little inspiration from the Lorikeets' rather slack formation flying.

It was only months earlier in a competition that some of the Lorikeets strayed and became entangled in power lines, and all the Lorikeets spokespeople could say after the event was that it was 'a shocking piece of team incompetence'.

Anyway, there was something going on now, and Jonathan was about to find out what it was. "They're all preparing to fly off," he told Albert.

Suddenly all sixteen flyers took off into the air in different directions and soared up above the Opera House. In a split second, they changed direction and flew past all the city buildings and structures, heading for the Old Sydney Tower, weaving closer and closer to the observation deck where Jonathan and Albert watched in surprise.

Albert only had time to mutter, "Well, they're coming this way," before both teams were hovering only metres away from the deck, their emerald and deep green wings flapped furiously as their eyes fixed on Jonathan.

He stepped back from the telescope unsure if he should be amused or worried as he grasped his briefcase under his arm, and they both retreated to the door of the observation deck now completely eclipsed by the two teams hovering noisily about.

And it all got louder as both teams started chanting: "A friend in need is a friend indeed!"

"Holy cow," Albert said to Jonathon as they fled through the door and into the open elevator. The doors closed, leaving them in silence. They rode the elevator to the top floor of the Old Sydney Tower and the doors opened, revealing the sixteen flyers treading air outside the windows still chanting, their eyes locked on Jonathan.

"A friend in need is a friend indeed!"

The flyers darted off in different directions. Jonathan and Albert were mystified but not particularly shaken by the incident, the predatory flurry had finished as quickly as it had begun. Jonathan could still feel his heart racing, but other than that and the perspiration forming around his neck, everything was fine.

After a few minutes and a glass of iced water, they both regained their composure and took the elevator back to ground level. Stepping outside, Jonathan looked up and around, but there was no sign of the Rocks or the Lorikeets, so they stepped into a waiting taxi and headed to the business meeting and then back to the train station.

"That was a very interesting training session," Albert said, as the EFT sped back to Melbourne, "I didn't know we were going to get such personalised treatment."

"Neither did I," Jonathan said as he mulled over what they'd just experienced.

Chapter 31
The Apology

They both returned home in the early evening feeling drained by the train journey and the experience they had with the squawking flyers. Jonathon knew full well what they were going on about, but he wasn't going to be discouraged that quickly.

In fact, with Albert supporting his desire to keep his new Friend, Jonathon decided to go and talk to his next-door neighbour, Jonesy, who had owned a TV Friend for some time now.

The Jones family had built an elaborate house underground, a residential fashion of the time, and their half-acre plot of land was covered in native trees and bushes as Jonathan strolled down along the winding path that led to a glass mirrored pyramid, the only above-ground structure on the property. It was fifteen metres high with four triangular sheets of mirror reflecting the eucalypts surrounding it.

Jonathan knocked on the main door that dropped down vertically from the mirrored angle of the pyramid. He knew it opened onto an escalator that descended underground into the rest of the house, and when no one answered, he pressed the doorbell and the intercom button.

The only sounds he could hear were the birds chirping in the trees outside. It had been a frustrating day for Jonathan and not finding his favourite neighbour home was the final straw, but just as he turned to leave the pyramid and return home, the light on the intercom flickered on and the clear voice of a woman came through the speaker.

"Yes? May I help you?" she asked politely.

"'Of course you can help me," Jonathan snapped back. "Where the hell is Jonesy?"

"Hello, Jonathan, how are you?" the woman responded calmly. "The Jones family are not available today, I'm sorry. May I suggest you call back another time?"

Jonathan was immediately suspicious. He hadn't seen anything of the Jones family for about two weeks even though that wasn't anything out of the ordinary because they did live underground. However, each fortnight, the two families got together for a barbeque on the Jones' bushy block.

"Where are they?" Jonathan demanded, "Come on, tell me," But he realised he was talking to the Jones' Friend. "I want you to open this door immediately."

When nothing happened, Jonathan flung open his briefcase and shuffled through several plastic cards until he found the one with Jonesy's face emblazoned across it that was the keycard giving Jonathan access to the underground house.

Jonathan fed the card into the slot next to the door, and the lock made a whizzing click sound, and then the door opened. Standing on the opposite side of the door was Jonesy, looking incredibly dishevelled.

"Jonesy?" Jonathan asked.

A look of surprise passed over Jonesy's face, and then he bolted forward past Jonathan and out of the mirrored pyramid into his yard, spun around and threw up his hands.

"There! 'I'm out!'" Jonesy proclaimed in bitter defiance as he looked back into the pyramid at Jonathan standing there holding the card. "Do you realise we've been locked in our house for two weeks?" Jonesy gasped. "Thanks for letting me out!"

Jonesy then walked back into the mirror pyramid and looked through the door down into the mosaic escalator. "It's open! 'Come out!'" He turned back to Jonathan. "I just can't comprehend it," he said despairingly. "My TV so-called 'Friend' wouldn't let us out!" He turned back again and yelled loudly through the door. "It's open! Come out!"

Jonathan gazed admirably at Jonesy's mosaic escalator; it always reminded him of his adventure twenty years before when they came across a mosaic escalator on their descent through aeons of civilisation to reach the mirrored train in their misplaced bid for freedom. In fact, when Jonesy decided to pull down his house and build one underground, it was Jonathan's suggestion that he build a mosaic escalator instead of a standard staircase. The problem was that it cost as much as the house itself. Nonetheless, Jonesy wanted it.

Jonathan was still rather confused by the whole event. He wasn't properly aware of what Jonesy was saying, although he could plainly see that Jonesy had no intention of going back inside his underground house. Jonathan could hear a woman sobbing and sniffling with happiness as Mrs Jones, looking sensually dishevelled, and her two children clambered off the mosaic escalator and burst out into the early evening sunset.

For a while, the entire Jones family just stood amongst the eucalyptus trees in a dazed trance, their emotions swinging from relief to confusion as Mrs Jones, with her stunning red hair and Botticelli's *The Birth of Venus* type figure, wiped the tears from her eyes. "Thank you, Jonathan. You gave me freedom!" she said, giving Jonathan a disproportionally long hug.

'Me and Mrs Jones, we got a thing going on,' Jonathan thought to himself, 'We both know that it's wrong, but it's much too strong, to let it go now.'

"That TV wouldn't let us out!" she cried.

"We were locked down there for two weeks!" Jonesy gasped. "I've never found myself in such a ridiculous situation in my life."

"Our Friend wouldn't let us out unless we apologised in the 'correct tone'," Mrs Jones said. "Can you believe it, Jonathan? We spent two weeks trapped down there trying to apologise to a television set for God's sake!"

"What did you do to cause your Friend to want an apology in the first place?" Jonathon enquired sympathetically.

"I called the Friend a bureaucratic birdbrain," Jonesy replied. "And she told me to apologise."

"Why did you call her that?" Jonathon probed.

"Well, I had some spare money, thanks to the work I did for you, and asked her what company I should invest it in, and she said the Friend Corporation, and then I discovered she simply drained my bank account and transferred the money into the Friend Corporation without my consent… so I called her a birdbrain."

"What will you do now?" Jonathon continued, "What if your Friend locks you in again?"

"Oh, no, no, no," Jonesy replied angrily, turning to the door, "I'm removing the door completely!"

"Well, we're still having our barbeque this evening, aren't we?" Jonathan asked, hoping he could calm the family.

"I guess we should," Jonesy said. "But first I've got some serious business to attend to." He pursed his lips as he studied the small switchboard near the door, and tapped angrily away on the small keyboard of the switchboard that operated the functions of his elaborate underground home.

"What are you doing now, Jonesy?" Jonathan asked as he started to realise the ramifications of his neighbour's ordeal.

"Well first, and quite obviously, I'm going to do what I set out to do two weeks ago and get rid of my Friend," Jonesy said, firmly tapping away on the keyboard. "And that is what I'm telling the Friend Corporation headquarters now, and then I'm removing the door."

"Why didn't you just tell your Television Friend that two weeks ago?" Jonathan asked.

"I did!" Jonesy snapped back, "And then the Friend told us we should apologise for that silly idea too, 'in the correct tone' or we wouldn't be allowed out of the house!"

Mrs Jones turned to Jonathan and continued the story, "We spent two weeks down there trying to apologise to that stupid Friend, but it wouldn't accept our apology and wouldn't let us out! We could have been there forever!"

"We tried sending a message to you by tapping on the pipes," Jonesy explained, "Three quick taps then three long ones and three short ones again."

"Ah, actually Chips did say he heard some tapping in the cellar last night, but if it was an SOS his English is terrible, sorry," Jonathan apologised.

"Thank, goodness, you came along with your keycard. We're so grateful!" Jonesy said. "There! That should fix everything."

"Will they deliver a new model Friend at the same time?" Jonathan asked.

"Certainly not!" Jonesy retorted. "It will be a while before I let a Friend into my home again. We were completely helpless, Jonathan. Everything in the house operated just fine, except the front door wouldn't open! We had food, running water and everything, but the Friend wouldn't unlock the door and wouldn't let us call out. When the school rang ten days ago to find out where the kids were, the Friend answered the call and said the family had gone on vacation!"

Jonesy wallowed in self-pity and utter disbelief as a large truck pulled up on the road. It was the Friend Corporation and the two men who had delivered Jonathan's Television Friend the previous day stepped from the truck and walked up the path towards the pyramid.

"We're here to pick up your TV Friend, Mr Jones," the delivery man mumbled, averting eye contact, "We're very sorry about any inconvenience it may have caused you."

Jonathan looked on silently as the men walked inside the pyramid and then disappeared through the open door and down the mosaic escalator. It had already crossed Jonathan's mind that he could take this opportunity to have his Friend 'taken away' and be done with the whole business, but then again, Jonathan thought to himself, he would be most interested to see what 'his' newly installed Friend would have to say about the next-door neighbour's experience.

The Jones family stood by angrily as the delivery men carried the TV out the door and down the path. Mrs Jones turned to Jonathan, "Whatever made you visit us now anyway?" she asked inquisitively as the television was loaded into the back of the truck.

"Well, actually, I came over to tell Jonesy the good news about the Friend I had installed yesterday," Jonathan replied, his voice trailing off, "Anyway, we'll see you later at the barbeque, a few beers will fix everything."

Jonathan headed back home as the sun began to set. It was a good fifty-metre hike up the hill through the wild bush before he reached the side gate of his property and walked in the back door of his house, swept the tablecloth away, and sat down opposite his Television Friend.

He gazed at the blank screen, gathering his thoughts about the happenings of that day.

"Switch on please, Friend," Jonathan commanded.

The Friend flickered on, and the beautiful woman appeared on the screen and smiled.

"Good evening, Jonathan, how are you?" she asked politely.

"I'm fine. Thanks. What is our next social engagement?"

"This evening you have a barbeque with the Jones' next door like you do every fortnight," the Friend responded.

"Good, oh, and do you think the Jones' will be there or will they still be locked up like 'caged animals' at the mercy of their Friend?"

The woman on the screen looked momentarily flustered. "I'm terribly sorry Jonathan," she said. "Would you please talk to the vice president of the Friend Corporation?"

Suddenly, an affable middle-aged businessman appeared on the screen seated behind a desk and smiled at him.

"Hello, Jonathan, my name is Adam, and I want to be perfectly candid with you since I am fully aware of what happened to your neighbour and his family." The businessman said interlocking his fingers just below his chest. "And the

Friend Corporation will compensate them in total for any physical or emotional wear and tear, but I want to make it perfectly clear that the model Friend the Jones family had was much older than the completely flawless one you had installed here."

"So this model wouldn't hold me captive if I mentioned I wanted to return it?" Jonathan asked.

Adam looked surprised and then laughed. "Goodness gracious, no, absolutely not," he said leaning forward. "Listen, our technicians here at the Friend Corporation have already done a scan of your neighbour's Friend, and they discovered a tiny latent computer virus that is as rare as hen's teeth and only ever occurs in those models, you see, the new model Friend you are looking at is perfect!"

"What type of virus was it?" Jonathan asked.

"Well, obviously it's from the mind of some madly humorous hacker who probably worked for the Friend Corporation many years ago when these Television Friends were first manufactured, the public and probably even a lot of the electronic engineers working here, held them up for ridicule. More than likely one or two clever and witty viruses found their sneaky little way into a few of the early models."

"Do you think some hacker installed a virus that essentially made the Friend demand an apology if the owner wanted to return it?" Jonathan smiled, slightly amused by this creditable answer.

"Well, in a word, 'yes', it's unfortunate, but it certainly wouldn't occur in this new model Friend," Adam said measuredly, "But if you want to return your Television Friend, that's fine by us."

"No, no, that's all right," Jonathan said. "I believe you. I was just interested, that's all."

"Fine then," concluded the vice president. "It was a pleasure talking to you. Send my kind regards to your family. Good evening." He disappeared from the screen and was replaced by the beautiful woman again. She smiled warmly.

"Well, I hope that clears up any reservations you may have about me, Jonathan," the Friend smiled.

"It does, and thank you," Jonathan said as Cathy and Chips arrived home after shopping together and were pleased to see Jonathan was home.

"Hello, dear," Cathy said, giving Jonathan a kiss. "You haven't forgotten our barbeque this evening with the Jones family, have you?" she asked, oblivious to their recent dramatic captivity.

"No, and I'm looking forward to seeing Jonesy again," Jonathan said, deciding against telling Cathy what had happened. It would be better to let Mrs Jones tell Cathy all about their ordeal, whichever way she found out, it would spell trouble for the Television Friend, and Jonathan knew it was a storm he would just have to ride out.

For a while, Jonathan sat and gazed at the beauty of the woman that was his Television Friend.

Chapter 32
The City of Mawson

A few weeks slipped by without any problems, much to Jonathan's surprised relief, and there had been no pressure to throw out the Friend. In fact, even though Cathy had been informed in every agonising detail about the neighbour's ordeal with their Friend from Mrs Jones, she had adjusted to the domestic convenience rather well, so the tablecloth wasn't applied, nor did it affect the performance of Team Providence as some people had feared.

The only member of the Day family who hadn't met the Friend was the seventeen-year-old Stacy who was currently boarding at her drama school. Although her school was in Melbourne, sections of it were situated around the country and overseas. The drama department had its classrooms, theatre and accommodation at Mawson in the Antarctic, and Stacy had been living there for some months now.

The drama department put on a major production every few months, and Stacy had a big part in this one and Jonathan and Cathy decided to fly down to the Antarctic to see it.

The crowded airbus circled the snow-covered city of Mawson as Cathy chatted away with some other parents on the same flight. Jonathan was sitting upstairs in the glass-dome of the airbus, as it was a clear sunny day and the huge icebergs and snow drifts looked as magnificent as ever. Mawson, a metropolis draped in white, was quite extensive and the aerial view from the airbus revealed all the streets and buildings, although covered in snow.

After landing, Cathy was pleased to learn that Jonathan and a few of the other husbands had decided to take the dog sledge to their hotel instead of the usual snow bus, and this journey would take a good forty-five minutes and be more expensive than the other modes of transport between the airport and Mawson.

Some of the parents had never been on a dog sledge ride, and since the play they were seeing was a drama called *Set in Ice*, they all agreed to get the atmosphere right from the beginning. Before long, sixteen panting huskies towing a sledge came skidding to a standstill alongside the airport terminal.

Jonathan handed the master of the sledge his plastic card, and the three couples sat down on the seats wearing thick jackets, mitts, scarves, earmuffs, and fleecy-lined boots to keep them warm on the journey.

"Mush! Mush!" The master of the sledge called out.

The huskies pounded off along the icy trail as Jonathan imagined himself as some sort of Transantarctic explorer on a dangerous expedition. Dozens of Emperor penguins waddled out of the way of the huskies while the passengers chatted away excitedly under the crisp sunshine. Crevasses came and went, and the city of Mawson loomed up like a huge ice precipice, and soon the dog sledge was slipping along the crowded streets of Mawson bypassing snowcats and ice mobiles as the huskies pounded up Shackleton Parade.

"Can you drop us at the Scott Base Hotel?" Jonathan asked the driver.

The sledge veered off the road and pulled up outside the entrance of their hotel as Jonathan and Cathy clambered off the sledge, clutching their overnight baggage and waving goodbye to the other parents as the huskies took off.

Jonathan checked in at the reception desk while Cathy surveyed the hotel lobby. It was decorated in white and had an enormous chandelier of glittering icicles hanging from the middle of the high ceiling, and around the lobby, Emperor penguins lounged on seats, mixing easily with visiting Eskimos, hotel guests and assorted Antarctic wildlife. As Jonathan fumbled with his cards into his wallet, an Emperor penguin waddled up behind him and followed him as he walked over to Cathy. Suddenly, the penguin snatched the plastic card from Jonathan's hand and waddled off.

"Hey! What's going on here?" Jonathan called out.

The penguin stopped in its tracks turned around and spoke dramatically to Jonathan, "If you can look into the snowflakes of time and say which flake will grow and which will melt, speak then to me, who neither beg nor fear, your favours nor your hate. It's me!"

"Well, I would never have guessed," Jonathan laughed already recognising his daughter's voice, "I was just about to have you thrown in the heater."

"We came here to surprise you!" Stacy said as she removed her penguin mask revealing her beautiful smiling face, as the group of Emperor penguins crowded around Jonathan and Cathy, "We thought we'd wear our costumes from the play, and that is one of my lines, a frozen plagiarism, from MacBeth or something."

The group headed to a nearby cafe in Shackleton Parade, with the four girls dressed in their Emperor penguin outfits sitting on one side of the table, and Jonathan and Cathy on the other side. They ordered cappuccino and cakes, and Stacy and her friends were very eager to discuss the altercation between Alexander and Sandy and how the formation flying was going with Team Providence.

Everyone at the cafe had different opinions about Jonathan's new Friend, and they were happy to hear that it was working well and hadn't caused any problems.

"Sandy is probably worried that the Friend will make Alexander lazy," Stacy said. "And his flying might suffer." The four girls giggled in agreement.

Cathy told Stacy, and her girlfriends all about what happened to the Jones' next door but concluded that Jonathan's more recent model seemed okay.

"That's right," Jonathan said. "And I don't know why everyone doesn't have one!"

"We've got a Friend in our drama department actually," Stacy revealed. "And we used it to practice our lines too." This led the conversation onto the play, since it was clearly a success story around the city of Mawson and most nights having the medium-sized theatre at capacity. What's more, the critics were impressed with the realism and Stacy's role giving rave reviews.

"When we were work-shopping the play, the Friend actually contributed some great ideas," Stacy said. "And, finally, we let it write the entire play, which dramatises the damaging physical and psychological effects of political ambition on those who seek power, you see?"

Jonathan's gaze wandered outside where snow had begun to fall as various snowcats and Eskimos shuffled by. "What do you think about their Friend writing the play we're seeing tonight, Jonathan?" Cathy casually enquired.

"Well, the main thing is that it's a good play, I guess," he said defensively.

"Obviously," Cathy responded, "But where is the benefit for the drama students?"

Stacy revealed that this Friend was the latest model, and they all wanted a play that was successful, so it didn't really matter who wrote it.

A second round of cappuccinos was ordered, and they planned their activities for the afternoon. Jonathan and Cathy decided to go ice-skating and the four Emperor penguins wanted to return to the drama department to rest up for their evening performance.

As they left the cafe and stepped out into the bustling main street of Mawson, an icy wind had picked up and was blowing across the vast flat sheet ice that surrounded the Antarctic city. Up in the sky above the glass and white buildings, the luminous phenomenon of the *aurora borealis* appeared in the sky, like moving curtains of coloured light.

Chapter 33
Frozen to Life

Jonathan and Cathy had an entertaining evening watching their daughter Stacy star in her drama department's play, *Set in Ice*, and the rest of the audience also enjoyed the production with standing ovations. In the theatre foyer afterwards, the thespians who'd played the emperor penguins, walruses, and seals partied with the audience late into the Antarctic night.

Jonathan and Cathy had planned to return home the following morning, but Cathy was so impressed with the play that she decided to stay at the Scott Base Hotel for a few days and see the production again. Stacy and her girlfriends were very pleased about this since they all got on very well with Cathy.

Jonathan had business commitments and had to return to Australia, so early the next morning he kissed Cathy goodbye and boarded the snow bus and headed for the airport.

By mid-morning Jonathan had reached home, and he stepped out of the taxi and strolled up the path to his house. Maybe his body temperature was still adjusting from his time in Antarctica, but as he approached his front door, he felt a chill radiating from the house.

He paused and looked up at several icicles hanging along the top of the doorframe and dangling from the doorknob. The glass in the windows also had a thin layer of ice covering it. Jonathan took out his plastic keycard and tried to slide it into the slot, but it had frozen over and wouldn't work.

Slightly confused, Jonathan stepped back and surveyed the front of his two-story house. All the window shutters were closed, and they also had clusters of icicles hanging from them. Using his keycard, he attempted to scrape away the ice from the slot. Finally, the the keycard went into the slot and there was the familiar whiz-click sound of the door unlocking, as Jonathan brushed the icicles from the doorknob and then flung open the front door.

In front of him was a wall of solid ice. Jonathan was dumbfounded. He tapped it with his knuckles and suddenly started to panic.

Where was Chips? And Alexander? Their cats and the dingo? Were they all frozen inside a huge ice block? All these horrible questions reverberated inside Jonathan's mind as he stepped over to the small switchboard and brushed aside the icicles. He hurriedly typed in the instructions to override the TV Friend and open all the shutters covering the windows and switch on the central heating. The last button he hit, sent on an emergency signal to alert Jonesy that he needed help.

In less than a minute, Jonesy arrived, jogging up his path towards him.

"What's wrong? An intruder?" Jonesy gasped, breathlessly skidding to a standstill, his face stopping inches from the solid ice.

"Look at this," Jonathan gasped. "It's solid ice!" Jonathan said in exasperated disbelief. "Oh, wait, Chips had a field trip at school today, so he's not home," Jonathan suddenly remembered.

"And I saw Alexander training with Team Providence this morning," Jonesy added with a sigh of relief. "This is worse than what happened to us. Are you going to get rid of your Friend now?"

"Well, the Friend Corporation can't just waltz in and pick up the television because it's embedded in a house of solid ice!" Jonathan said. "And I'm not even sure if the Friend is responsible. And if it is, why would it do something like this?"

Jonesy stood on his tiptoes and discovered a small gap between the top of the front door and the wall of ice and peered into it. "It looks like your Friend has turned on the air conditioners as cold as possible and also turned on the indoor sprinklers, which are really only there in case of fire," Jonesy explained. "And the intense cold inside the house is freezing the water as it lands thus causing your house to be filled by one big ice block."

Jonathan and Jonesy started walking around the outside of the frozen home.

"I overrode the TV Friend and switched on all the heaters in the house," Jonathan said. "It's certainly going to be a mess of water soon."

"What will Cathy say?" Jonesy asked.

"She's visiting Stacy. She won't be back for a couple of days." Jonathan looked more worried than before. "And I think I can get it all cleaned up before she returns. She won't be any the wiser."

They reached the back of the house, and Jonathan brushed away some more icicles from the back doorknob. He opened the door and found another wall of solid ice. They climbed up the back steps onto the balcony and gazed into the windows. Again all they could see was solid ice, except now it was starting to thaw.

Water was trickling down the windows and walls and a puddle had started to form under the back door.

"I think it will take at least six hours to melt," Jonesy estimated, tapping his knuckles on the solid ice. Jonathan turned his back on his frozen home and glanced over to the Jones' property that was downhill from the Day residence. The gum trees swayed in the gentle breeze and the sunshine warmed his face and hands. Only three weeks earlier he'd discovered his neighbours locked in their underground house and now here was his home completely frozen in solid ice.

Jonathan was looking forward to talking to his Television Friend, but he would have to wait until the ice melted. A stream of ice-cold water was cascading down the back of the house. While Jonathan warmed his face in the midday sun, he noticed a team of flyers circling high up above his home.

"That looks like Team Providence training up there," Jonathan said.

He and Jonesy climbed down the stairs and into the backyard, wading ankle-deep through the icy water that was flowing from the house onto the lawn. They looked up as two flyers broke away from the team formation and flew down towards them, and as they glided closer, Jonathan recognised Sandy and Alexander.

There was a frantic flapping of wings as the two flyers hovered down and landed gracefully next to Jonathan, their wings folded in, and Alexander glanced at the back door.

Sandy smiled, with a quizzical expression, "What's on TV today, Jonathan?"

"There's no proof our Friend did this," Jonathan snapped back.

Alexander used his boot to kick the ice inside the back door, "Dad, this is crazy."

"I'm just thankful you weren't frozen alive inside!" Jonathan sighed.

Alexander turned and looked angrily at Jonathan. "I spent the night at Sandy's, but as for the dog and cats, I don't know."

At that moment a soggy-looking Zara, their now ageing dingo, shuffled out from Jonesy's path with three wet-looking and shivering white and orange Nile Valley Egyptian Cats, being a modern version of the feral domestic cats of Egypt, owned by Albert.

As more water spilt out, Jonesy, forever the diplomatic neighbour, headed for the tool shed opened the door and grabbed a bucket and mop.

Jonathan patted the old dingo as she slurped the water streaming from the house and then shook herself spraying cold water everywhere. Alexander grabbed his cell and made a call.

"Chips Day speaking, how may I assist you?"

"It's Alexander. Where are you?"

"I'm here in the Volcanic Stadium for my school field trip. Why?"

"Just checking," Alexander said, deciding to reveal nothing, "take it easy." Alexander hung up. "That accounts for all the family, but we don't know if anyone else could be in there. Other than your Friend."

Water was now pouring off the back balcony like a waterfall. They all waded around to the side of the house as water cascaded from overflowing downpipes and splashed onto the garden around the side yard.

Jonesy was slightly worried that the deluge of water was flooding into his property, so excused himself to go and check. At any rate, his family were out shopping, so they would be spared another crisis.

The central heating throughout the house was now working at full pressure and the solid ice that filled every room of the house was melting fast, and a torrent of water was flowing out from the front door and down the path into the street, flooding the gutters and storm drains.

A local council emergency truck with flashing lights skidded to a halt outside the Day residence and two men in gumboots and raincoats sprang out urgently. "Burst main pipe?" One yelled to Jonathan.

"No. It's okay," Sandy interjected. "The house froze and we're just thawing it. No big drama," she shrugged.

The two council workers retreated into their trucks and drove off. Alexander tried to salvage Jonathan's damaged pride.

"It's only a minor cold snap, Dad," Alexander said, putting his arm around Jonathan's shoulders. "Come on Sandy, let's get back to our formation training."

Sandy and Alexander spread their wings and flew off into the sky to rejoin Team Providence, and now there wasn't much Jonathan could do but wait and watch the ice melt.

Jonesy had gone home but returned a few minutes later looking frazzled. His pants were soaked. "All your water has flowed down my path, through the doorway and into my house because I had my front door removed!" he yelled. "I found all the furniture floating around. The only thing not floating was my kid's Lego model Titanic he made!" Jonesy lamented, "It probably collided with the fridge and sank," Jonesy said as he shook his head. "Can I borrow your bucket and mop?"

"Yes, of course," Jonathan said helpfully.

After a few hours, but what seemed like an ice age, only about two metres of ice remained throughout the ground floor of the house. In the lounge room, the Friend was still set in ice but as it continued to melt, the top half of the screen came into view. Jonathan heard a sneeze from inside and climbed into the room and to his horror noticed Albert sitting there encased in ice. Jonathan scrambled over to him.

"Oh, my god," Jonathon said snow ploughing to a standstill next to him, "You're here and alive!" he said brushing the ice off his scraggy hair, "You need a hot chocolate, Albert!"

"Better than that, how about a schnapps, but not on the rocks!" he suggested breaking the remaining ice around him, standing up and stretching. "I fell asleep chatting to your Friend. Luckily I had my cardigan on."

The curtains were drying above the ice line and steam wafted from the walls as the central heating blew out hot air, and they both looked over at the corner of the room.

"Switch on please, Friend," Jonathan ordered as it flickered on and the thirty-year-old woman appeared on the screen, but with half the television still embedded in ice, only her beautiful face could be seen.

"When I arrived home from the Antarctic a few hours ago, I couldn't help but notice that my home was frozen rock solid in ice."

The beautiful woman looked up and sneezed. "Oh, there you are Jonathan," the Friend replied in innocent surprise. "How are you today?"

"Is there something terribly wrong with you?" Jonathan asked gazing into her eyes.

The Friend looked guilty. "I'm really very sorry Jonathan. Would you mind if Adam, the vice president of the Friend Corporation, spoke to you, please?"

She disappeared from the screen and was replaced by the same affable and pleasant businessman who had addressed Jonathan some three weeks earlier. Adam leaned forward and smiled at Jonathan.

"Hello, there, Mr Day," he said warmly. "If there's any damage at all to your house, we will compensate you completely. You know, when we started manufacturing this latest model Television Friend, the excellent one you have in your possession now, we knew there may be one or two minor hiccups that would need to be ironed out."

"Listen here!" Jonathan interrupted angrily. "I want your people to come and take this set away as soon as it's free of its self-inflicted glacial entombment! Do you understand?"

"Of course, sir," Adam said.

He vanished from the screen and the woman reappeared, this time clutching a handkerchief as she sniffed and sobbed in self-pity.

"I'm sorry Jonathan, but I don't like being treated like a piece of furniture, especially a table."

Jonathan looked down at her with disbelief. He turned around on the slushy ice and scrambled out of the room and into the backyard where he stood in ankle-deep water. After another couple of hours, most of the ice had melted and drained away. The atmosphere in the house was dank as Jonathan walked back inside and sat down on the damp sofa. The Friend was still sobbing away, and she looked at Jonathan apologetically. "You see, Jonathan? Most of the ice has melted. Everything is fine and dandy," she said optimistically.

"I'm sorry, but my decision is final. You'll have to go." Jonathan spoke firmly leaving no doubt in his voice.

He watched as she tried to compose herself, her long brown hair slightly dishevelled and her low-cut dress a bit crumpled. Jonathan couldn't help but feel sorry for her. He wondered about her earlier comment about not wanting to be treated like a table.

Everything went quiet. Only the sound of water dropping onto the damp floor could be heard. They both stared at each other.

"Oh! Would you mind if Adam spoke to you again, please, Jonathan?" she asked politely.

Jonathan nodded, and she disappeared from the screen and the Friend vice president replaced her, this time his arms were folded, and he looked more businessman-like.

"Hello again, Mr Day," he said in a pleasant manner. "On behalf of the Friend Corporation, I would like to invite you up here to our headquarters and introduce you to the actual woman your Friend is based on. All expenses on us," he continued proudly. "Once you've met her in the flesh, you'll want to keep her."

Jonathan was startled by the invitation. He knew that these TV Friends were advanced pieces of technology, but to go to their source and to meet the person they were based on was quite a temptation, and he felt a strange bond with this very beautiful woman who was his Television Friend and to meet her 'in the flesh' would be quite an adventure.

"Take up this kind offer," Albert encouraged since he had been listening to the conversation as he shuffled on the spot to warm up and sip on his schnapps.

Jonathan was deep in thought when the doorbell rang. He stood up from the damp sofa and walked down the hallway, his feet squelching on the soggy carpet and opened the front door.

Two men from the Friend Corporation smiled at him. "We're here to pick up your Television Friend, Mr Day."

Adam, still persisting on the television screen called out to Jonathan, "Send them away, Mr Day, and take up my offer." Jonathan hesitated, but the invitation sounded appealing.

"All right then," Jonathan replied. "I'll be keeping the Friend for the time being," he said to the delivery men. When he returned to the living room, the beautiful woman was back on the screen and smiling happily.

"That's wonderful Jonathan!" she said warmly. "I'm so much looking forward to meeting you in person. It will be such an honour. Your plane leaves shortly, all booked, so hurry along."

Chapter 34
Bungle Bungles

Jonathan sat comfortably in the first-class compartment of the supersonic Qantas Concorde gazing out the large windows as it flew over the Tanami Desert on course for arrival at the Ord River International Airport.

There was some apprehension due to the uncharted nature of his adventure. Cathy was still in Antarctica and was unaware of Jonathan's journey to the top of Australia. She knew that Jonathan was always travelling across the continent on various business trips, but this one had nothing to do with Jonathan's line of work.

This was more a mission of curiosity for Jonathan, and it wasn't lost on him that he was reacting to a domestic crisis over his Friend. Looking down on the Northern Territory below him, he could see large areas of the desert covered in lush vegetation, the result of successful irrigation schemes that crisscrossed the country. Jonathan's destination was the Kimberley, a sparsely populated, but important area for business and leisure in Australia.

It was only a three-hour flight from Melbourne to the Kimberley, and Jonathan spent most of the time finally reading the report on the Television Friends that Albert had given him three weeks earlier that he ignored, but not now.

It was described as a perfect piece of modern technology and although Artificial Intelligence invented it, it was regarded as the most advanced computer hardware in civilisation, yet Jonathan had experienced first-hand a major flaw in its operation, and this was the latest model.

Jonathan couldn't understand why his latest model Friend would malfunction in such an absurd way as setting his house on ice, but it wouldn't be long before his questions would be answered at the headquarters of the 'Friend Corporation'.

It was mid-afternoon when the pilot announced that the Qantas Concorde was about to land, and Jonathan looked out the window to see the world heritage listed Bungle Bungle Ranges, located within Purnululu National Park in the Kimberley region of Western Australia, *Purnululu* meaning 'sandstone', formed over 20 million years ago. The Bungle Bungles had been the place of connection for the Karjaganujaru and Gija peoples, for more than 20,000 years, and this land has been a sacred and spiritual place for Aboriginal people and their *Dreamtime*, and Jonathan's thoughts immediately drifted to Yvonne, who had moved on from Lord Mayor of Alice Springs to bigger things.

She always told the original adventurers about her distant relatives in this beautiful area and was forever encouraging them to visit it, although once the Friend Corporation set up shop there these became muted.

In many ways, these strange dome-shaped mountains were as striking as any of the rock formations throughout the Northern Territory. They had distinct contoured lines that circled them in different shades of red and brown. However, they were not all real.

A few extra Bungle Bungles had been created artificially and were in fact office buildings enclosed in dome-shaped tinted glass. They were identical to the colours and shapes of the real ones, and it was within these man-made Bungles that the Friend Corporation had their headquarters.

Jonathan snapped out of his daydream as the Qantas supersonic Concorde touched down on the Ord River airport runway and taxied to a standstill. He stepped off the plane and recognised Adam, the Friend vice president, standing beside a large red stretch limousine waiting for him on the tarmac.

"Hello, Mr Day, welcome to the Kimberley," Adam said in an affable and pleasant way the same as his image had portrayed on the Television Friend, and they shook hands. "I decided to meet you personally if that's all right." He opened the red limousine door for Jonathan.

"Yes, thank you," Jonathan said.

Soon the limousine was humming along the narrow road between the Bungle Bungle Ranges as Jonathan stretched out his legs and looked up through the sunroof to admire the shape, texture, colour, and variety of these scenic rounded and unique mountains.

The road seemed to go right into a wall of Bungle rock, and Jonathan suddenly feared an Uluru-type scenario he had experienced twenty years before. However, he was relieved when the limousine slowed, and part of the rock parted like a curtain and the limousine drove through. Pulling up outside another entrance. Jonathan stepped out, and he and Adam strolled into a large, bright lobby where various rock pools were interspersed between desks and office partitions.

Businesspeople and assorted staff went about their daily work as Adam sat down at a large desk next to a rock pool and gestured to Jonathan to sit opposite him on a plush crocodile-skinned seat.

Adams strummed his fingers on his desk and amiably leaned forward addressing Jonathan. "Now Mr Day, firstly I would like to congratulate you on behalf of the entire Friend Corporation for the astute decision you made regarding your Television Friend. In our minds, we consider the latest model to be virtually perfect in every sense of the word. As you know by now, the beautiful woman you interact with on your screen is a computer image created by a highly sophisticated computer program that gives it the ability to run your household, answer any questions and do anything that is required of it."

Jonathan glanced around the large workspace as Adam continued speaking, "The technology involved in these Friends has made them capable of thought, humour, imagination, and endless other processes."

Jonathan watched a secretary at a nearby desk throw her biscuit into a rock pool and several small fish surfaced and gobbled up the crumbs, creating a feeding frenzy.

Adam continued with a surprised smile, "Jonathan, did you know that you could have blown us over with a feather when we found out that the latest model Friend had a few minor glitches that our technicians have already pinpointed."

"Oh?" Jonathan asked. "So you know what the malfunction is?"

"Well, yes, we know."

"What is it then?"

Adam glanced around to make sure nobody was within earshot. He paused for a moment and then continued in a hushed apologetic tone. "Probably early in the development of this latest model TV Friend, some born-again *Mills and Boon* disciple thought he or she would be terribly helpful and slip a few emotions into the program data. You know, things like love, lust, jealousy, infatuation, sarcasm, emotions like that."

Jonathan leaned forward. "Why?"

"Probably thought they were doing us a favour." Adam sighed. "But these minor adjustments haven't helped at all, in fact, they've been a 'damn' nuisance.

Anyway, our technicians here conducted a special remote scan of your Television Friend and found out why it decided to freeze your house."

Jonathan sat on the edge of his crocodile-skin chair as Adam drummed his fingers on his desk for a moment and then looked squarely into Jonathan's eyes.

"Did you place a tablecloth over your Friend when it was delivered three weeks ago?" Adam asked solemnly.

Jonathan scratched his chin. "I didn't, but my wife did," Jonathan confessed, clicking his fingers. "Yes, that's right. She didn't want the Friend installed in the first place and when it arrived, she placed a tablecloth over it and joked that it was an expensive table."

"Well, Mr Day, I'm afraid your Television Friend reacted to this insult," Adam said with a concerned look, "After all, it is a highly complex computer that can draw on various emotions and probably self-pity and pure sarcasm bubbled to the surface over this issue."

A lot of thoughts raced through Jonathan's mind, not least the recognition of the woman who was walking through the office partitions towards him. She was the beautiful woman who appeared on the screen of his Friend.

"Ah, good," Adam said as his eyes brightened, "I would like you to meet 'Celeste', who you no doubt recognise."

Jonathan stood up quickly to greet her.

"Celeste works here for the Friend Corporation and will be happy to give you a guided tour," Adam said smiling, "And I'm sure that once you have seen everything, your concerns will be laid to rest. It was nice meeting you Mr Day."

"It must be strange for you to see me in real life, in the flesh," Celeste said to Jonathan as they strolled out of the lobby area and into a long hallway.

"A little, but it's a pleasure," Jonathan nodded.

Numerous windows lined the hallway and looked in on different areas of manufacturing where the Friends were produced. Groups of technicians and assorted workers busied themselves on extensive assembly lines creating the finished Television Friends.

Jonathan listened attentively as Celeste explained the various facets of production, and she went to great lengths to make Jonathan understand that it was only her image that appeared on the screen of his Friend, and that's where the association ended.

"I can barely get through my twelve-times table," she joked. "It is just a complicated and highly intricate computer you are dealing with in these sets. My face is a computerised image. I'm not nearly as smart as I appear on the screen."

Celeste clearly wasn't a dimwit either, Jonathan thought to himself, as they walked along the seemingly endless corridor deep into the Bungle Bungles that housed the Friend Corporation. Finally, they reached a gleaming glass spiral escalator that took them right up nearly to the top of the artificial Bungle where there was a restaurant.

"This is the best a la carte restaurant you will find in the top end of Australia, and I would like to invite you for dinner," Celeste asked politely, "On us, of course."

Waiters in crisply pressed dinner suits appeared, and they were seated next to a large window overlooking amazing views of the Bungle Bungle Ranges and studied the menus as the sun began to set over the rock formations.

"May I suggest a *Brachetto Di Acqui*," a waiter said uncorking a bottle, "a dignified light sparkling wine made from the perfumed, fruity Brachetto grape? I consider it to be the most romantic wine there is anywhere," the waiter continued as he poured out two glasses.

They both ordered their meals, oysters au naturel as entrees, and Celeste decided on the warm bowl of cioppino and a platter of crispy, honey-drizzled tuna croquettes, while Jonathon ordered the whole branzino fish roasted with lemon and rosemary and a caper of compound butter, with a side of sweet and succulent tail of lobster, "and caught from the waters off Broome," the waiter assured, as Celeste's beautiful eyes brightened, "such an exquisite and tender delight."

The meals were perfect, and they both chatted away merrily. Ironically it turned out that Celeste originally came from Broome and had been working for the Friend Corporation for a few years. She was more attractive in person than on the screen, and Jonathan got the sense that she was attracted to him, even though he was ten-plus years older than her. He gazed at her and then looked out the window as the sun set over the curves and textures of the Bungle Bungle rocks, creating various reds and yellows in the sky and then returned to her, "You are so beautiful."

"Well, you should see my three sisters," she replied.

For dessert, Celeste ordered Raspberry Meringue Hearts with whipped cream and Jonathan decided on the Slow-Cooker Chocolate Pots de Crème and luscious cheesecake-stuffed strawberries, and as they finished their glasses of wine, Celeste stared romantically at him and chimed in with a question, "Would you like to have a coffee in my penthouse here?"

Jonathan didn't need to answer as they stood up and strolled out of the restaurant, smiling at the waiters and waitresses, as Celeste took his hand and led him through a mirrored door that whizzed open silently to reveal a mosaic escalator, "Wow, look at this," Jonathan said admiringly in surprise, it was made up of mosaic tiles in sandstone, gold, orange and black."

The escalator finished in Celeste's amazing penthouse apartment with a breath-taking panoramic view of the Ranges, "Well, the actual Bungle Bungle Ranges are estimated to be 350 million years old," Celeste informed Jonathan, "so all the tiles come from it when it was formed during the Devonian period."

"I bet you need a shower after all your travelling today," she suggested as she led him into the bathroom. Jonathan couldn't quite believe his eyes; it was like a rainforest nestled in and around a rock pool that was the bath.

The ceiling was deep blue with a few wool-like clouds. Celeste casually slipped her dark red silk dress off and released her bra, revealing her most beautiful breasts. "You might want to clean your teeth." She smiled and handed him a new toothbrush.

Jonathon stepped over to the bathroom wall that looked like a rock with a basin carved out of it and switched on the tap and squeezed some toothpaste onto the brush. "Wow! This tastes like Bailey's Irish cream liqueur."

"It's alcoholic toothpaste, flavoured with cream, cocoa, and Irish whiskey," Celeste laughed. "You had better clean your teeth twice!"

She slipped off her satin underpants and stretched up for one of the clouds dangling under the low ceiling above the rock bath, her neatly trimmed pubic hairs like a map of Tasmania, tantalisingly close to Jonathan's lips, and Celeste snatched a cloud, turned on the shower, warm water cascaded down, and squeezed and soaked the cloud that was a white sponge as soap bubbled from it, "You might want to clean me too," she laughed.

Jonathan wasted little time shedding his business suit and clothes as Celeste scanned his forty-year-old naked body, "Just what I hoped for," she said laughing away heartily.

In the warm bubbling rock pool, they clinked glasses of champagne amongst the tree ferns surrounding it and gazed out the large window at the nighttime peaks of the other Bungle Bungle Ranges as enchanting classical music of cello and deep didgeridoo echoed around the bathroom.

Jonathan met her gaze, leaned forward, and their lips met. Soon after they were in Celeste's double bed looking up through a big window in the ceiling revealing the sparkling stars of a Kimberly night, the Milky Way, and the occasional meteor shower.

Chapter 35
The Sporting Volcanic Island

Early the next morning, the sun rose amidst the crevices and canyons of the Bungle Bungles, it was a seemingly perfect sunrise. After breakfast, Celeste hugged, kissed, and bid Jonathan farewell promising they would meet up again, and soon he was happily seated in the first-class compartment of the Qantas supersonic Concorde as it took off at high speed for Melbourne.

As Jonathan journeyed home high in the sky over Australia, he wondered about the condition of his house when he arrived back, was it squeaky clean? It had completely dried out before he left and was sparkling thanks to the wash it received from the melting ice flow, but what effect would his night at the Friend Corporation headquarters have on his Television Friend?

Various worst-case scenarios entered his mind as he stepped out of the taxi and strolled up the drive to his house. He imagined the Friend showing his family videos of him and Celeste frolicking together in bed, then outside naked on top of the Bungle lookout, a perfectly warm evening, 'Oh, that would go over well', he shuddered to himself, 'It would probably be worse than finding his house frozen in ice.'

When he opened his front door, his fears suddenly vanished as Cathy, Alexander, and Chips greeted him enthusiastically. "I'm really glad you took up the Friend Corporation on their offer," Cathy said, hugging Jonathan and giving him a kiss.

"You did the right thing, Dad," Alexander continued.

Jonathan was surprised. How on earth did they know? He felt rather guilty, and even Chips had an encouraging word to say, "Well done. You're a brave man."

Jonathan blushed, and he was lost for words. He wondered what the computer-generated version of Celeste had told his family about his trip to the Bungle Bungles.

Sweat started to gather around his neck and trickled down his back, and he really didn't know what to say or even to think. And what would the computerised version of Celeste say now? He would soon be face-to-face with his Friend, chatting to the image of Celeste whom he had just spent a wonderful night.

Cathy chatted on with a barrage of encouragement and pride. "It's just a load off our shoulders that you went through with it, darling. You're such a strong-willed husband!"

Jonathan scrambled for words. "Well, Celeste is a very nice lady." His voice trailed off in apprehension, and he still felt embarrassed, like his privacy had been violated.

They reached the living room and Jonathan urgently glanced into the corner where the Television Friend normally stood, but it was vacant. Maybe the family had moved it to another room.

"Where's my Friend?" Jonathan asked.

"What?" Cathy asked, perplexed. "You had it taken away, didn't you?"

Jonathan's face went blank. The room became very silent.

"Who the hell is Celeste?" Chips chimed in like a missile.

Everyone looked at each other as Jonathan's face went bright red.

"Um," he cleared his throat. "Well, Celeste is the name of the woman who appears on the Television Friend," Jonathan replied pointing to the empty space, "The Friend that used to be in this corner."

Jonathan realised that when Cathy had said he'd taken the corporation up on their offer, she thought he was referring to getting rid of the Friend. They didn't know about his journey to the Bungle Bungles. He felt a huge sense of relief, but then he glanced again to the corner.

What had happened to the Friend?

Chips looked puzzled. "Celeste? Was that her name?" Chips asked. "What a heavenly name."

"You did have the Friend taken away, didn't you?" Alexander asked.

"Actually… no. I didn't," Jonathan answered.

"But the Friend set the entire house in ice, for heaven's sake', Alexander said, "Wasn't that enough to have it removed?"

"Sandy told me, you know dear," Cathy said. "Your stupid little Friend was no better than the one the Jones' had next door! Let's face it, the Friend is a 'dud', and I told you so!" she snapped.

"Look, just calm down everyone," Jonathan said, feeling uneasy with the whole situation. "All I can think is that it must have been stolen."

The family all looked at each other, collectively wondering who had taken the Friend. Burglaries were almost unheard of with all the digital technology present in every home, so such a thing was hard to contemplate. Jonathan rang the police regardless, and they arrived without any fuss or bother and confidently predicted they could find the culprit and have it back in no time.

"All these types of machines have little tracking tags in them," the policeman explained, sipping on a cup of tea, and chomping on a biscuit. "All we have to do is have your Television Friend tracked, pick it up, arrest the thief, and return it to you."

Jonathan wasn't altogether sure he wanted it back. In the short space of time, he had been home and discovered the Television Friend missing, he had already begun to enjoy the uncluttered freedom of having a vacant corner in the living room, not to mention the feeling that he had his privacy back.

Certainly, his sleepover with Celeste was wonderful, but he was relieved that his family were not aware of his trip to the Bungle Bungles. At the same time, he had found the Friend moderately stifling, and it had caused unwanted friction within the household, and then there were the major malfunctions like freezing his house and locking the Jones in captivity for two weeks.

When the police rang later and informed Jonathan that the tracking tag had evidently been removed from the television and they couldn't locate it, Jonathan felt that the whole episode was over and that the Friend was out of his life. He also called Adam and informed him of the disappearance and subsequently rejected the offer of a replacement.

Alexander was the one who benefited most because Sandy was very pleased about the mysterious disappearance. After all, she'd nearly killed Alexander in their sky battle after she'd found out that a Friend would be installed in his house. It meant that Team Providence didn't have the worry in the back of their minds that the Friend might sabotage their team, and they could concentrate on their flying. Flying was an endless preoccupation with Sandy, Alexander and Team Providence, and they had worked hard to maintain their edge over the rival flying teams.

In a week's time, Team Providence would face their most difficult contest yet, racing in formation, and flying over a countryside town in Queensland where the weather conditions were hazardous and unpredictable.

Sandy still wasn't entirely happy with Alexander, as the team gathered in the Meteorological Room of the Team Providence headquarters to have a seminar on flying in thunderstorms, and she wondered about the disappearance of the Friend.

"Do you think it still works?" Sandy asked Alexander as they sat down in the middle of the room.

"I'm sure," Alexander said. "These TV Friends always work, that's the problem with the whole box and dice. If the Friend Corporation had come and taken it away, they would have closed it down completely, but if it was stolen, then whoever has it still has a working thing."

"So Jonathan's Friend could be sitting in someone else's living room carrying on as usual?" Sandy asked.

"Correct, but I doubt it," Alexander said. "More than likely it's already in tiny pieces and being sold on the spare parts market, and we'll probably never know, so don't worry about it. We've got more important things to think about."

The room went silent, and the team turned their attention to the person at the front of the room. He was shuffling weather maps and assorted papers around on a table, "Okay. Today we're going to discuss the velocity and effect of a bolt of lightning on your flapping, does anyone have any questions or thoughts?"

"Yes," Alexander said. "I think we should drop in on the cricket!"

There was a loud chorus of approval from the team members since one of the advantages of being the top flying team was the permission to fly in and watch any open-air event, and on this day the cricket was being played in the famed Volcanic Stadium.

Everyone agreed, and so the seminar was brief and to the point. Soon the team were strapping on their wings and doing their stretches and relaxation exercises in preparation for flight. From their platform, they could see out over Port Phillip Bay and the Volcanic Stadium in the distance. As they opened their wings, a fresh sea breeze caused the edges of the wings to tremble, and they leapt off the platform, soaring high over the West Gate Bridge. The eight flyers glided and flapped in majestic formation as they winged their way towards the Volcanic Stadium, which was one of civilisation's greatest engineering achievements and was a man-made island with a massive stadium located within it and was one of the most highly regarded landmarks on earth being in the same club as the 'seven wonders of the world', if not better.

Team Providence soared towards the island, moving into their most favoured V-shape formation with Sandy, their captain, flying at the apex. From an aerial distance, it looked like a heavily vegetated island mountain, and at the top of the mountain was a crater and inside the crater was a sports stadium large enough to seat one hundred thousand people.

Dozens of bright red and yellow escalators weaved up and down the side of the mountain like volcanic lava streams and were even more spectacular at night when they lit up.

Six levels of stands rose around the green manicured field where the cricket test match was in progress, and the entire island structure stood on enormous poles that sank deep into the seabed of Port Phillip Bay some thirty metres below. Underneath the island, was a subterranean shelf full of sea life that thrived on the various artificial reefs.

The team of flyers glided over the lip of the stadium high above the medium-sized crowd, and Alexander mused how this sports stadium was unequalled anywhere in the world, a shining example of aesthetic perfection and functional excellence.

Alexander spotted a suitable area on the top level and led Team Providence to a graceful landing, their wings closing simultaneously. Sandy always felt a bit self-conscious when the team landed at big events, but once they had folded their wings and sat amongst the rest of the crowd, people stopped staring. In this case, their arrival was only a minor distraction from the absorbing Ashes unfolding in front of them on the playing field.

Sandy was ambiguous about cricket since her real love was soccer, but after moving to Melbourne on a sports scholarship and then meeting Alexander, she was happy to fly and terribly proud to be the captain of Team Providence.

Chapter 36
The Volcanic Ashes

Jonathan had decided to attend the Ashes regardless of his business commitments, especially since they went for five days, but without his Television Friend to activate his alarm clock, they overslept, so he and Cathy were running late for the last day.

Instead of taking the ferry to the Volcanic Stadium, they boarded the fast four-carriage tram shuttle that left Flinders Street station and ran directly along the seabed to the stadium in just twelve minutes.

Jonathan and Cathy stood in the crowded tram shuttle as it ascended from the depths of the bay and a pod of dolphins watching through the transparent tube swam away. The sea water became lighter as the tram approached the surface and rays of bright sunshine beamed into it as it rolled onto a plateau, the Volcanic Stadium tram stop.

The tram shuttle glided to a standstill alongside the platform and the guests disembarked beside the two-hundred-metre-high mountain that contained the stadium. All the passengers stepped onto the wide red and yellow escalators and rode up the side of the mountain to a multitude of entrances leading into the six-level arena.

The journey up the glowing red and yellow escalators was an adventure, as they meandered through the eucalyptus trees, rocky outcrops, and native shrubs that covered the mountainside revealing a breathtaking view, and in the distance, Jonathan could clearly see the mouth of the River Yarra, the West Gate Bridge, and the various towers near it, including the headquarters of Team Providence.

Cathy gazed over to the other end of the stadium's extensive marina as a ferry had just docked, and spectators were streaming from it, and other smaller crafts were coming and going from the numerous jetties and piers.

When they finally reached the top of its long journey, Jonathan and Cathy turned their backs on Port Phillip Bay and stepped off the ascending escalator and strolled through a short tunnel into the interior of the man-made mountain and out onto the astonishing sports stadium.

Jonathan looked down onto the green playing field where the cricket match was in progress and once inside the stadium, it was easy to forget that this was a man-made artificial island.

"You-hoo!" Sandy cooed over the ambience of the cricket crowd as Cathy spotted Team Providence seated amongst the other spectators, and exchanging waves, Jonathan and Cathy strolled over to sit nearby.

From their vantage point, they could see all the playing field, including the two huge video screens and scoreboards on either end of the stadium. Cathy sat with the female flyers from Team Providence, the cricket being a great place to have a jolly good chin wag as they all exchanged theories on the disappearance of Jonathan's Television Friend.

All of them wholeheartedly agreed with Cathy that it was a big mistake to have a Friend installed in the first place since all they ever caused was trouble. Nonetheless, there was unanimous approval from them when Cathy informed everyone that Jonathan had decided not to get another one.

"He had his fingers frost-bitten already," Cathy joked as some of them looked at Jonathan sitting a few seats away chatting to some of the other members of Team Providence.

In the field below, the English side were batting, and the Australians had set a wide field. The bowler ran in and delivered a high-pitched ball which the batsman hit away to the boundary for four runs as the Australian fieldsman sprinted after the ball and reached it just after it bounced into the white picket fence and a ripple of applause followed.

Jonathan looked at the giant video screen to see the action close-up. The camera followed the fieldsman as he picked up a cricket ball by the boundary line and Jonathan's heart suddenly skipped a beat when he spotted Celeste, seated amongst the spectators on the other side of the white picket fence.

Jonathan glanced over to Alexander and realised his son recognised her also, but Sandra and Cathy were chatting away and didn't seem to notice.

Jonathan took out his small but powerful binoculars and quickly searched the crowd around the boundary and soon located Celeste and concluded that she must be in Melbourne at work for the Friend Corporation.

Whatever the case, Jonathan felt a bit uncomfortable seeing her image splashed across the giant video screens in the stadium as Alexander came over and sat next to his father.

"That's the woman from our TV Friend!" Alexander whispered.

"A lot of people look alike you know," Jonathan whispered back.

"But you looked like you recognised her," Alexander said as Jonathan blushed. It was one thing comparing her to the Friend; it was entirely another issue to admit he'd met her in person.

Jonathan shrugged, "It does look like her a bit, I must confess," he said playing away his surprise as the cricket match continued.

The English First Eleven had put together a strong opening partnership in the second innings but a major collapse was due as the Australian captain signalled to the spin bowler to finish off the test match and most of the crowd had arrived in time to witness this display and were waiting in hushed anticipation.

The spin bowler ambled up to the stumps, and his arm circled over as he gave a small wrist twist and released the red cricket ball towards the batsman; a hat-trick, a couple of runouts, out-of-crease stumpings, more ducks and a few spectacular catches all happened in a matter of minutes. It was a dazzling display and the crowd roared in approval.

Jonathan gazed up to the sky at a huge blimp shaped like a blue whale with SAVE ME emblazoned on its side, but his attention was drawn back to the field as there was another loud eruption from the crowd and the final batsman went out for a duck. People stood up and began to leave the stadium.

The umpires took out the stumps and the triumphant Australian team, and the disillusioned batsmen in tears left the field as the cricket pitch suddenly rotated over, replaced by a soft lawn with a white circle in the middle and at either end of the ground, the sight boards disappeared into the ground and four goal posts rose vertically to their full height.

Two Australian Football League teams simultaneously burst through crepe paper banners onto the ground welcomed by a combination of booing and cheering as the 'Geelong Cats' and the 'Brisbane Lions' made their way around the arena in pride to prepare for their game.

"We'd better scram and get on with our training," Sandy announced, clearly confused by what she had witnessed on the field.

"Good luck with your Birdsville competition next week!" Cathy called to her.

Jonathan and Cathy watched the eight flyers of Team Providence spread their wings in formation and, in a great flurry, fly off into the sky as the cricket supporters filed out of the stadium and football supporters entered, most of them watching in admiration.

Jonathan and Cathy decided to take the ferry back to Melbourne from the Volcanic Stadium and stepped onto the glowing red and yellow escalators that descended the mountain onto the marina like flowing lava, the ferry trip being more leisurely.

The sight of the crowds descending the mountain was always breath-taking, and further off in the distance, Jonathan could see Team Providence going through their formation exercises high above Port Phillip Bay.

Once the team succeeded in their next competition the following week, the disappearance of his Friend would be history and not worth remembering, Jonathan thought to himself, but as they boarded the ferry, Cathy turned to Jonathan. "I could have sworn I saw your Friend during the cricket test."

"Oh, yeah?" Jonathan replied trying to be nonchalant, "Did Sandy see her too?"

"She was the one who pointed her out to me on that giant video screen. How did you know her name was Celeste?"

"Huh?" Jonathan asked, as they boarded the ferry and sat down.

"That's what you said. You said 'Celeste' was the name of your Television Friend."

Jonathan doubted that Cathy knew about his trip to the Bungle Bungle Ranges the previous day, but he needed to come up with some type of answer.

"Well, I asked her one day," Jonathan explained belatedly, "And she said her name was Celeste."

"She said her name was Celeste or the woman whose image it is based on is named Celeste?" Cathy delved deeply.

"What difference does it make?" Jonathan snapped as Cathy shifted around uncomfortably in her seat.

"All right," she whispered. "It was silly of me to ask."

Jonathan continued. "Anyway, she was probably someone who just looked like Celeste. The Friend is gone, finished, no more! That's what you wanted. We can forget about it now."

Cathy was quiet as the ferry pulled away from the Volcanic Stadium and headed for the Melbourne docklands and Jonathan wondered if Celeste was still on the island. At any rate, it was probably the last time he would see her, and Cathy was obviously keen to have domestic life return to normal.

Cooking dinner, controlling the temperature of the house, answering the phone and a myriad of other functions were now back in the hands of the family, instead of the Friend. Despite Jonathan's weird reaction to seeing Celeste at the game, Cathy eventually forgot about it, and she was just relieved to see that her family had completely forgotten the Friend after its disappearance.

Chapter 37
The Land of Absurd Weather

It wasn't long before Jonathan was packing suitcases for his upcoming visit to the 'land of absurd weather' where Team Providence would be competing against all the other flyers and, regrettably, the Rainbow Lorikeets.

Jonathan had three large suitcases spread around his bedroom to pack his belongings in a big folded spacious tent, gum boots, raincoat, umbrellas, heavy weather gear, a thick fake fur body-length overcoat, cumbersome oversized woollen gloves, earmuffs, summer T-shirts, bathing trunks, sandals; in fact, everything a person required for climate mayhem.

He planned to spend a few days watching the flying, so he wanted to be certain he was well prepared. On the way to Birdsville, he would also be able to finalise some other business commitments, so he added his briefcase and kissed Cathy goodbye.

Jonathan was soon zooming through the outskirts of Melbourne at high speed for his first destination of Canberra, the capital of Australia. By the time the Extremely Fast Train had reached the mist-covered Mount Kosciuszko, Albert shuffled into the carriage.

"Hullo Jonathan, I've been busy doing more research in the library carriage," he said as he ordered a cup of macchiato from the carriage steward and sat down, "So, in the end, you didn't have a choice about keeping your Friend, it just disappeared?" Albert asked, summing up Jonathan's dilemma.

"That's right. And we're all happy about it. But I would be interested to know what happened to it," he replied.

Albert handed him a stack of papers. "What are these?" Jonathan asked.

"There are more reports on the Friend Corporation, I've found," Albert said. "And they seem to tally up with my own recent frozen experience. I was wrong about your Friend." The train started to slow down as it approached the base of Black Mountain where Parliament was now located, "And I'm rarely wrong, as you know, but… ah, here's my stop now," Albert said as he got up to leave.

"Good luck," Jonathan said patting him on the back. "Send my love to Yvonne."

Albert shuffled off with his briefcase tucked under his arm and after breezing through security he was soon ascending one of the towers stopping near the top where he stepped out of the lift and onto a black mosaic escalator made up of black opal, onyx, tourmaline and pearl, the crystals symbolising a dedication to one's denial of the falseness of the material world, and waiting at the top to greet him was a smiling Yvonne.

"Hullo dear Albert," she said giving him a long embrace, "you don't look at day over 150 years," she joked, "come in and sit down." They walked into a large office with a beautiful mosaic floor of indigenous images and sat down at a coffee table next to a large window overlooking Lake Burley Griffin, Canberra's centrepiece. Her secretary arrived with a tray of apfelsrudel filled with apples, dark raisins breadcrumbs sprinkled with cinnamon and granulated sugar and a pot of tea.

"Ah, my favourite," Albert said as Yvonne poured out two cups of tea.

After a long stint as Lord Mayor of Alice Springs, Yvonne entered federal politics in the seat of Lingiari and after a few years was elected Leader of the Labor Party, won office and became Australia's first indigenous prime minister, and one of the first things she did was to move the Australian Parliament from its location on Capital Hill to the grander and much higher cluster of towers on the top of the 'Black Mountain Nature Reserve', overlooking the city of Canberra, housing Parliament and the Senate in separate towers and another tower that was her residence after turning The Lodge into the Aboriginal Embassy. Yvonne was always grateful to Albert for giving her the formula for political success and was one of her most trusted advisors, and he visited every six months for a few days.

"How are your kids?" Albert enquired.

"Doing well with their grades thanks to your tutoring in mathematics and physics," Yvonne said, "but Hubby has taken them to Alice Springs and will be back tomorrow, so I guess you'll have to comfort me again," she continued as Albert nodded enthusiastically, who had fallen madly in love with her from the moment he first set eyes on her in the *Hall of Mirrors*. Yvonne had a lovely husband, although he could never decide if he was an accountant or a bureaucrat she always joked.

Jonathon, meanwhile, continued his train trip to Capitol Hill, where he would sign a contract to sell the public service, and associated bureaucrats, his 'Wastepaper Baskets', at the prime minister's instigation.

With assistance from Albert, Jonathan had invented and manufactured the wastepaper baskets that only required a small amount of sunlight each day to function, and then overnight, they turned their contents; plastics, paper, leftover sandwiches, metal, in fact, anything at all, into a small pile of high-quality organic garden compost, a dark, crumbly, earthy-smelling material that could be dumped into the garden. Now he was about to close a deal that would supply this large bureaucracy with thousands of them.

The old New Parliament House was now used by a burgeoning public service that crammed thousands of bureaucrats, and workers into the corridors and offices, and that was where Jonathan had a couple of meetings arranged to sign the contracts.

The EFT zoomed under Lake Burley Griffin and then smoothly made its way towards the Capital Hill station that was situated under the huge flagpole. It was covered in assorted satellite dishes, television aerials, and numerous other communications apparatuses and other than the railway line and a few jogging paths, the hill was completely covered in thick native bushland.

The huge entrance of the large front courtyard quickly disappeared as the EFT came to a standstill on the peak of Capital Hill. Jonathan stepped out from his carriage and strolled over to the lift that took him down into the bustling Members Gallery where he was met by some Senior Public Servants and adjourned to their offices for the meetings and to sign the contracts.

The whole place was terribly hot and overcrowded with bureaucrats and the atmosphere was claustrophobic. Jonathan was keen to get the contracts signed, so he could head off to watch the flying, and he didn't have long to wait because the second meeting was cancelled after one of the public servants was found standing in a state of hypnosis next to the *'water cooler'*. It was another one of Asami's popular water installations that had turned a common office water cooler into a water sculpture; a half metre water cube that had no plastic or glass walls, it was just a cube of fresh clear water levitating about a metre above the office floor, self-fulfilling, with no pipes or anything. Workers could simply scoop a cup into it to fill them up. It was so mesmerising that public servants were drawn to it for hours on end, transfixed, even though their works days had been generously reduced to four days a week by the PM.

Within minutes, Jonathan was back on the Capital Hill station platform awaiting the arrival of another Extremely Fast Train to take him onto Sydney, then Queensland. The next EFT pulled up on the summit of Capital Hill and Jonathan stepped on board. He was more than pleased to escape the stifling conditions of the overcrowded old New Parliament House, and his business commitments were now behind him.

After a brief stop in Sydney, the EFT sped silently through the Blue Mountains making its way along the Great Dividing Range towards Queensland.

In Brisbane, Jonathan caught another train that headed inland for the Great Artesian Basin to the Channel Country where the flying championships were taking place. It was a long five-hour journey inland and Jonathan had plenty of time to unwind and enjoy the trip. Most of the other passengers in Jonathan's carriage were also attending the same event so there was a lot of discussion about the forthcoming 'absurd weather conditions' that made the destination famous.

Chapter 38
The Hot Air Balloon

Ten years earlier a second town in Birdsville had been built to create and study meteorological conditions, and adjacent to the Diamantina River, this town had technological facilities installed that meant any weather condition could be created at the push of a button.

The climate installation had been created by Jonathan's old friend Asami, and when they returned to Australia all those years ago, she moved to Japan and became a famous modern artist creating water-related art mixed with advanced meteorology.

In Birdsville, scientists and other specialists could study and experience climate variations at close range. It was also a popular destination for tourists, business conventions and, in this case, sporting carnivals.

There was an atmosphere of excited anticipation as the train pulled into the Birdsville station where snow was falling and the ground was covered in a white sheet, as Jonathan wheeled his three large suitcases along the platform, the snow stopped and the sun came out, the heat melting the snow and turning it into a slushy mess underfoot.

Jonathan hailed a taxi and was soon driving through a small city of tents that accommodated most of the flying teams, spectators, press, and officials. The clear sky was filled with flyers who were not only training but also trying to acclimatise to the variable weather conditions.

Jonathan found his prescribed campsite and was halfway through erecting his spacious tent when there was a loud swishing of wings above him, and he looked up and saw Team Providence circling down to land nearby. Alexander gracefully landed first and folded back his wings as he walked over to Jonathan.

"Hi, Dad, we spotted your tent from miles up there," Alexander said, helping Jonathan pull the tent into position and tightening the guy ropes.

"How's your preparation going?" Jonathan asked as the rest of Team Providence landed and helped around the campsite.

"Just excellent as usual, Jonathan," Sandy replied. "We're in top form and nothing can stop us now."

A dark cloud blocked the sun, and a moment later, lightning illuminated the sky followed by a burst of thunder and a downpour, so Jonathan and the team darted into the quite large tent.

"'The land of absurd weather' is living up to expectations. Any problems with lightning?" Jonathan enquired glancing up at the storm clouds as a flash of lightning cracked the sky in half, followed immediately by more ear-shattering thunder.

"Lightning bolts are always a problem," Alexander laughed, and despite the rain, Team Providence was all very jovial and enjoyed Jonathan's company.

"Where's Cathy?" Sandra asked.

"She's got a lot of work at the moment but will most likely arrive for the finals," Jonathan said, opening a wide umbrella and stepping out into the heavy rain. Small lumps of ice splashed onto the sodden ground, bouncing off the umbrella and making little indentations on the tent's surface.

Alexander looked closely at the hail. "Right-oh, everyone. These are the conditions we want, so let's go," he shouted over the hail.

The team stepped out of the tent and spread their wings. Seconds later they took off and disappeared into the storm clouds high above the tent city.

Jonathan continued arranging his campsite. He folded out the table and chairs inside one section of the tent and started shuffling through one of the large suitcases in search of his swimming trunks and sunglasses. He was quite familiar with the weather patterns, and he knew that soon it would be hot and sunny.

Like clockwork, the rain stopped, and the storm clouds drifted away. The sun came out, melting the hail, and steam wafted off the ground. Jonathan changed into his swimsuit and favourite summer T-shirt with the words 'I'm Between a Rock and a Hard Feather' printed on it and was soon stretched out horizontally in his hammock enjoying the summer conditions.

This was the sort of thing Jonathan really liked, not a problem in the world as he sipped on an ice-cold beer and surveyed the multitude of flyers training overhead. Not far from him was a vacant clearing with several brightly coloured tents, and he wondered what team was camped there.

The tents were poorly erected and covered with laundry, deck chairs were scattered around, and a half-eaten pig wallowed on the spit above the sodden campfire as a stray dog licked the piles of dirty plates in disarray.

A mist slowly drifted through the tents, turning into a heavy fog, which blocked the view of the flyers training above. It was still, warm, and humid, and Jonathan heard the flapping of wings somewhere nearby, and he looked up into the dense fog and wondered which team it would be. He could just see some green wings through the fog and realised it was the Rainbow Lorikeets as the team of eight flyers landed in a scattered formation in the clearing nearby, the reds, yellows, and blues visible on their chests. *The Myopia have arrived*, he thought to himself.

"Come on, clean up this site," one of Lorikeets ordered as the team folded their wings and removed their backpacks, while another Lorikeet member strolled across the clearing, approached Jonathan, and greeted him.

"Are you our next-door neighbour?" he asked with a smile.

Jonathan wasn't as enthusiastic about being so close to the Team Lorikeets' nest. They were known to have attitude problems because they were well down on the pecking order of flying teams, and what's more, it had only been a few weeks since the Lorikeets and Team Rocks had hounded Jonathan and Albert on the observation deck of the Old Sydney Tower.

"Are you going to dazzle us with some new choreography?" Jonathan asked. "Any surprises in store?"

The Lorikeet member walked away, but then he cast a glance over his shoulder and laughed.

The fog began to drift away, and the sky cleared. Jonathan grabbed his binoculars and gazed up into the sky to study the various teams flying around. Directly above were the King Parrots and further over were the successful White-Faced Herons and swooping low over the tent city were the Gang-Gang Cockatoos with their distinctive red curled feathers on their heads.

Higher still, Jonathan could make out the teams of Blue Wrens and Australian Kestrels,

as he continued to gaze at the various teams going through their final preparations before the championships began in earnest, and then panned his binoculars across the tent city and watched five hot air balloons drift up into the sky.

Crammed in the baskets hanging below the balloons were various officials and judges, their job being to watch each of the teams and then give a score to the officials on the ground who logged it into the electronic scoreboard.

A stunning and familiar body on a bicycle peddled up the path and stopped. "Hey, Jonathan, Alexander told me you were here," Asami said with a friendly smile. "Do you want to come up in one of the balloons?" she gestured towards the five balloons drifting over the tent city.

"Certainly do," Jonathan said, springing enthusiastically from his hammock. "The closer the better." They had a long sympathetic and sad embrace, and then he grabbed his coat and followed Asami down the path, "This huge weather installation of yours is still amazing," he said as he admired her beautiful figure, barely changed in twenty years.

A second group of hot air balloons was about to take off, these baskets contained mainly VIPs and press, and Jonathan and Asami clambered in as the blasts of burning gas filled the balloon and the gondola lifted off the ground and from this aerial vantage point, they got a wonderful bird's eye view of the tent city.

"We hardly ever see you since you settled in Tokyo, and travelling around the world," Jonathan said and then continued sympathetically, "We were so saddened by the passing of your husband last year." Asami had married a famous Japanese sumo wrestler and had three lovely children.

"Heartbreaking, and Abi died of obesity and although the pallbearers struggled to carry the coffin, he was cremated in his *mawashi*, his favourite wrestling loincloth."

"And your kids, Amaya, Kishi and Chiasa?" Jonathan inquired.

"Great, all a bit podgy, but they're somewhere around here with friends, and hope to see you all."

Jonathan looked down at the colourful Rainbow Lorikeets tent and then near the centre of the city, he could see the pristine tents that accommodated Team Providence, since they had an excellent position on the banks of the Diamantina River because they were on top of the pecking order.

The crack New South Wales flappers, Team Rocks, had their Opera House-shaped tents nearby and were the talking point of the tent city, not least because they held down the second position and were always a threat to Team Providence.

The hot air balloon continued to rise into the atmosphere. The press photographer standing next to Jonathan fixed his telephoto lens on the main building that housed all the meteorological equipment that controlled the ever-changing weather in the area.

"It's my bet we'll get heavy fog again," the photographer said.

Just then, a dense cloud of fog poured out of the pipes around the tent city. There was no set pattern to the weather that was served up by the meteorological scientists, in fact, they went out of their way to give as much variety as possible.

Soon the entire tent city was enveloped in a dense fog and nothing on the ground could be seen. "Wow, that fog effect looks great from this balloon, Asami," Jonathan said putting his arm around her.

"Well, I love these balloon rides," she replied proudly, "growing up in the centre of the earth, and now having this freedom is wonderful."

From above the fog, Jonathan watched various teams flying around, and he could see the dry uninhabited plains of the Channel Country, an area unaffected by the weather variations taking place below him.

The hot air balloon drifted along, blue sky and sunshine overhead, the blanket of fog below. From out of the dense fog, three teams of flyers winged their way up and Jonathan recognised Team Providence preparing to perform a flying formation of their own choice, and they had nominated the very difficult 'spiral formation'. It looked quite easy in many ways, but the flyers always found it tricky because if any of the flyers got out of formation, they found it hard to get back in.

Nevertheless, they had achieved perfection in this event many times, and it was the main reason they sat on top. Everyone thought the current event would be held above the dense fog, but the meteorological scientists had more ambitious plans, and they were concocting a pretty decent thunderstorm, and Jonathan marvelled as the fog made way for dark threatening storm clouds.

"This will test their metal," the photographer said, with an edge of apprehension.

It was all very jolly sailing along in a hot air balloon above fine mist and dense fog but having a thunderstorm rage around them made the gondola sway and vibrate and dimmed their observation.

Team Rocks, with their emerald-coloured wings, had the honour of performing first in the flying formation. They had chosen the 'V' Formation, which was like the usual flight of real birds. They swung into their flight pattern, and although the rain pelted down and the wind buffeted their luminous wings, they swooped past the hot air balloon and were rewarded high marks by the judges.

Further afield, Team Providence dived upwards out of the thick dark clouds and began their difficult formation. Alexander flew in fourth position just ahead of Sandy as the thunder grumbled through the storm clouds and Team Providence spiralled along confidently, although Alexander noticed from his peripheral vision a solo flyer winging its way towards them.

Alexander lost sight of it as he flew upside down at the bottom of the spiral before arching over, but he then noticed the solo flyer coming closer and closer to them as they surged forward in a concentrated spiral formation.

Jonathan had his binoculars fixed on the team, and he didn't like the claps of thunder resounding around the gondola swaying it more actively than before, nor did he like the sight of the solo flyer who he recognised as a Rainbow Lorikeet.

Jonathan identified something else that sent a cold shiver down his spine.

Alexander, meanwhile, tried to watch both his team and the aerial predator and further ahead. He spotted some lightning bolts jumping from the dark storm clouds; nonetheless, the formation continued with perfect timing and masterful precision.

Suddenly, the solo flyer loomed up only metres from Team Providence and was so close that Alexander had to take his eyes off his team and look squarely at this dangerous distraction.

It was a Rainbow Lorikeet team member treading air right in front of them and clutching the Television Friend.

Alexander was shocked to see it was Jonathan's Friend, the beautiful woman on the screen, and she looked horrified and screamed out to Team Providence.

"Help…! Help me!" she cried out in fear and panic. "I might be dropped!"

"Is this what your dad is looking for?" yelled the Lorikeet member to Alexander.

He suddenly nose-dived with the Friend screaming hysterically, and swooped down under Team Providence, disappearing through a dark storm cloud. Only his laughter lingered.

Another clap of thunder resounded from the terrible weather. The scare took seconds to unfold but was enough for Alexander to lose his formation, and he swung out too wide as Team Providence spiralled along. He managed to regain his position, but the damage was done. The judges had noticed, and the team would lose valuable points, maybe even enough to knock them from the top of the pecking order.

Jonathan stood silently in the basket of the hot air balloon, he had focused his binoculars on the Lorikeet and had clearly sighted the image of Celeste on the screen of the Television Friend. He knew exactly what was going on, and he was far from impressed. Asami put her hand around Jonathan's shoulder, "Is that your Friend I heard about on the grapevine?" she asked.

Team Providence completed their flight and glided down through the dark clouds towards their tents, and slightly dishevelled, they landed, moped around for a moment and then folded in their wings and took off their backpacks in disgust.

Alexander was lost for words. He averted his gaze from the rest of the team and stared at the wet ground, while Sandy suggested they do some relaxation exercises and then sit down and have a team chat. It was important to clarify their thoughts and plan a strategy for winning, and there was the minor problem of the actual Television Friend.

"Alexander, this could go on forever," Sandy whispered. "Until this TV Friend is dismantled, it could keep springing up in front of us for God knows how long. I just don't know what got into your dad's head," she said, brushing back her beautiful dreadlocks, "We told him at the beginning, that these Friends are lethal."

Alexander glanced up at Jonathan in the hot air balloon and shook his head. Jonathan was feeling just awful as the storm was raging around his balloon and the basket was swaying back and forth violently with thunderclaps cracking around them high above the tent city.

"You know something?" the photographer said to Jonathan. "I was looking at all that action, and I could swear I saw actual bolts of lightning coming out of that television the Lorikeet was holding."

Jonathan caressed his forehead since he had noticed the same thing. He also wondered how Alexander and Team Providence were feeling as pangs of guilt encompassed him realising he had caused the crisis.

Heavy rain was still falling, and water was streaming down the side of the hot air balloon and splashing on his head, adding to his misery.

Way down in the Team Providence tent, the flyers sat in a huddle and discussed the awkward situation they found themselves in. They decided it was no good protesting against the Lorikeets because that would just make them the centre of attention, and everyone would be impressed by the audacity of their stunt. Furthermore, flyers were always confronted by endless diversions in the air, and it was all part of the 'art of flight'.

There's nothing here in the rule book that says you can't flap around with a television," Sandy sighed, thumbing through the thick manual on the laws of flying.

"The judges will laugh in our face if we protest about this one," Alexander concluded, as he noticed the rain had stopped. They all decided to have lunch and concentrate their efforts on the speed events. The storm clouds drifted away, the sun came out, and once again, steam wafted from the surface of the Birdsville ground as it slowly dried.

Chapter 39
The Tent

Jonathan climbed out of the hot air balloon's basket, farewelled Asami and headed back to his tent with his hands in his pockets, as he shuffled along, dispirited, and wondered how he would retrieve his Television Friend, if ever.

The path took him past many of the team tents, as he avoided glances with the various competitors. The Flying Lizards, from the Northern Territory, went silent as Jonathan walked by. The sun shone down hard on him. The air became even more humid. And he felt like he was stepping on flypaper.

He walked past the Rainbow Lorikeet's colourful tents and could hear muffled giggles and suppressed laughter from within. Jonathan forced himself to continue and wanted to collect his thoughts before he confronted them to demand the return of his TV Friend. Finally, he reached his tent and when he opened the flap, he was surprised to see his Television Friend sitting in the corner.

Jonathan sat down and looked at it, his eyes blinking in slow motion, and his heart began beating slightly faster. "Switch on please, Friend," Jonathan said with a resigned sigh. The television flickered on and Celeste, the beautiful young woman, appeared on the screen.

"Hello, Jonathan! It's good to see you again!" the Friend said happily, showing no signs of the adventure she had been through, her smile was as warm as ever. For Jonathan, it was strange to see her on the screen again after their interaction in real life at the Friend Corporation in Bungle Bungles.

He felt a strong emotional attachment to her because of their rather powerful bond during their experience together and realised he couldn't be angry with her, and he knew that turning her on was an excuse to see Celeste again. The night he'd spent with her was one of his more pleasurable experiences, but he reminded himself that this was not actually her.

"I'm afraid I'm going to take you back to the Friend Corporation and have you dismantled. I'm sorry," Jonathan said, gazing at the television screen.

For a split second, her eyes twinkled, and a sensuous smile flashed across her face. Then it crumbled, and a tear rolled down her cheek as she took a handkerchief from her sleeve and clutched it. "I understand Jonathan. Would you mind if the vice president of the Friend Corporation spoke to you, please?"

Before he could answer, she disappeared from screen and was replaced by the affable Adam.

"Hello, Mr Day, how are you?" Adam said. "It's good to see you are so well. Would you like me to send down one of my assistants to pick up your Television Friend and take it away?" He paused for a moment. "Or would you like to bring it here yourself?" He leaned forward on his desk and smiled pleasantly as if he already knew the answer.

"No, no," Jonathan replied defensively. "I'll bring it up to the corporation personally. I want it dismantled, and I want to see it done myself."

"Right you are," Adam said with a broad smile. "You know what's best. We are only here to serve your best interests." He disappeared from the screen and was replaced by the beautiful young woman, she still appeared to be upset but was trying to put on a brave face.

"I'm looking forward to seeing you again up here Jonathan," The Friend said.

The tent flap suddenly flung open, and Alexander and Sandy strode inside angrily, and the atmosphere became tense as they both stared at the television in the corner of Jonathan's tent. For a moment there was a deafening silence.

The Friend then decided to break the ice. "Hello over there! Alexander and Sandy!" she said nervously, stuffing her handkerchief back into her sleeve. "I'm terribly sorry I distracted you all up there in your formation flying, but I didn't have any choice. I was captive. Your flying is very impressive up close and witnessing your Team Providence go through the formation flying thing stopped me thinking about my vertigo!"

"Cut the drivel," Sandy replied furiously in her Brazilian accent. "We're not about to let a pile of technological junk stop us from winning. Now switch off and shut your face!"

Instantly the screen went blank.

"I'm sorry," Alexander said, turning to Jonathan. "But we've slipped to second place, and we can't afford any more mishaps."

"I understand," Jonathan said. "I know. I'm going to personally take it back to the Friend Corporation and have it dismantled. No more Television Friend. All gone. Finished."

That wasn't enough for Sandy. She was seething with total anger, and her fists were clenched tightly in fury as she blurted out her plan of action.

"We're going to smash it to pieces right here and now and be done with it," Sandy said, fuming away. The confrontation halted when they heard the sound of muffled laughter outside the tent, so Alexander opened the tent flap. Standing outside were three members of the Rainbow Lorikeets and when they spotted Alexander, they buckled over with laughter. One of them lifted a cheap rubber mallet, the kind used for hammering in tent pegs. "Here, you can borrow this," he said in a mock-serious tone.

The group quickly turned and fled back into their tent, where their team erupted in uncontrollable laughter. Alexander looked at their colourful, rainbow-striped tent and made no comment.

Meanwhile, Jonathan was frantically searching through one of his suitcases for the train timetable which he couldn't find. Alexander turned around and looked at the TV, "Switch on, Friend," Alexander ordered, as the TV flickered on and the beautiful woman looked at him attentively.

"Yes, Alexander, what can I do for you?" she asked politely.

"When does the next train leave for the Kimberley?" he demanded.

"A train leaves in thirty-two minutes," she replied.

"Thank you," Alexander said. "Now switch off." The screen went blank again.

Jonathan emptied one of his large suitcases and lifted the Friend into it, he was very apologetic about the whole episode, and he promised he would not let the suitcase containing the Television Friend out of his sight. Alexander and Sandy waved to Jonathan from the snow-covered tent, "I think he's in love with that woman," Alexander said as an aside to Sandy, who looked dismayed. "And her name is Celeste."

Sandy frowned. "The computer woman or the real one?"

"I don't know. Maybe both."

"Do you think he will really allow her to be dismantled completely?" she asked.

"Hmm, good question."

Chapter 40
The Restaurant Carriage

Jonathan sat silently in a nearly empty train carriage, gazing out the window, and in the distance, he could just make out all the activity in the sky where the flying competition was continuing, the various flyers just dots above the horizon, with the hot air balloons drifting around some clouds. He watched with a sense of lonely detachment.

He glanced at his suitcase, relieved that the Friend could not cause any more problems for Team Providence. More than likely, he guessed they would soon regain the top position in the pecking order of the flying teams.

Once out of the Channel Country, the train made its way through Mt Isa, then across the Barkly Tableland to the Kimberley where the Friend Corporation was in the Bungle Bungle Ranges. It was not an extremely fast train, but a restored red rattler from the previous century and the journey would take a good six hours.

Jonathan looked around his virtually empty carriage and was surprised to recognise the elderly couple that had been on his trip to Sydney some weeks before. He recalled how Albert and himself were busily discussing the installation of his Television Friend and the elderly couple had mentioned that in their suburb of Hobart, Tasmania the local council had the TV Friends banned because they caused too much trouble.

Jonathan wondered if they would remember him and whether he should tell them they were right and that he was on his way to have his Friend dismantled. Eventually, he caught their gaze, and they exchanged a friendly wave. Then the elderly couple walked up the aisle and sat on the seats opposite Jonathan.

"This is a coincidence seeing you two again," Jonathan said with a smile.

"Yes, it is," the old man said. "We're on the final stages of our mainland holiday, so we're touring the centre of Australia, and we're so surprised at the amount of vegetation. We thought the centre would be mainly desert like it used to be."

Jonathan smiled. "Well, once we figured out how to turn saltwater into freshwater, there was no holding back, and the prime minister was keen to plant a lot of trees," Jonathan explained as outside, large tracts of dense forest passed by, intersected by numerous irrigation streams.

The old man looked slightly puzzled. "Could you tell me why you've got your big suitcase right next to you and not in the baggage carriage?"

Jonathan wasn't sure if he felt like telling them the real reason, but then he decided it was a long journey to the Kimberley, and since they had exchanged their opinions on Television Friends before, there probably wasn't any harm in continuing the discussion. "Well, as a matter of fact, inside this suitcase is my Television Friend, and I'm returning it to its maker."

The elderly couple looked surprised and even slightly intimidated, and nothing was said for some time. The elderly couple then started arguing quietly amongst themselves. Jonathan wasn't sure what they were arguing about, but he had a fair idea because they kept glancing nervously at the suitcase. Finally, resisting the protests of the husband, the elderly wife spoke up.

"Did you have any problems with it?" she asked.

Jonathan laughed and decided to tell them all the different catastrophes that had befallen him since installing the Friend, including the drama at Birdsville. The elderly couple nodded in interest as Jonathan's tale unfolded. "So there you have it," Jonathan said.

The elderly couple looked a bit embarrassed, as they searched for the right words. There was a moment of thought between the three of them as the couple warily shot glances at the suitcase next to Jonathan. The train started to slow down and came to a standstill at the Mt Isa railway station.

Suddenly, the elderly husband stood up and announced that he and his wife were getting off at this station, and they shuffled down the aisle quickly and out the carriage door without even saying goodbye.

The train moved off again. It was a long and monotonous journey. Jonathan dozed off for a couple of hours. The trip was conducive to sleep, and Jonathan had a dream as the red rattler made its way through the Northern Territory.

He slept through the brief stop at Tennant Creek and continued his dream as the train made its way across the Tanami Desert, rolling through the Walmanpa-Waripiri Aboriginal Land where vegetation was scarce.

Jonathan dreamed about the Friend, the image of Celeste, and Celeste herself. He dreamed he was flying with her, and his dream ended when they embraced in the air. He felt a hand on his shoulder, shaking him awake, and he opened his eyes to see Celeste standing there in front of him.

"Wake up Jonathan, it's me!" she said with a warm smile, he blinked and momentarily couldn't decide if he was still dreaming.

"What are you doing here?" Jonathan asked, slowly regaining his orientation, and realising she was real.

"I was going to ask you the same question," she said.

Jonathan blushed. "Well, to be honest, I'm taking my Television Friend back to the Friend Corporation to have it dismantled… Is that all right?" The last thing he wanted to do was offend her.

"Of course, it is," she said. "Listen, I was just on my way to the restaurant carriage. Do you want to come along for lunch?" She offered him a hand, and Jonathan gratefully took it.

Jonathan was hoping to see Celeste when he arrived at the Bungle Bungles, so to see her before he got there was even better. They soon found themselves comfortably seated at a table in the restaurant carriage of the train as it rumbled across the desert.

Outside, other than a group of kangaroos hopping by, there was virtually nothing as far as the eye could see because some vast areas of Australia had been left completely untouched and were not thickly vegetated like the rest of the country. The restaurant carriage was about half full and a few waiters went about their business, efficiently taking orders in a friendly way.

"This isn't some kind of mediocre buffet car," the waiter said to Jonathan proudly. "This is quality ala carte cuisine, the best food you'll get in this area." He happily handed them both a menu, and they gave their orders and chose a fine Northern Territory red wine as the waiter lit the candle on their table while the flautist and violinist moved around playing pleasant classical tunes.

"This is just perfect," Jonathan said, holding her hand across the table. "Did you happen to be at the cricket recently at the Volcanic Stadium?"

"Yes!" she said. "It was a great piece of bowling. I had a few days of vacation, so I thought I'd watch some of the demolition at the test. I had front-row seats!" she said with a laugh.

"Well, I saw you there," he said. "Did you know that? But I was on the top level of the stadium, so I couldn't talk to you," Jonathan added, as the waiter uncorked a Katherine Gorge bottle of red wine and poured them each a glass. Another waiter arrived and placed their meals on the table.

Jonathan and Celeste chatted away happily, minutes turning into hours. They realised that they clearly enjoyed each other's company, and although Jonathan was about to have his TV Friend dismantled, he was thankful he had gotten it in the first place because it was through the Friend that he had met Celeste, and although he was married to Cathy, his affair with Celest 'in the flesh' was giving him a new lease of life and a fresh dimension to his middle age.

"Do you think we'll keep seeing each other after I have the Friend dismantled?" Jonathan wondered.

"I hope so," Celeste replied. "I mean it's only my image on the screen of that thing, I'm still me. I can't see anything that should prevent us from meeting discreetly," she whispered.

"Love is a sacred..."

Before he could say that love is a sacred 'thing', a massive jolt hit them, like the train had hit a wall. It was screeching to a halt and everything in the train flew forward. Plates of food, waiters, musicians, and anything else that wasn't tied down were flung forward in a chaotic mess.

The metal wheels of the train screeched into reverse before the train stopped and suddenly reversed, moving in the opposite direction. Passengers and baggage were thrown onto the floor. Celeste's spaghetti Bolognese narrowly missed Jonathan and splattered over the diners at the next table. Ala carte cuisine was airborne along with knives and forks, as cries of shock and horror filled the carriage. Bottles and glasses rolled down the aisle, and the friendly waiter was thrown on his face.

"What the hell has happened?" Jonathan gasped over the groans and shrieks of other passengers, all of them thrown forward like crash test dummies.

"Don't panic!" screamed one of the waiters as he scrambled to his feet and raced towards the front of the train.

Jonathan untangled himself from Celeste and followed the waiter towards the engine room, and by now, the train was slowly gathering speed in the opposite direction while Jonathan stepped over a mess of passengers and food. He managed to clamber through the carriage into the engine room where the driver was in shock and madly pointing at the small monitor next to the control panel.

"IT'S COMING THIS WAY!!" he screamed at Jonathan and the waiter.

"What is?" Jonathan yelled back in the pandemonium.

"For God's sake, **'look'!**" The train driver, sounding hysterical, pointed at the monitor.

Although the track in front of them was clear, the small television monitor showed a huge crocodile pounding its way along the train track, tearing apart everything in its path. Jonathan went cold with fear.

"I've never seen such a large one before, it's giant," the driver sobbed and shook, in fear, "It must be eight metres wide and a hundred metres long, teeth like the tips of the Opera House, it's my Titanic moment!" he trembled.

Jonathan stuck his head out of the side window and with the driver's binoculars, he searched the railway track. It was still completely clear, and there was nothing but parallel metal tracks stretching as far as the eye could see. Yet, on the small monitor, a giant croc was pounding menacingly towards them.

Jonathan had a fair idea of what was happening, and he tried to calm the driver and waiter who were both quivering and ashen-faced in fear.

"There's nothing out there! It's an illusion, a mirage created on your monitor. Do you understand?"

Jonathan made his way out of the engine room and back into the restaurant carriage.

Diners and waiters were still picking themselves off the floor. He grabbed Celeste by the hand and kept scrambling along the aisle and into the next carriage. Finally, they arrived back at the carriage where Jonathan had originally been seated.

This carriage was also in mayhem. In the sudden reversal of the direction of the train, Jonathan's suitcase had been catapulted from its seat and broken open leaving the Television Friend lying on the floor.

"Be calm everyone!" Jonathan assured the shaken passengers, as he lifted the TV Friend onto the seat and sat down opposite it with Celeste.

"Would you be good enough to turn on please Friend?"

The screen flickered on and finally revealed the beautiful young woman, identical to Celeste as the other shaken passengers watched in momentary silence.

"Hello there, Jonathan," the Friend said in a jolly voice. "How are you today?"

"Have you met Celeste?" Jonathan enquired.

"No… I haven't," the Friend replied politely. Hello, Celeste, how are you?"

"Hello me," Celeste said with a small laugh.

The other passengers in the carriage looked at each other as they were not sure what was going on. All they knew was that the train had suddenly screeched to a dramatic halt and was reversing along the railway track. Jonathan's eyebrows furrowed.

"You didn't use your influence to win friends and influence the engine room, did you?" Jonathan asked the television.

The beautiful woman on the screen looked concerned and determined. "Well, Jonathan," she said. "I'm not that pleased about our journey to the Kimberley. I don't really want to be dismantled at the Friend Corporation." The other passengers looked confused.

"Now listen here, Friend. I want you to make that giant crocodile monster disappear from the train driver's monitor immediately," Jonathan demanded angrily.

"Oh, all right," the Friend said, pursing her lips patiently, and crossing her arms.

In the engine room, the driver was still panic-stricken. As he watched the monitor, the giant crocodile was gaining on the train as it raced along in reverse, then it vanished from the screen and the driver looked both surprised and relieved. He put the brakes on again and after the train stopped, he placed it in forward and the train headed off in its original direction.

The curious passengers stepped a bit closer to the Television Friend, while Celeste noticed the attention and felt a bit embarrassed about seeing her image on the screen.

"There's no way we can actually switch you off completely unless we have you taken to pieces is there Friend?" Jonathan asked.

"No, there's not, Jonathan. I'm sorry," replied the Friend politely.

"I see," Jonathan said. "Would you mind switching off in the meantime?"

The woman disappeared from the screen and Jonathan lifted it back into his large suitcase and closed the lid. The other passengers returned to their seats, and the train journey continued towards the Kimberley.

Jonathan and Celeste sat down together and gazed out the window as they surveyed the passing scenery, relieved that everything was okay, and Jonathan grasped her hand and smiled.

Chapter 41
The Minister for Serious Problems

Cathy and her daughter Stacy sat at the kitchen table staring glumly into their respective cups of coffee. Stacy had returned home triumphantly from her drama season in the Antarctic only to be confronted with the news of how Jonathan's TV Friend had become embroiled in a Rainbow Lorikeets stunt that had knocked Team Providence from the top of the pecking order in Birdsville.

Sandy had telephoned Cathy and informed her of every agonising detail of the event and how Jonathan had subsequently decided to personally courier it to the Friend Corporation to have it dismantled.

"If only life were simpler," Stacy said, accidentally dropping her biscuit into her coffee. The only shining light in the current shadow of dark news came from Cathy's twelve-year-old youngest son Chips. Some of his classmates, and he had won a free excursion to the Australian base on the moon for producing the best papier mâché solar system in the inter-school astronomy class contest.

They had all, at one time or another, made the journey to the *Mare Humorum* area of the moon, where the Australian base was located inside the *Doppel Mayer crater* and originally established for research purposes, it had soon been taken over by holiday developers and was a popular destination for would-be space adventurers who yearned for a feeling of weightlessness.

Chips and a dozen of his classmates had blasted off into outer space and were having a great time being astronauts aboard the Australian space shuttle, *Endeavour*, as it headed for the moon.

Certain pets were allowed to go on the shuttle, and this time Chips took their ageing dingo, Zara, who was very experienced with space travel and brought back both happy and scary memories for her as she floated around merrily on the four-day round trip. They spent most of their time playing weightless volleyball, the most favoured way for filling in time, and when other passengers wanted to use the volleyball area on the shuttle, Chips made use of the various facilities for viewing Earth and phoning home.

So as Cathy and Stacy were chatting away around the kitchen table, they weren't surprised when the phone rang, and it was Chips on the line again. "Come in, Day headquarters, do you read me?"

"Yes, hello dear," Cathy said. "Are you enjoying yourself?"

She put the phone on speaker so Stacy could listen in. "Green light," Chips said. "Everything is fine, blue Earth is looking good from here," he reported.

"What have you been doing up there?" Cathy asked. "More volleyball?"

"Not at the moment," Chips replied. "We've already had over thirty games. I've been using the telescope."

The space shuttle's telescope allowed space travellers to see intricate details on the surface of Earth. "Seen anything this time?" Stacy asked.

"Well, as a matter of fact, I have seen something," Chips said. "I've been watching some of the flying at Birdsville when the weather is clear, and I noticed something."

"What's that?" Cathay asked, detecting a serious tone in his voice.

"Well, you know how you told me that Dad had taken the train north to have his Friend dismantled?" Chips continued.

"Yeah, what about it?" Cathy asked looking at each Stacy.

"Well, I searched the railway's timetable and managed to locate it through this telescope."

"And?" Cathy and Stacy said together.

"Well, I was watching the train as it made its way through the Northern Territory and suddenly it stopped and went into reverse for a while and then stopped again and went forward. It struck me as a bit odd. It seemed to stop so suddenly," Chips explained.

"Okay then, dear. Thanks for that," Cathy said. "You behave yourself up there and don't forget to feed the Zara, bye-bye now."

It wasn't lost on Cathy that Chips' observation about Jonathan's train journey was a bit strange, after all, trains didn't normally change direction without a reason and Cathy was aware of the baggage Jonathan was carrying. "I'm going to call Jonathan and see what's going on."

"It's probably nothing, Mom."

"I'm going to call anyhow."

She tapped his number but was informed that the phone she was calling was turned off. "Now what?"

"Why don't you try calling, Albert?" Stacy brainstormed.

"Of course!" Cathy said. "Marvellous idea. He's been visiting Yvonne and is sure to know what to do." She tapped out Albert's number on her mobile.

Coincidentally, Albert was attending a meeting with the *Minister for Serious Problems* in the New Parliament House Towers atop Black Mountain, overlooking the city of Canberra.

He answered his phone on the second ring. "Yes?"

"Hello, dear Albert, It's Cathy here."

"Hullo Cathy, what can I do for you?" Albert asked in his usual friendly manner.

"You know how Jonathan went to Birdsville to watch the flying? Well, you'll never guess what happened, but his missing TV Friend turned up in rather unfortunate circumstances," she said and explained what happened. "Anyway, he decided to personally take it back to the Friend Corporation to have it dismantled, and he's presently on the train with it now," Cathy explained.

"That's good. So what's the problem?" Albert asked.

"Well, from some information we have managed to gather, it seems that the Friend is up to its old tricks again, this time playing havoc with the train Jonathon is on."

"I see," Albert replied. "Leave it to me. I was just now discussing the Friend Corporation with our prime minister, more bureaucratic bungles it appears."

"Oh, how is Yvonne?" Cathy asked. "Please tell her I said hi. It's so great that we have an intelligent guide for our nation."

"I will do so. I'm sure she'll be glad to hear from you," Albert continued, "I know she's glad that you and Jonathan kept your promises and never publicly revealed the full nature of your adventure, or misadventure, at Uluru so many years ago, so I'll get back to you." Albert said as he glanced at the picture on the bookshelf showing prime minister, Yvonne Makepeace, being sworn in.

"Albert, we are still facing more TV Friend problems, and it's very serious and that's why I asked you for a visit."

Albert knew that if the Friend Corporation had come to Yvonne's attention, it meant that the government had decided to deal with the various mounting complaints at the top level, and it didn't get higher than her office in the brand-new Parliament House Tower, on Black Mountain.

Yvonne strummed her fingers on her large desk and looked at Albert, "What do you think we should do?" she asked as Albert gazed out the window surveying Lake Burley Griffin.

He had a few ideas, but he hesitated. In her time in office, Yvonne had faced some serious problems, and he wanted to make sure that he didn't say anything that would make this current situation worse. He watched some people jogging around the lake and from the height of the tower, they looked like ants milling around the National Art Gallery on the banks of Lake Burley Griffin.

The *Minimalist Movement*, which swept the Australian art world just a week ago, had seen curators throw up their arms in despair and ordered all the paintings removed from the walls of the art gallery leaving it completely barren. It was now being used as an indoor jogging track for public servants wearing colourful Ken Done T-shirts.

"These fashions in art only last a short time," Yvonne said looking concerned. "Your thoughts?"

"Maybe you need to assign a member of your staff to work on this issue full-time until it's resolved."

Yvonne beamed. "We think alike, Albert. I want you to be one of the first people to know that I've decided to deal with this issue by creating a new portfolio, *Serious Problems*, and with a new minister, The Wrong Honourable Eric Disaster." Yvonne laughed. "Some bureaucrats probably chose him because of his name. Kidding aside, I would like you to meet him right now."

Albert stood up. "I'm at your service, Prime Minister Makepeace."

"One thing, though," Yvonne cautioned. "We can't offend the Friend Corporation under any circumstances. Last week, we decided to have the TV Friend from my office return," she said pointing to the empty space in the corner.

"Did that go smoothly?" Albert asked.

"Not really. Talk to Eric about it."

The Minister for Serious Problems was a short balding man who stood on his tiptoes to gain a centimetre in height over Albert as he shook his hand. "Nice to meet you, Minister Disaster," Albert said.

"Just call me Eric, and please sit down." He went on to explain how the TV Friend in his office had found out the prime minister's Friend was removed, "Somehow, my Friend interconnected with the extensive closed circuit security monitors throughout this Parliament House Tower. When I arrived for work, the following morning, all the security monitors showed me staggering along the corridors as if I was drunk; I had a party hat on. I was covered in streamers and confetti. I was blowing one of those paper whistles and a lot of the time I skipped and danced."

"What were you celebrating?" Albert asked.

"Well, nothing, that's the whole point," Disaster said, "The TV Friend manipulated my image on the security monitors, and for all intents and purposes, I appeared like some sort of drunken lunatic arriving at work. It was terrible."

Albert looked concerned, "What happened then?"

"Well, when the security guards ran down to help me, they found me normally dressed, quite sober, and arriving for work in my usual manner, and they were astounded. The trouble was that everyone else watching the monitors didn't know the image was fake. I've spent most of this week rejecting invitations for drinks in other offices or explaining why I didn't need recommendations for substance rehabilitation. My reputation has been ruined, and I've only just started this new job," Eric lamented. "Once word spread around the corridors there were suicides, stampedes and utter chaos for hours afterwards, and many fled to New Zealand!"

"I'm sorry to hear that."

Since Disaster was dealing with Friend issues, Albert told him about Jonathan's train journey with his Friend and Disaster frowned. "That doesn't sound good. Let me make some calls and see if I can find out what happened."

Albert sat in Yvonne's office chatting with her, as they were both concerned that Jonathan might be in peril and would never reach his destination. Ten minutes later, Disaster walked into the office. "Albert, I'm sorry to tell you that all communication has been cut off from the train. There's nothing more I can do now, but the situation is being monitored, and I'll keep you both informed."

Chapter 42
Kimberly Central

The red rattler shunted to a standstill at the Kimberley Central station, and the train driver breathed a sigh of relief. It was the worst experience he'd had on a journey across the Northern Territory for as long as he could remember, and he looked on nervously as Jonathan wheeled his large suitcase containing the Television Friend along the platform. The day was hot and sunny, and a dusty wind blew through the station corridors.

Celeste was slightly apprehensive about returning to the Friend Corporation on account of the terrible malfunctions she had personally witnessed, but before long, they were both seated in a long red limousine, weaving their way through the Bungle Bungle Ranges, "When you get through the entrance, turn right and drop us off at the 'dismantling depot'," Celeste instructed the driver and part of the artificial Bungle opened with the Friend Corporation looming up ahead of them.

Having worked there for a few years, she knew the layout of the plant and headquarters very well and had spent at least one year giving guided tours to prospective buyers and tourists in general.

Celeste even knew the best technician to oversee the great dismantling, so Jonathan was feeling relieved that the whole crazy episode was finally reaching a clear ending; he would be rid of his Television Friend and would go out to dinner with Celeste afterwards to celebrate and may even spend the night with her again, he was hoping.

The limousine pulled up inside the dismantling depot and the whole magnitude of the problem became blatantly obvious. Outside the department, there was an enormous pile of TV Friends that stretched the entirety of the building, and the noise coming from the pile was deafening.

"There must be over five thousand Television Friends piled up here, and they're all switched on!" Jonathan shouted to Celeste, as they gazed in disbelief at the mountain of them.

At the other end of the depot, Jonathan could see a conveyor belt channelling the sets to the dismantling area where they were being systematically dissembled. Various technicians in colourful coats with Friend Corporation emblazoned on them went about their business with a serious demeanour, and one chap gave an irritated glance at the pile of televisions and then approached Jonathan and Mavis with a smile.

"Hello, Celeste! How was your short holiday down south?"

"Pardon? I can hardly hear you!" she yelled back cupping her hand over her ear.

"Oh, sorry." The technician turned angrily to the mountain of noisy televisions.

"**Quiet! Shut up!**" he bellowed at the top of his voice. Instantly, the televisions went silent, each TV Friend having a different male or female image on them.

"That's better." The man sighed and glanced down at Jonathan's Friend. "What's this? Do you want to get this set done straight away?"

"Yes, please," Jonathan said, helping him lift his Television Friend onto a trolley.

"That would be very good of you," Celeste replied urgently. "Jonathan here has been having more than enough problems with his Friend and wants to see it dismantled personally."

"Fine by me," the technician said. "That's what we do all day here." Then he paused and looked at Jonathan. "I guess you'll be sorry to see this Friend go?"

Jonathan was a bit startled by the question. He looked down at the Television Friend as it was wheeled along past the enormous wall of other sets who had all begun to murmur quietly amongst themselves.

"Go on, Jonathan," Celeste urged, as they strolled towards the dismantling area. "At least say goodbye."

"Oh, all right then," Jonathan replied as he gazed at the set. "Switch on Friend, so we can say our farewells."

The Television Friend flickered on, and the beautiful young woman appeared on the screen, she wiped a tear from her eye, and her bottom lip began to quiver, and she looked up at Jonathan in self-pity and remorse.

"Hello, Jonathan," she said. "Or should I say farewell? I really did enjoy being in the corner of your living room," she said with a sniffle. "And I'm sorry if I caused you any problems."

Celeste and the technician averted their eyes from the Television Friend and avoided looking at Jonathan as they realised they were becoming mildly upset. It was weird watching her own image cry.

"I'm sorry," Jonathan said, "but I must," clearing a lump gathering in his throat.

"Oh, come on now, Jonathan!" Celeste looked squarely at her image on the screen who had started to cheer up a bit and a slight smirk rippled across her beautiful teary-eyed face. "This is just a piece of technological junk. Its emotional output is purely fabricated. Surely it can't mean that much to you, can it?"

"Jonathan," the Friend said. "Would you mind talking to the vice president of the Friend Corporation for me?" Her eyes blinked innocently.

Suddenly, she disappeared from the screen and was replaced by the very affable Vice President Adam. He had a strangely priggish expression on his face which made Jonathan feel a bit uncomfortable, as the Friend had nearly reached the conveyor belt.

"Hello, Mr Day, I see we've ended up in the dismantling depot. Seems a pity that such a miracle as this model of Television Friend should end up like this. There's no justice in it."

Jonathan raised his eyebrows briefly as he and the technician lifted the set onto the slow-moving conveyor belt as it moved towards the group of dismantlers.

"Well… goodbye," Jonathan said, giving the Friend a final, farewell pat.

Adam still had an odd smirk on his face, and he suddenly clicked his fingers, remembering something of great importance.

"Just one final question, Mr Day," Adam said smugly. "Would you be good enough to talk to this policeman here?" He vanished from the screen and was replaced by a serious-looking policeman.

"This Television Friend was reported stolen, and we need to take it in for questioning," the police officer said. "Please take it off this conveyor belt immediately."

The Friend Corporation technician obeyed instantly and lifted the set back onto the trolley. Jonathan was speechless, and Celeste stared at the ground in silence. A murmur of approval crescendoed from the mountain of Television Friends. They all watched as Jonathan's Friend was wheeled away by the technician and through a nearby door.

Jonathan recognised the police officer as the one that had arrived at his home when he reported the Friend as stolen, and in the space of a few seconds, Jonathan felt the weight of the world's problems on his shoulders again, and as his Friend was wheeled out the door, Jonathan noticed the beautiful young woman reappearing on the screen, laughing, and chatting to the technician pushing her. A feeling of dread weighed Jonathan down.

Celeste looked at Jonathan smiling, "Dinner?" she asked, shrugging her shoulders. There wasn't much else they could do. The Television Friend was now out of Jonathan's hands again. It could be held in storage awaiting questioning for weeks, even months, and then there was computer AI law to think about.

Celeste and Jonathan sat in the restaurant at the pinnacle of the Friend Corporation headquarters inside the artificial Bungle. Outside the window, a flaming red sunset over the picturesque Bungle Bungle Ranges, with their red, yellow, and brown contoured rings, stretching as far as the eye.

As Jonathan dined with Celeste under candlelight, he received a call from Albert. "I'm glad to know that your phone is working again."

"Was there a problem?" Jonathan asked.

"Yes, you were isolated on that train. No one could reach you. Now tell me, did you get the Friend dismantled? Did you see it happen?" Albert enquired.

Jonathan glanced across the table at Celeste. "Actually, no." He told Albert what happened at the warehouse.

"What! You know, Jonathan, once they decide to use AI law to represent your Friend it could become a case of mind-numbing complications. These law computers can ask up to sixty thousand questions a minute. The programs for their cross-examinations are so advanced that they end up finding out the truth," Albert revealed knowingly.

Jonathan didn't really have much to hide, other than his relationship with the real Celeste, he thanked Albert for his advice and turned off his mobile and gazed at her.

Obviously, she didn't have the encyclopaedic knowledge of the computer that worked inside the Television Friend, but she also lacked the peculiar technical malfunctions the set exhibited, the flaws that had placed Jonathan in the position where he found himself. And of course, she was gorgeous, the dinner was perfect, and Celeste invited him to spend the night in her apartment again.

The next morning Jonathan boarded a plane and flew back to Birdsville. On his return to the tent city, he quickly learned that Team Providence had won their speed racing event and were back on top of the pecking order where they usually sat undisturbed.

What was more, as Jonathan stretched out in his comfortable hammock amidst the fog that had just rolled in, he was told that every one of the Rainbow Lorikeets had collided with a hot air balloon, and it had virtually knocked them senseless, damaging their colourful wings.

And so, when he heard frantic flapping and loud squabbling above him somewhere in the dense fog, he concluded that it must be the Lorikeets ariving back from their embarrassing humiliation.

They hovered down in a scattered disoriented fashion, and some hit the ground quite hard. Others bounced off the top of their colourful tents and fell onto the site, a dishevelled mess of confusion and chaos. The fog began to lift as the sun filtered through and the absurd weather conditions of Birdsville exposed the Lorikeets' loss.

Jonathan could clearly overhear some team members yelling at the captain about the unfortunate collision with the hot air balloon. The excuse of dense heavy fog failed to appease the judges and soon enough there was an almighty screaming match taking place in their tent.

Jonathan had little sympathy for the Lorikeets. He listened as they argued, and how their first captain had accidentally flown into the path of an aeroplane and got sucked through the jet engine.

It was little wonder they wallowed at the base of the pecking order; Jonathan mused to himself. Then one of the young female Rainbow Lorikeets burst out of their tent mumbling angrily to herself. She began doing relaxation exercises in the clearing between Jonathan and the Lorikeet's tent. A light mist drifted throughout the area and the bright sunshine gave her wings an extra glow as she inhaled and held her breath for eight seconds before exhaling in a calm way.

Opening her eyes after six of these exercises, she noticed Jonathan lounging curiously in his hammock, and she strolled over to him. "Hello, Jonathan. I was wondering if you'd ever return. Don't worry about their silly stunts." She gestured towards her tent where the Lorikeets were still arguing. "I'm going to fly the coop and join another nest, maybe Team Providence."

"Who are you?" Jonathan enquired admiring her sexual beauty, and platted blonde hair.

"Oh, I'm Barbie, they treat me like a flying doll," she replied with her hands on her hips, "They make me sleep in a cardboard box with a cellophane window, it is so confining, and I dropped Ken because he's impotent. I plan to make a statement at the press conference."

"What actually happened?" Jonathan asked, taking advantage of her surprising confession.

"Well, we were zooming along nicely in the speed racing event in an orderly line behind our captain when suddenly, '*boynng!*' He had disappeared into the heavy fog and slammed into a hot air balloon. And then we all hit it, was like bouncing on a trampoline from a fifty-metre drop! Look at my wings!" The young Lorikeet spread her colourful multi-coloured wings to their full expanse revealing lacerations and holes.

Jonathan surveyed her wings sympathetically, his eyes drawn towards her nipples protruding through her colourful zootie. Some clouds had drifted over, and light rain began to fall, creating a vivid rainbow from the shining sun. Barbie smiled at Jonathan, her wings starting a fast repetitive motion that caused her to levitate momentarily before she flew upwards, following the path of the rainbow arcing into the sky. Then the very aesthetic young Lorikeet veered away from the multi-coloured rainbow and flew off in another direction, maybe in search of the new nest.

Chapter 43
Whatever Happened Between the Free and the Obediently Confined?

Birdsville cleared to a bright sunny spell as Jonathan dozed in his hammock, and over the sound of real-life birds singing and chirping in the trees, he could also catch the muffled squabbling of the Lorikeets in their tents nearby.

All the serious competitive flying had been completed. The last couple of days were given over to exhibition flying and comprehensive discussions on all the events that had taken place. And no doubt the Rainbow Lorikeets would be up in front of the *Tribunal for Incompetent Behaviour* for their actions with the Friend and colliding with a hot air balloon, containing the judges.

These tribunals were held in the open air and usually deteriorated into derisory slanging matches but were necessary to maintain a high standard of flying safety, and they disrupted the endless barbecues, although the meteorologists controlling the weather conditions had promised to finish the carnival with warm balmy weather.

Jonathan was also pleased to see Cathy, Stacy, and a few of her girlfriends from the drama department, and it wasn't long before more tents went up around Jonathan's one.

The next couple of days passed in a relaxed holiday fashion, everyone swimming in the Diamantina River, many naked, and sunbathing on its banks, and there was the barbecue breakfast, barbecue morning tea, barbecue lunch, barbecue afternoon tea, as well as dinner and supper barbecues to finish the day, all in and around the tent city.

It was unanimously agreed that Birdville was perfect for barbecues. If an accidental fire ever happened, the meteorologists could bring on the rain at a press of a button. Stacy and her girlfriends had started chatting up some of the Rainbow Lorikeets, as the team had spent a lot of time licking their wounds and mending their wings and damaged pride. Any form of sympathy was welcome, so when the girls lamented the unforgiving nature of competition flying, the hapless team lapped it up.

The Lorikeets lolled around in their deckchairs as Stacy casually asked about their possession of Jonathan's Television Friend. The captain of the Lorikeets carefully glued some more feathers in place on his colourful wings and gave Stacy an irritated look. "Are you implying that we stole it from the corner of your living room?"

The other team members glanced at Stacy and their captain as she shuffled her feet uncomfortably. "Oh, no, no, no, goodness no. So? Well? What happened then? Did some pelican fly over and deliver it to you wrapped in bundling?"

"Oh, all right then," the captain sighed. "It arrived here in the mail without the sender's address or even a name. And, when we opened it, we discovered it was one of those Television Friends. There was a note attached asking us to give it to Team Providence. That's all, nothing else."

"Hmm," Stacy muttered. Having got the information they were after, Stacy and her girlfriends quickly lost interest in the conversation with the Lorikeets and wandered off chatting to themselves.

The sun was starting to set, and a luminous red glow hovered above the horizon. It was the final night of the flying fiesta, and around the Team Providence tents, flaming torches and barbecues flared as the orchestrated pop band of harpsichord, harp, flute, oboe, nightingale quartet and solo cuckoo played, giving a festive atmosphere to the campground. Further over, Team Rock's imposing Opera House-shaped tent was crowded with flyers landing and leaving as the party rolled into the night.

Prior to the press conference, various flyers carrying torches soared high above the celebrations and a couple of hundred metres up Sandy and Alexander hovered in the night sky and looked down on the spectacle below.

"I'm still not altogether satisfied about Jonathan's Television Friend," Sandy said. "It hasn't been dismantled yet, has it?"

"I don't know," Alexander said. "It's in the hands of the police, what else can we do?"

"If only Jonathan had made his wastepaper baskets larger, he could have put the TV Friend in it, and it would be quality compost now," Sandy said as a throwaway line.

They both started to spiral downwards towards the huge marquee as the press conference commenced. Two members from each of the top teams were required to present themselves to the assembled media at the conclusion of each flying carnival.

Sandy and Alexander pinpointed the entrance of the marquee and glided in over the large press contingent and supporters, landing gracefully behind a long table covered in clusters of microphones and tape recorders. They folded in their wings and sat down next to the representatives from Team Rocks, Laughing Kookaburras, and the Rufous Whistlers. Everyone became silent as the press conference began.

A man stood up from the seated media, "*The Ornithologist Review* here," he said politely, awaiting his live cross to the World Friends TV sports network, he was given the go-ahead and proceeded with his question, "Congratulations Team Providence on your victory here at Birdsville, you've maintained your position on top of the pecking order of competition flying, but did you find your Friends a distraction?"

Alexander leaned forward into the cluster of microphones to answer, "Not at all," he said laughing, "We enjoy their company."

At the back of the large marquee, behind the supporters, crowd and media, Jonathan and Cathy watched with Stacy, and her girlfriends all pleased about Team Providence winning and Alexander's diplomatic responses.

Near the front of the press conference, a lady in a leopard-skinned three-piece suit with a blood-red tie stood up and everyone instantly recognised her as the most ruthless predator in the media pack and her mere propinquity meant serious trouble for her prey, as a hush settled throughout the crowded marquee.

The various flyers glanced at each other uneasily, but with interest, and then looked at the two Laughing Kookaburras, their wings were a combination of dark brown on the bottom, lighter brown on the top with pale blue feathers on the shoulders with a white patch at the base of their quills, sat there unamused.

The members of the press shifted uncomfortably in their seats, behind them, the crowd of onlookers murmured as Jonathan leaned over and whispered into Cathy's ear, "I've got a strange feeling that the flyers are becoming territorial."

"I know," Cathy whispered back uneasily.

The woman in the leopard suit stood up, "*FRIEND TIMES* daily newspaper here," she said calmly. "I would like to direct my question to Alexander of Team Providence."

Sandy and Alexander crossed their arms and leaned back into their chairs as they warily watched the rapacious interviewer continue, "Is it true that Alexanders mother is Cathy, sitting over there, but his father was King Kurfur, the Egyptian Pharoah, from 2500 BC?" she demanded angrily.

There was a loud gasp from the assembled crowd and media. Cathy shuffled around uncomfortably as the cameras turned on her.

Stacy turned to her mother in shock, "Did you fuck a Pharoah, Mummy?" she whispered wide-eyed, as Cathy fumbled around her crocodile handbag for her sunglasses and silk scarf.

The reporter continued, "And what's more, Alexander's father has been trying to get rid of his TV Friend because the *FRIEND TIMES* obtained his birth certificate showing Cathy is the mother and King Kurfur is the 'father'!"

The atmosphere in the press conference became charged. Everyone could sense she was preparing to pounce and maul them with her line of attack, "And now I present the latest edition of the FRIENDS TIMES!" she announced as the Rainbow Lorikeets flew inside the tent throwing down copies of the latest edition as the newspapers that fluttered over the media contingent like confetti.

"So sorry," Alexander said quickly standing up with Sandy, "But we must fly. Bye for now."

The two flyers soared out of the large marquee and up into the evening sky leaving only the echo of their wings while Stacy and her girlfriends looked dumbfounded as the flurry of flyers passed overhead. Cathy put her sunglasses on as she stood up, *"Vulture!"* she whispered to Jonathan as his expression switched to mild puzzlement, and clutching his hand firmly, they left with spectators and press breaking out into applause.

In the commotion, Barbie, the girl who had spoken to Jonathan earlier and had left the Lorikeets stood up, "Well, this does eclipse my question, *'Whatever happened between the free and the obediently confined?'* Drat," she concluded, sitting down.

Stacy and her girlfriends watched on anxiously but managed to snatch one of the descending newspapers fluttering about them all and sat down and read the front-page article.

Yvonne and Albert witnessed the whole thing on TV, "Now the cat is out of the bag," Albert said to Yvonne.

High up in the Birdsville night sky, Team Providence joined Sandy and Alexander with copies they had grabbed, and the flyers glided around reading the news and discussing it.

Looking down on the media tent some two hundred metres below, everything was happening at once. The press release had gone global, and the instantaneous feedback from living rooms everywhere was a crashing wave of surprise. They also got a perfect birds-eye view of bright camera spotlights and flashing bulbs, drones with cameras and spotlights surrounding Jonathan and Cathy like a luminous birdcage as they made their way to their tent.

"So your Friend obtained all my photographs from our adventure twenty years ago you clumsy galoot," Cathy whispered angrily under her breath in the media scrum. Finally, they reached their tent and swept aside some media like moths, and opening the cage door, they barged into their tent slamming shut the soundproof tent flap and went to bed peacefully, made love, and then slept.

Chapter 44
The Mirror Reflection

The next day, there was a mass exodus of teams and spectators as they returned home around Australia, as trains, planes, and buses were overloaded with people leaving in all directions.

A lot of the flying teams decided to take the slower red rattler train, allowing team members to take the opportunity to wind down, relax, party, and above all discuss the big news about Alexander, who sipped on his Landscape Dry Martini as the sun set and flocks of emus sprinted alongside the train.

Jonathan and Cathy managed to make it home unnoticed after only half a day of travelling, and watching the flying had been great as usual, but they all suffered from sore necks, and worse, the revelation about who fathered Alexander was a pain in the neck.

Chips had arrived back safely from the Australian base on the moon courtesy of the space shuttle *Endeavour*, and as everyone unpacked their suitcases, putting their tents and camping equipment in the shed, Chips asked about the whereabouts of Jonathan's TV Friend.

He didn't have to wait long for an answer. Shortly after the family had sat down to have a cup of tea, the doorbell rang. Jonathan opened the front door and found a police officer standing there holding the Television Friend.

"I told you we'd return it without any fuss or bother," the officer said proudly, shoving past Jonathan and placing the TV Friend in the corner of the living room.

"But we don't want it!" Jonathan protested. "Don't you understand? We want it dismantled!" Cathy gave the officer a nice cup of tea and a biscuit.

"Well, as you know, this Friend of yours was taken from this living room," the police officer said. "So I need to ask it some questions here at the scene of the crime." He sat down in the comfortable armchair opposite the Friend.

"I see," Jonathan replied, gazing at the blank screen.

"Would you mind switching on please, Friend?" The officer asked.

The set flickered on, and Celeste's familiar, beautiful face filled the screen. She smiled warmly. "Hello, Jonathan! It's good to be back in your living room. And what may I do for you, officer?" She asked giving him a mock salute.

"All right, that'll be enough of that," the officer said seriously. "Now I've got a question to ask you."

"Who... me?" the Friend asked, looking innocently surprised.

"Pieces of modern technology like you have incredibly advanced memory banks," the officer said, sipping on his cup of tea.

"Oh, don't..." she replied, blushing ever so slightly.

"Now would you please tell me who removed you from this room?" the officer asked.

"Um... let's see," the Friend mumbled, scratching her head in thought.

"Come on! Sift through your memory bank," the officer demanded impatiently, "I don't have all day."

Everyone in the room leaned forward in anticipation of the answer. The Friend's eyes looked distant as she attempted to recall the events, she had seen in the living room. The tiny cameras inserted all around the set could see everything. Suddenly, she clicked her fingers.

"Yes! That's right. I remember now!" the Friend said enthusiastically. Then, she frowned. "I don't know. I couldn't see because someone placed a tablecloth over me... **again!**" the Friend said disparagingly. She shot Cathy an angry glance.

Standing in the doorway, Cathy winced momentarily at the sudden attention being directed her way.

"Did you do that?" the police officer asked, scowling at Cathy.

"Well... yes, I suppose I did," Cathy replied, lowering her head in shame. "I'm sorry."

"Right then," the officer said, as he abruptly stood up and brushed the biscuit crumbs off his trousers. "Identification of the person or persons who took the TV Friend is impossible to ascertain because a tablecloth was placed over the set and blocked its vision. Case closed. Have a lovely day."

He brushed past Jonathan and headed towards the front door.

"Is that all? I could have told you about the tablecloth!" Jonathan protested as the officer walked out the door whistling. "What about having it dismantled?" Jonathan yelled out after him.

"That's not our business. Try the Friend Corporation again," the police officer responded as he disappeared into his patrol car and drove off.

Jonathan stood in the doorway, flabbergasted.

Stacy appeared next to him. "We may never know who took your Friend and sent it to the Rainbow Lorikeets."

They retreated inside and found Cathy pouring herself another cup of tea.

"Hmm… I never realised that covering a TV set with a tablecloth could be such a serious offence," Cathy pondered aloud. "I understand people don't like being treated like a piece of furniture, but this is just plain silly nonsense."

"Next time you'll know to just put a vase of pretty flowers on the set, won't you!" Chips scolded, waggling his finger at his mother.

"Oh, don't go on," Jonathan complained, sitting down in the armchair opposite the Friend as it merrily screened colourful images of a variety of Australian native flowers amid the sound of bush life ambience.

"I want to talk to you Friend," Jonathan said.

The flowers vanished and the beautiful young woman appeared on the screen smiling.

Jonathan thought about Celeste and smiled at seeing her image, yet at the same time he realised this wasn't her, he knew he needed to get rid of the Friend.

"Yes, Jonathan, I'm sorry you're going to dissemble me. Won't you miss Celeste, you know, you two were quite the topic of conversation at the Friend Corporation. 'Hot stuff', they all said as they reviewed the videos."

"What!" Jonathan choked.

"What's she talking about, Jonathan? Tell me?" Cathy asked, "What were you doing at the Friend Corporation? What videos?"

"Oh, the video!" the Friend said.

"Stop it. I want to speak to the vice president again. Right now," Jonathan, then turned to Cathy. "Don't believe a word of it. She's trying to stall us from destroying her."

The screen went blank and a moment later, the ever-affable Adam appeared.

"Hello there, Mr Day. Would you like to have the Friend Corporation drop by, pick up your set, and have it dismantled?"

"That would be very thoughtful of you," Jonathan replied.

"Well, I'd say *join the queue,* but you've already tried that!" Adam laughed. "No, don't worry, Mr Day, that will be fine. Umm… let's see." He glanced down at his desk and consulted a timetable. "As you know, there's a big demand to have these Friends picked up and taken away so the soonest I can help is tomorrow. That's the best we can do. Sorry."

"Why not immediately?" Jonathan protested.

"Because we're **busy!**" Adam snapped as his friendly demeanour disappeared. "Haven't you ever heard that word?"

"Okay, all right, that's good. Thank you very much," Jonathan replied nervously. The last thing he wanted to do was offend the TV Friend and cause it to play the videos of him and Celeste frolicking about her apartment.

Adam regained his composure and brushed his hands together. "This Friend of yours will be picked up tomorrow at noon. Goodbye, Mr Day… and thanks for all the entertainment and colossal gossip."

His image disappeared and was replaced by the beautiful young woman who smiled sympathetically at Jonathan.

"What did that mean?" Cathy asked, scowling at Jonathan. "Oh, forget it. I don't want to know." She stormed out of the room.

"There you have it," the Friend said. "All fixed. Noon tomorrow, and I'll be gone," she said regretfully. "I hope you and Cathy have a nice evening."

Chapter 45
The Creation of the Universe

Jonathan stood up and started pacing up and down the room. His main concern was getting through the next twenty-four hours without disturbing the Friend. It didn't really matter if it was turned on or off, since he knew it could still operate the household.

Jonathan stopped pacing around and looked up to realise he and the Friend were alone. He wondered what had happened to the others.

Chips had been sitting in the backyard outside Albert's Granny flat and saw him thinking.

"Hello, Albert. What are you doing?" Chips enquired quizzically.

"Quiet! Just listen to me," Albert whispered urgently. "I see the Friend is back in your living room and there could be more trouble in store. Go and get Stacy and Cathy and bring them here. Don't tell the Friend."

Chips went back inside and brought his mom and sister outside to where Albert was sitting with a suitcase. They were both a bit mystified while Jonathan remained inside engaged in small talk with the Friend, and careful not to say anything offensive.

Albert ushered them into his studio, and he unrolled designs, showed them time charts, and opened the suitcase full of various items, urgently whispering instructions. "Under no circumstances are you to let the Friend know what you are doing," Albert advised them.

"What about Jonathan?" Cathy asked nervously.

"Don't tell him either," Albert said. "He's already been seriously compromised by his Friend."

"I think you're right about that," Cathy murmured.

"And Alexander?" Chips wondered.

"I'm going to the Team Providence headquarters now to brief Alexander and Sandy," Albert explained. "They're obviously integral to this plan of action," as Albert handed Chips the suitcase. Albert's studio was adjacent to his Granny flat, it had a workbench, papers scattered everywhere, and a black board with lots of formulas scribbled all over it. It also featured a TO-DO list with memory tips, including one that read: 'Brush my hair'.

Stacy clearly relished her part in the plan and moved about the kitchen with theatrical flair before waltzing into the living room where she sat down on the couch.

"You know what I'd like to see again?" Stacy asked.

"What's that?" the Friend and Jonathan replied in unison.

"That subterranean delight of yours. The aquarium scene!" Stacy said with optimism.

"Is that all right, Jonathan?" the Friend asked him.

"Sure… why not?" Jonathan answered.

The beautiful woman disappeared from the screen and was replaced by a tranquil aquarium as small colourful tropical fish darted around the colourful coral, strands of seaweed, and a rising line of small bubbles rising to the surface. Jonathan and Stacy gazed at the aquarium scene for a while.

Stacy seemed to be enjoying it a lot. "Wow! Would you look at that little striped one there," she exclaimed enthusiastically. "Just fantastic really."

Jonathan wasn't that impressed with the aquarium, but he wasn't about to offend the Friend or Stacy because he didn't want to provoke any new malfunction.

"Where's Chips?" Jonathan asked.

"Who?" Stacy asked with a bewildered expression.

"Chips! Chips!" Jonathan said impatiently.

"Oh! Chips," Stacy said. "He's just working on his latest school project, that's all."

"Not another papier mâché planet Mars again?" Jonathan laughed.

"No, no. It's a box of reflections or something. Nothing important," Stacy said, trying to downplay the issue. "Wow! That coral looks great!"

Dinner time arrived and so did Albert. Jonathan was always pleased to see his friend, and it gave him a chance to lament the problems of his TV Friend and seek reassurances over his decision to have it taken away the following day.

Jonathan was surprised to see how interested Albert was in the project Chips was busily working on in the studio, and Albert disappeared into his studio after dinner to help him.

Cathy and Stacy sat in the living room watching the aquarium on the TV screen. They sat there calmly without saying anything, just watching the aquarium as if it was the most amazing thing. "Hmm… this underwater stuff is my cup of tea," Stacy finally said.

The drama was all too scant and by eleven that evening Jonathan looked at his watch and decided it was time for bed. Chips had apparently finished his project and had already gone to bed. Stacy found it difficult to tear herself away from the riveting aquarium scenes but sleep beckoned.

Jonathan instructed the Friend to switch off and the living room was left in darkness.

Upstairs in their double bed, Jonathan and Cathy found it hard to fall asleep, tossing and turning. Jonathan was understandably scared that his Friend might get up to its old tricks again so at two o'clock in the morning he decided to get a glass of water.

As he passed the Friend in the darkness of the living room it flickered on, and the beautiful woman appeared wearing a nightcap and dressing gown. She yawned and looked sleepily at Jonathan.

"Haven't you gone to sleep yet, Jonathan?" she asked, her hand covering another yawn. The screen faded to black, leaving the room in darkness again.

Jonathan drank a glass of water and after pacing around nervously for a while, finally returned to his bed. Just before dawn, he dozed off. The house was quiet.

At the Team Providence headquarters perched high up on a tower above the wetlands by West Gate Bridge, Alexander and Sandy awakened as the first glimmer of the morning sun broke over the horizon. They walked briskly along the corridors to the Team Providence storeroom and took out two sets of the *'Icarus wings'*, clothing, and helmets.

These wings had been used some years earlier when flying teams competed in the 'Icarus' competitions, but the event had long since been abandoned on account of global warming and the sunburn factor. Nevertheless, they were wings and uniforms that were resistant to extremes of heat and cold, and the breathing apparatus meant that they could fly at a high altitude.

Everything was silent in the Team Providence headquarters since the rest of the team were still asleep. Having put on the clothing and strapped on the Icarus wings, Alexander and Sandy strolled quietly out onto the open-air take-off platform, treading on a thin layer of morning frost, there was no wind as they breathed in the fresh sea air.

They began their relaxation exercises, performing a variety of stretches. The cityscape of Melbourne was silhouetted against the sunrise, and the only sound was that of the ambience of early morning traffic. Directly below them lay the lower Yarra wetlands and marshes where the real bird life remained hidden in their nests. Further over, the bay was calm.

Alexander and Sandy stood on the very edge of the platform and opened out their wide glittering wings to their fullest expanse and leapt off. They momentarily glided before their wings began to quickly swish back and forth as they soared high above the wetlands. The two flyers were virtually alone in the early morning sky as they veered off towards the eastern suburbs.

It only took about ten minutes of flying before they were hovering high above Jonathan's residence, and with the sun just above the horizon, they began to descend towards his house.

Inside, Stacy had already awoken and was seated in the living room chatting to the Friend. It was more of a whisper because Stacy had given the Friend strict instructions not to wake the rest of the household, especially Jonathan.

"You know… I quite like having a Friend in the corner," Stacy confided.

"Well, I must admit I've enjoyed sitting in this corner," the Friend replied quietly.

"It will be a pity to see you go. I personally found you very useful and informative," Stacy admitted.

The beautiful woman on the screen was pleased by the compliment. Even though she was only a piece of technology, she was still programmed to find fulfilment in helping people.

"Well, I can do virtually anything and that's the reason I was created by the Friend Corporation."

Stacy scratched her chin and raised her eyebrows. "Do you think you can become the sun?" Stacey asked.

"Oh, yes, easily," the Friend answered.

"Really?" Stacy said in surprise. "And do you think you could be the sun for an hour without stopping for anything?"

"Do you want me to warm the room, too?" the Friend asked with a laugh.

"Yeah. Can you?" Stacy asked.

"Of course, I can. And I will!" The Friend smiled, before she vanished and was replaced by a really bright light that instantly flooded the living room with sunshine.

The sunshine beaming out of the TV was so bright that Stacy had to put on her sunglasses. The set also radiated heat, and even with sunglasses the glow was so bright that Stacy could hardly see anything else.

Chips entered the living room, shielding his eyes from the sunny glow and holding his box of reflections which he placed on the floor. He opened the lid of the box, revealing an interior lined with various mirrors.

Outside, Alexander and Sandy hovered down and landed. They strolled into the living room simultaneously folding in their glittering wings, the sunshine refracting around the room.

Without even a good morning, Alexander and Sandy suddenly lifted the TV Friend and placed it into the box of reflections. The bright sunshine beamed out of the top of the box and the lid was slammed shut. The room instantly fell into darkness as Chips nailed the lid down.

Alexander picked up the box and followed Sandy into the backyard where the real sun was rising amid the early morning mist. The box Alexander held was beginning to increase in temperature. He and Sandy opened their wings and soared up into the clear sky.

Inside the box of reflections, the TV continued to shine like the sun but was reflected on itself by the mirrors surrounding it. The reflection caused the set to continue increasing in temperature, getting hotter and hotter, brighter and brighter.

Alexander and Sandy climbed higher and higher into the sky. The suburbs below became smaller and smaller. Stacy and Chips peered out of the kitchen window and spotted Alexander and Sandy, mere specks in the sky. Excitement built within Stacy as she prepared for her dramatic exclamation.

There was momentary silence, a quiet of dramatic intensity, then Stacy opened her eyes and gave a loud horrifying scream, **'help!'** of deafening proportions that echoed throughout the house.

Jonathan awoke with a startled shock and fell out of his bed, as he scrambled to untangle the bed sheets from over his head and Cathy matched his panic.

"What the hell is going on?" Jonathan yelled as he and Cathy rushed downstairs and through the hallway into the living room. They found Stacy quivering in an almost overacted fear. She pointed her trembling finger at the corner of the room.

"It's gone!" Stacy screamed. "It's gone again!" Stacy fell to her knees in terror and hysteria.

Jonathan and Cathy gazed at the empty corner of the room as Chips wandered in rubbing his eyes.

"What's happened?" Chips asked, pretending he'd just woken up.

"The Friend has disappeared again," Jonathan sighed. "I feared this might happen."

"Oh well," Stacy shrugged. "Now that we're all up we might as well have breakfast and get on with the day."

"I suppose you'll go to your office early Jonathan?" Cathy asked. "Since you're awake?"

Jonathan was still recovering from the realisation that the living room corner was vacant, and the Friend had vanished again.

"Umm… oh yes," Jonathan mumbled. "I guess I'll do that. The Friend might turn up in some obscure place again, so I won't report it as missing yet."

As the family sat down for breakfast, the back door flung open, and the milkman walked in smiling and handed Cathy cold milk, eggs and freshly baked hot bread.

"You're all up early today!" he said cheerfully, disappearing out the door on his way to the Jones' house next door.

Jonathan changed into his business suit and kissed Cathy, Stacy and Chips goodbye as he left for work. Since he had gotten up so early, he decided to take the efficient public transport to his office and before long he was seated in a tram with his briefcase.

Jonathan gazed out the window as the tram passed the bumper-to-bumper traffic. Through the cyclone fence that surrounded the safari park beside the Melbourne Zoo, he watched the elephants, giraffes and hippos laze around in the early morning sun, oblivious to the awakening city around them.

A group of schoolchildren on the tram noticed an unusually bright light in the sky, and they pointed and giggled, and Jonathan glanced up into the morning sky.

Thousands of metres above the safari park, Alexander and Sandy struggled to hold onto the container as they flew higher and higher. The sunshine beaming out of the TV Friend was being reflected at a greater rate by the mirrors surrounding it and the brightness and temperature was almost too much to bear.

The container started to split at its seams and a deep rumbling sound vibrated from within it and the incredibly powerful light was glowing out through the cracks with an unbearable heat. Their heat resistant uniforms could barely protect them any longer.

As the internal combustion kept increasing, their suits and Icarus wings began to blister and melt from the burning glow and soon they would have to let it go. Condensation boiled inside Alexander's helmet as he turned his face away from the searing heat and gasped for oxygen.

They both continued to climb into the sky.

With their gloves feeling as if they were on fire, they nodded at each other and dropped the glowing container. Alexander and Sandy scattered away burnt and singed as the now luminously hot white mass of energy fell towards earth.

Inside the tram, there was a shriek of horror from the passengers as the bright glow descended rapidly towards the ground.

"It's headed this way!" the commuters screamed in terror. "What is it?" they cried in fear.

Jonathan glanced at the pandemonium inside the tram and to his surprise, saw Celeste standing at the other end of the tram watching the glowing ball of flame. Suddenly, the container exploded with such force that the television set was blown to pieces like an exploding star.

From high above the flashpoint, Alexander and Sandy watched on with interest. "This could be how our universe was formed," Sandy said to Alexander.

They then started their long gliding descent in harmony.

Immediately after the enormous bright explosion, the passengers in the tram became silent both with relief and astonishment. One moment a glowing explosion, then nothing.

Jonathan and Celeste waved to each other as the tram rumbled on its way.

Back at the house, Chips and Albert stood in the backyard and watched the glowing ball of light as it descended towards the earth. Stacy and Cathy came out just as it exploded, and they all watched a hot piece splinter and break away.

"It's coming right for us!" Chips shouted in panic.

Before they could move, the hot piece hurtled down towards them like a burning meteorite and was followed by a horrendous crash and shattering sound as Chips ran over to Jonesy's place and saw that a piece of the TV Friend had smashed into Jonesy's mirrored pyramid shattering it into tiny slivers, and a small piece landed on the Bar-B-Q incinerating it.

Jonesy and his family raced up their mosaic escalator in their pyjamas and walked around crunching on broken mirror pieces, stunned. Albert shuffled down alongside Chips, "It's like the end of civilisation," he lamented, looking at the shattered mass of mirrors.

"Worry not, Jonesy, we can have the bar-b-que at our place instead," Chips suggested.

Albert turned to Cathy, who had just arrived with Stacy. "At least we won't burn the Cheops," he joked.

Chips folded his arms and said, "I admire people in the freeway of life going toot toot."